Pretty Lies

Astrid Scott Series

Blake Blessing

Blake Blessing

Pretty Lies

Blessing, Blake
Pretty Lies: Astrid Scott Series #1

Cover: Simply Defined Art

Editing: Heather Long

Proofread: Zoe's Author Services

Formatting: Rainbow Designs

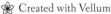 Created with Vellum

Chapter
1

This school was smothered in lies.

But what school wasn't?

The picture on the screen captured Silver Ranch High School's most darling sweethearts. Smiling at each other, saccharine sweet, like no one would ever understand their secret love, or even existed for that matter. But I knew the truth. Just this morning Bella had been blowing the star basketball player in the girls' bathroom. How do I know? Because I had a front row stall when they slammed through the door, believing they were alone.

I pulled up my feet, pretending I wasn't there, and those fucktards never even thought to check the stalls. It was awkward with my pants down, because let's be real, I had just finished peeing, and I didn't want to get coined the resident outcast the first week of school for pissing off the in crowd. Did I mention the guy she blew was not the boy in the picture?

My feet squeaked over the course material covering the seat of my bay window.

I should be thankful the jock only lasted about four minutes. I thought teenage boys were supposed to have better stamina than that. I rolled my eyes.

The next picture in my phone was their backs as they left the bathroom, the jock's hand clutching her ass like it was a pot of gold. Luckily, the guy, Trent I think was his name, definitely had a case of the moans and groans. When he was making his big finish, I was able get on the toilet seat, bring my pants up —which was necessary in case I fell — putting me in a great position to snap a picture over the top of the stall once they were on their way out.

That was my thing. Ever since I could remember, I'd been snapping photos of people when they didn't realize I was watching. It sounded creepy when I put it like that, but I swear it wasn't that weird. I found you can make people believe anything you want them to based on how you take the picture. The angle, lighting, expression. All together these things made up something compelling I found addictive.

Gestalt principal, I believe. The whole was greater than the sum of its parts. See, I paid attention in class.

Three days in this hellhole of a school and already I could point out the kids that had it all, the kids that had nothing, and the kids that lied. Not verbally, but with their image. These were the kids who came across as perfect, making everyone jealous of their girlfriend or boyfriend, their grades or popularity. But I saw the truth in their body language, the despair in their eyes. I knew, because I saw it in myself every freaking day.

Swipe left to the next picture. This was of the little girl a few houses down. She was the epitome of childhood inno-cence, light and bubbly. All sunshine and puppy tails. But everyday she went home to a place that barely had enough food to put on the table.

"Astrid!" A reedy voice bellowed from the first floor.

A trill of dread shot down my spine, because I had to go downstairs.

My bedroom door taunted me with new plastic glow-in-the-dark stars stuck to the back. They winked at me, taunting me about how I would go downstairs to see what Mother Dearest needed. My worn, suede boots, clicked against the old wooden floor when they hit the ground as I left the window seat.

Shoving the cell phone in the back pocket of my jean shorts, I tugged my gauzy sweater tighter around my body. I'd rather stab myself in the ear with a fondue fork than spend any time with the woman who bore me, but unfortunately that wasn't an option.

"Astrid! You have two minutes to be downstairs." My mother took on a shrill tone.

With the second call, I gained a little more urgency. The door creaked like a squeaky dog toy, signaling to anyone in the house, I was on my way. As I pounded down the steps, I was amazed by how many pictures were hung up on the walls already.

We'd only been in the house two weeks, but my mother wanted to be the best Suzie Homemaker on the block.

If I took her picture right now, she'd be the epitome of a woman with purpose. Clunky velvet heels that were currently the height of mom fashion, paired with a simple, dark blue dress that was mildly form fitting, falling to her knees. She'd be chopping salad for dinner, arranging the greenery in nice little bowls for me, her, and dad. The perfect mom. The perfect wife.

Lies. All of it lies.

"What's up, Mom?" I stuffed my hands in my pockets, rocking back on my heels.

Mother turned around, leaving a scattered pile of

lettuce on the island behind her. A deep frown line marred her forehead and I knew it was only a matter of time until she talked Dad into getting Botox. Not that we had the money for that.

"Astrid, did you get the chicken from the store like I asked?" She swiped small, fly away strands of hair off her forehead with the back of her arm.

My heart started to thump to the beat of the washing machine currently on the last spin cycle. She must have thrown shoes in the wash with all the banging coming from the laundry room.

"I, um. I thought you said this morning you were going to stop at the store on the way home." I didn't know how I could mess up like this so much. I could already tell she was going to flip in T minus two seconds.

"No, that's not what I said, you stupid girl. I had to work the late shift today. I specifically asked you to get the chicken so dinner wouldn't be late tonight. How many times do I have to tell you something before you do it right?"

Her words smacked against me like small pellets of shame.

"Sorry, Mom. I'll go right now." I snatched my keys out of the frog dish we kept in the kitchen, heading around her and straight to the back door.

She sighed like I fucked the world up and took baby Jesus with me on my merry way to hell. "I need the chicken in twenty minutes or dinner's going to be late. I won't cover for you with your dad. He'll know exactly why we aren't eating when he gets home."

I mumbled my goodbye and jogged to my car, ready to get out of there. My car beeped as I opened the door, my yellow and green lei swinging.

My mom and dad. I'd probably spent way too many

hours picking over their personalities and what made them tick. Or why they treated everyone like they were less substantial.

My aimless pondering of their relationship and personalities was pointless. Heaven would throw a party at the Gentlemen's Club before I had any substantial answers. Dad was a preacher and good ole boy from South Carolina and Mom was a southern bell from West Virginia. They met when they were in college at United Presbyterian at some kind of church function.

There were Bibles and fruit punch, like the regular nonalcoholic kind, and all kinds of sweater sets. Apparently it was love at first sight, and they've been married ever since. Their love wasn't blatant and obvious like so many other couples, but maybe that was because of my dad's beliefs? It was hard to believe sometimes. Why stay married if you weren't head over heels in love with someone?

Other than not having a deep, churning love for each other, their marriage was a decent one. They seemed to get along well enough, but they had a knack for making people feel like they were about two inches high. It wasn't reserved for me solely, but I definitely bore the brunt of it.

The day before had been my eighteenth birthday and I was counting down the months until I was able to go my own way and make my own mistakes. Nine months. I was hoping this was one of those times where it went much quicker than it felt in the moment. My luck, it would take three years until graduation.

Even when the time came, if I tried to make my own way, how would I support myself?

This year I was going to make a plan. Some miraculous way I could get out from under the toxic world I was living in.

The local grocery store was two blocks away from our house, which I guessed was convenient enough. It shared a parking lot with a small-town mechanic shop named Tacky's Tires. The thing about small cow towns outside of city limits, there were weird names attached to every store. No big chains for Silver Ranch. Little mom and pops places only.

I pulled into the parking lot, tracing the cracks I swore could have swallowed small cats. In fact, I was so focused on the picturesque quality of the pavement that I hadn't seen the light pole right in front of me. In fact, I missed it completely, until I hadn't missed it at all.

The car jerked and the thunderous clap of the bumper meeting the light pole echoed through the car.

"Oh, shit. Oh shit." I chanted as I slammed the car into break, hopping out to get a look at what kind of damage I wrought on my brand-new car.

My parents were going to kill me. This was my conciliatory present for not making a stink when we moved. Although, making a fuss was never a real option. I was sure mom would have stripped me down with a tongue lashing, or three.

I cautiously walked to the front, my hands covering my eyes because I wasn't ready to see my freedom wash down the rusty, hair-ridden drain.

A warm breeze whispered over my face and my shirt danced around my thighs, taunting me. On the count of three, I whipped my hands away from my face.

"Fuck!"

An old, blue haired lady stared me down from two rows over. She muttered to herself, shaking her head before turning away.

Yeah, yeah. I know. I'm what's wrong with America's Youth today.

I crouched down to inspect the busted headlight on my Jeep. It wasn't the newest or coolest car, but it was *my* very first one. My fingers longingly touched the cracked plastic covering the bulb. At least that part remained intact.

"Goodbye, Freda. I shall miss all the good times we didn't get to have together."

"Freda's such an unsexy name. Why didn't you go with Stacy or Veronica? Maybe even Devon."

A rough teasing voice cut through my moping and I turned to look over my shoulder.

The sun was setting right behind the guy's head so I couldn't make out his face. From what I could see, he was tall, and wearing baggy clothes.

"Freda was the name of my favorite cat when I was a kid. Now it's the name of my favorite car."

"Huh." He moved closer and whistled through his teeth. "I have to say, that's some spunk you have there. I've never seen anyone accost a light pole just for giggles."

"What?" I scrunched up my nose, with one hand shielding my eyes. "You know I didn't do this on purpose?"

"You must really think I'm stupid. I was joking. No one ever joke with you before?" He raised an arm to scratch the back of his head, the tone of his voice saying maybe *I* was the one that needed help.

I did need help. I needed a way to get out of the life I was destined to lead.

A good little woman. Degree in business or something *practical*. Married to a nice man that followed in my dad's footsteps. My stomach churned just thinking about it.

Nah, that wasn't the life I was going to live, even if it killed me.

"*You* must think I live under a rock. Look, I'm just stressed. This is a new car and when I take it home, my parents are going to lock it up, and I'll never drive Freda again."

Heat hit the back of my eyes and I held my breath, willing it to go away. We'd only been in town two weeks and even though I didn't know this guy, and would probably never see him again, I hadn't wanted him to think I was a cry baby.

He crouched down beside me and inspected the pieces of the headlight.

"That's not horrible. I can fix this right up for you." He tilted his head my way and my eyes widened.

Holy ear of Van Gogh.

Our heads were only a few inches apart, giving me an up close view of just how stunning this guy was. His dirty blonde hair was buzzed short and he had an edgy, dirty look to him. My eyes drifted down his body and realized why his clothes were so baggy. He was wearing a jumpsuit.

Beck was stitched in bright red over the white patch on his chest. When my eyes flicked back up to his, they were smoldering, daring me to lean in. Where was my phone when I needed it?

"Beck. That's your name." I blurted out.

The corner of his mouth hooked up at the corner. "Yeah, you? You must be new around here."

"Astrid. I just moved here with my mom and dad." I gulped, getting nervous under the intense power of his gaze.

"High school?" he turned deeper into me.

"Senior."

Beck sighed with a dick smirk on his face. "Jail bait." He sat back on his haunches, looking over his shoulder for a second. "Listen. Get your shopping done. I'll fix this up for you real quick and your parents will never be the wiser."

Hope brightened the world for a paltry second. Then it faded away. That wasn't going to work. What was I supposed to pay this guy in? Creepy stalker pics? Yeah, no. No one was interested in the lies like I was.

"I don't have any extra money. My mom doesn't let me have a job while school's in." Desperation clung to my very being, but I knew I couldn't pay for it.

"I'll take care of it. It's not an expensive fix anyway. I can count this as my one good deed for the year."

The almost moment we shared evaporated but I still bounced on my knees. I shouldn't take this guy up on the offer. But I was going to. New town, new school. The last thing I needed was to make my life hell by taking the bus as a senior.

I'd find a way to pay this guy back. Maybe I could babysit or something around the neighborhood.

"Thank you." I beamed at him and shot back to my feet.

My door was still wide open from where I jumped out like a crazy woman. Beck was picking up the pieces of the broken light when I grabbed my wallet from the console and the keys out of the ignition.

I kicked the door shut and faced the mechanic.

"Thank you. Thank you, thank you. I won't be long, maybe ten minutes." My smile wobbled as I started toward the grocery store.

"The keys?" He tapped once on the hood of the jeep.

"Oh yeah," I twisted to toss the keys to him. Then second thoughts weaseled their way into my mind. Could I trust this guy? If I thought my parents would be angry now, it would be so much worse if my car was stolen.

No, I hadn't gotten any strange serial killer vibes from him. I believed he was a mechanic at Tacky's.

Beck caught the keys in midair, flashing a dimple as he stood there watching me. I stared back, mesmerized by the sexy working man thing he had going on. I didn't see that very often in boys my own age.

He quirked a brow, his grin spreading to engulf the lower half of his face.

I squeaked and spun around, racing toward the front. What the hell was wrong with me, staring at him like he hadn't known I was there? But he did. And it was totally awkward.

Shaking my head, I picked up a basket after I passed through the automatic doors. The back of my neck burned for me to turn around and see if he was still watching, but I forced myself to keep walking until the doors were out of sight. I instantly relaxed and headed toward the meat section.

The aisles were packed with the after work rush. I dodged around working mothers in their expensive heels and modest blouses, and the working men with old jeans speckled in dirt and grease. A cacophony of annoying beeps filled the air.

It was barely over ten minutes when I paid for the chicken and walked into the night. Warm air kissed my skin and a shiver ran down my spine as I adjusted to the outside temperature.

My car was no longer in the parking lot so I went to Tacky's Tires. The tail end of Freda peeked out from one of the bays. If the stars aligned in my favor, Beck would be done and I could head home. My night would be hell if I was late with the chicken. And by hell, I meant the snide comments and irritated huffs I'd be subjected to all night.

Freda was the only car in the garage and it was silent except for some tinkering around the hood. I knocked twice on the door to signal my arrival.

"Beck?" My fingers skimmed the side of my baby as I walked around to the front. Beck was wiping down the new light with a cleanish rag, bobbing his head to whatever music played in his earbuds.

I stepped back out of his view and opened the camera on my phone, snapping a few pictures I could study in more detail later. Taking pictures became this weird obsession that developed when I got my first phone. Body language was a fascinating thing and I loved to study the story it told from the privacy of my own room. And his story intrigued me.

Satisfied with the quick shots, I shoved the phone in my back pocket and moved back into Beck's line of sight. This time, he looked up and jerked one of the ear buds out.

"Hey, you're just in time." He smoothed a hand over the shiny new light.

My fingers tightened over the plastic bag as it set in that I really wasn't going to get in trouble for this. I smiled and asked, "How much would this have normally cost?"

"Don't worry about it, it's on me." He stood, tucking the rag in the back pocket of his suit.

"Fine, but I'll bring you cookies or something. I can make a mean cinnamon chocolate chip cookie."

"I won't turn away cookies." He patted his stomach, then handed back my keys. "It was nice to meet you, Astrid."

The keys were warm from his pocket, a library card the

only thing on the keychain. I'd have to add some personalized keychains soon.

I shuffled to the door, determined to avoid any more awkward silences. My gaze met his as I was pulling my legs inside the jeep.

He opened his mouth to say something, but a loud crash came from the back of the shop. I glanced toward the back entrance as a skinny, disheveled woman fell through. She clumsily shoved matted hair away from her face as she tugged on her misbuttoned shirt, that was only half tucked into her pants.

"Ma, what are you doing here?" A vein stood out in Beck's neck as he twisted like he was going to go to her, but then turned back to me. "I think it's time for you to go. Don't worry about cookies or any kind of payback." He shut my door and went to his mother, grabbing her shoulders to hold her up.

Heat hit my cheeks at being so thoroughly dismissed. I got it. Family problems were the worst, but the abrupt change still stung.

To soothe my pride, I turned on Green Day's American Idiot album for the ride home.

Chapter 2

The night went about as great as the evening started. Dinner was late regardless of getting the chicken there on time. Dad ignored Mother Dearest while we ate and she, well, she made plenty of comments on how I never listened and how I wasn't going to make anything of myself if I couldn't use common sense. All things that made me want to go Lizzy Borden on her ass with my fork.

Now at seven in the morning, the parentals would just be getting out of bed. The downstairs was completely dark, only the hum of the refrigerator could be heard. My gaze flitted to their bedroom door as I quietly slipped on my shoes. I breathed easier when the fresh morning air hit my lungs and I jogged down the steps.

School started at seven forty, and it was only a ten-minute drive to school, but I liked getting there early. No one seemed to stare as much when you were already inside the school. None of that cliché crap where students all stop and gawk at the new kid, picking apart their ride and choice of clothing for the day.

I whipped into a spot at the back, far away from the other two cars in the lot. The school was a regular high school, nothing fancy or modern, and the lawn was well manicured because half of the school district fell over the rich side of town. My family fell right in the middle. We weren't poor, but we would probably be on the lower end of middle class.

It wasn't a big deal, we made it work. I worked in the summer and bought all of my school clothes. That was actually a perk, because I could get what I actually liked. If it were up to my mother, I'd be dressing in sweater sets and khaki pants.

The door popped open easily and my steps echoed in the hallway as I headed toward my locker. First period was conveniently located next to the library, so that's where I'd spend the next thirty minutes. I grabbed my books and slammed the door shut.

Shoes squeaking down the hallway caught my attention and I glanced through the strands of my hair. I tried not to be super obvious I was watching but I had just shut my locker. Frayed edges of stray papers were sticking out of my math book, I fidgeted with those so I wouldn't be the weirdo kid facing the locker.

Four guys in gym shorts and wife beaters were strolling down the hallway like they owned the school. Hell, they probably did. Like every school, the jocks reigned at the top.

Someone said something funny because they busted up laughing, and one of the guys broke away to make some skating motion down the hallway.

"Dude, that party last weekend was killer. You think Remy will be able to host them on the reg?" The guy closest to me asked.

"Her parents are divorced now, so good chance." Another responded.

"You would not believe the things she did with her

mouth." The first guy moaned under his breath. "Little Remy got some practice somewhere this summer."

They were passing directly behind me, and my shoulders relaxed, because soon I could disappear into the shelves of books.

A shoulder collided with the locker next to me, scaring the ever-loving crap out of me. I jumped a foot in the air and backpedaled away from whoever invaded my space. Hands clasped my shoulders, stopping me in my tracks.

The guy in front of me leaned against the locker with his arms and ankles crossed, a cocky smirk gracing his lips. Nice, the four jocks decided I was a fun distraction. I'd seen him around. Brent, I think his name was, was a senior. The hands never left my body, instead sliding down to cup my arms. When I glanced up, a red head with a curly fro and gap-toothed grin stared down at me.

"You're the new girl. What's your name? Aslin, or Anna, or something?" The red head pursed his lips in concentration.

Note to self. Duck lips was not an attractive thinking face.

"Astrid." I pulled away from his grasp but he held strong.

"What's with the flowy pajama pants. Are those the in thing, right now?" Curly asked.

"It's boho."

"The training room is empty for a while, want to go with us and get to know each other better?" Smarm smothered his voice like southern gravy over fried chicken.

Like I would ever put out just because I was the new girl. Yeah, no.

"I don't think so. I have somewhere to be, anyway." I pulled away again, but the guy's fingers dug into the meat of my arm. "You need to let go." My voice lowered to barely above a whisper and my pulse sped up.

"We're having fun. Want to welcome the new girl. Hasn't anyone given you a warm welcome yet?" Brent pushed off the lockers.

"No, I can't say I've had a welcome quite like this, and sorry, but I don't want this one either." I snark and stomped down on red head's foot.

"Shit, you bitch!" he released me, and I immediately sidestepped the group, turning to face them.

The other two guys were hanging back looking uncomfortable. No, only the shrimp of the group looked nervous as he glanced up and down the deserted hallway. The other was at least half a head taller than the other three, with dirty blonde hair and blue eyes. He didn't look uncomfortable; he was massively angry. His hands were clenched into tight fists at his sides and he was sending giant stabby daggers at curly and Brent.

"Don't come near me again. Any of you." I made eye contact with each guy.

Brent and redhead pierced me with a look that said *I will end you*, shrimpy blushed like he wasn't sure how he got here. Then there was Ragnar. Not really, I didn't know what his name actually was, but with his blond hair and blue eyes, he reminded me of a Viking. His thunderous expression also lent to that outcome.

I backed up slowly at first, testing to see if they would follow me. Brent and redhead started to take a step forward but Ragnar punched an arm out, knocking red head into Brent. He muttered something too low for me to hear and shook his head. Then they stopped and whispered back and forth.

Taking advantage of their distraction, I spun on my

heels and ran toward the library. Did running make me look like a coward? Yeah, maybe. But I did not like being the center of attention and even more, I hated being the object of other's jokes.

And those guys, they were trying to one, get some, and two, turn me into the next victim of their games. No thank you.

The library here was something pretty amazing for a high school. I swore it was almost as big as the auditorium, with shelves so high, a ladder was needed to pluck the highest books. There were comfy chairs arranged in nice seating areas dispersed throughout the space. I got what the school was trying to do here, encourage a college like setting to prompt the students to hang out and study. Luckily for me, most of the kids didn't step foot in here. At least, they hadn't this week when I was finding refuge among the dusty pages.

I plopped down on a cracked leather chair in the corner, next to a window overlooking the lawn. Students had begun to filter into the parking lot, milling around and talking to their friends. My phone was still in my back pocket so I shifted sideways to grab it. The first thing I did was pop open the camera app and scroll through my pictures.

Beck filled the screen and I paused. I had forgotten I'd taken these pictures of him. The angle of the camera had caught him almost in side profile, but not quite. Calm contentment radiated from the picture as he wiped down the car. It was a good picture.

I played with the filters and color settings until it was a warm, comforting picture. Whenever I looked at it now, I'd wish I could hang out with him and bask in his mellow vibes.

Before I knew it, the bell was ringing, signaling first

period. I gathered up my things and headed for the door. My phone buzzed in my hand and when I checked it, a smile sliding over my face.

Stace: Hey girl. What's up?

My previous school was my home for four years, from eighth grade through eleventh. I had one friend and that friend was Stace. Where I loved to catch people unaware, she loved to track people online and stalk their social media accounts. We've joked that between the two of us, we should open a private investigation firm when we graduated. Who knew, that could be the plan that gained my independence.

Astrid: Going to class. Where you should be rn

"Oof," the air rushed out of me as I collided with a guy by the door.

My phone flew out of my hand and slid over to the wall with a thump. Papers and books flew everywhere, but not from me. They were from the guy I accidentally crashed into. I scrambled around, trying to help him pick up his things but there were so. Many. Papers.

"I'm so sorry. I didn't see you." His features were hidden but he had a thick head of light brown hair that was slightly wavy on top. Thick, black framed glasses covered his face. When he glanced up his lip curled in a disgusted sneer.

Well, excuse me.

"If you were paying attention to what you were doing rather than looking on your phone this wouldn't have happened. We're going to be late now. It's assembly day. So, thanks." Sarcasm dripped from his words.

What had been embarrassed remorse, catapulted into

right bitchiness. "What the fuck ever. If you had been watching you could have side stepped me easily. I wasn't running any sprints."

I shoved all the papers I had gathered to his chest, then snatched my phone with an extra huff, leaving him alone on the floor.

It was a freaking accident. He acted like I stomped on his pocket protector while burning his favorite instruction manuals. Whatever, I tried to apologize and do the nice thing. If he wanted to be a dick about it, I wouldn't go out on any limbs to make nice.

Homeroom was teeming with teenage pheromones as I skated through the door. I made it right before the bell rang. Assigned seats had me sitting in the back, thankfully. My bag thumped against the floor as I sat. People still chatted and stood in half circles while they waited for the teacher. Although, homeroom was so lax at this school, yesterday the teacher never even showed up before the next bell rang.

A short, stout man opened the door and poked his head in, the fluorescent lights reflecting off his bald head. "Listen up, hell spawn. The pep rally is about to start in five minutes. I've marked you all down. Go ahead and make your way toward the gym."

He stood back, holding the door open. Good thing, because there was a high chance he could have been trampled by these over anxious students. The room was completely cleared in thirty seconds, leaving me to hurry behind them.

The trick to staying under the radar was generally staying in the middle of the masses. Don't be the first to walk in, and don't be the last. That way you blend in with everyone else. After that point, you can settle in the back shadows.

Drums, trumpets and whatever instruments were in the marching band played upbeat music, hyping up the team spirit. My old school had pep rallies too, but the scene I walked into seemed off the charts. The band stood on either side of the court as students climbed the bleachers. Cheerleaders and jocks all congregated in the center of the gym, waiting for the fun to begin. Would they be performing for us? Making us feel all bright and shiny, happy to be a part of this school?

Gag.

I climbed to the middle of the bleachers and sat on the end. I opened my camera app and snapped some pictures of the floor and then some of the people around me. I'd gotten pretty good at being inconspicuous the last couple years. If I smiled and pretended to take a selfie, no one would ever notice. And yes, I looked ridiculous but I got the pictures I wanted, so at the end of the day, it didn't bother me any.

An air horn blared through the gym and for once, everyone shut up. The crazy intense energy ratcheted even higher as the crowd leaned forward. Whatever was about to happen, they were stoked.

A tapping on the microphone echoed around the room and when I glanced down at the podium placed in the center of the court, the guy I bumped into was there, red faced and flustered.

Well, shit.

Chapter 3

"Good morning, students of Silver Ranch High. As most of you know, my name is Jonah Perez, and I'm the current student body president. With this new year, we wanted to start things off right, and what better way than to have a SRHS style pep rally." He cleared his throat and the red in his face turned a deep shade of tomato.

The poor guy looked super uncomfortable up there. I was also pretty sure the papers he dropped were his notes, because he sounded a little lost and robotic.

"Just a few announcements before we get the fun started. Nominations for student leadership positions will be collected during homeroom on Friday, and clubs will officially resume September fourteenth. There are two new clubs, Chess Club and Magic Club. If you are interested in joining, please contact Alicia Haven. Now. The sports of Silver Ranch. We have the Football team," Jonah threw an arm out to encompass a group of burly guys in oversized jerseys.

At his introduction, they roared and flexed their arms. Even from this distance, I could see the veins sticking out on their necks and forearms. *Yes, fellas, you are the epitome of masculinity.*

The crowd of students went crazy over their show, spinning blue and white handkerchiefs in the air. On the floor, the guys arranged into a loose diamond formation and proceeded to dance, in a poor imitation of the cheerleaders.

They wrapped up their cheer with more yelling and fist pumps. Jonah stepped back up to the podium. "Thank you, football team for that impressive display. Although not supported through the school, we have the local hockey team, the Grizzlies," Jonah tossed out his arm to the opposite side of the gym.

These guys were more professional athletes and less drunk college frat guys. They still did the whooping and stomping but they were way more reserved about it. It must have been a thing because they moved into their own formation, and I recognized the four guys from this morning. These boys were front and center, with Ragnar in the lead position.

Music filtered through the speakers, and when the beat dropped, so did my chin. These boys could dance. Like legit dance. Giggles bubbled out of me, and the girl sitting next to me scowled. They had skills, but something about big Viking Ragnar, breaking it down to a Post Malone song was hilarious.

After the hockey team it was the dance team, then the cheerleaders. Another hour of pumping us up before they sent us back to class, which was coincidentally the beginning of third period.

A goofy grin adorned my face as I headed down the hallway. I wasn't expecting to enjoy that as much as I had, I couldn't deny it was a good time. And while I would never want to be on the court, viewing from the bleachers was just fine.

My locker was on the way, so I stopped to swap out

some books. There were kids walking around with a damned turtle shell on their back, holding all their books and notebooks for each class. No, thank you. I valued my good posture and healthy spine.

By the time I got to fourth period, I was actually pumped. Art class. Undoubtedly, it was my favorite class of the day. I sucked at still life and anything hand drawn, but I loved being in the atmosphere of art. And I loved photography.

There was something so calm and accepting in any art teacher I'd had. Everyone in my mom and dad's world were posers. It was all about status. Who had the better paying jobs, who had the better connections. And most importantly, who gave the biggest donations at church. Ironic, since Dad didn't make that much and neither did Mother Dearest.

With Dad, the ability and willingness to donate were the most important qualities in a person. I was sure Mother Dearest had a list of the deepest pockets in the congregation and which ones had sons similar in age.

"Astrid! What put that pout on your face? Are you a pout pout fish with a pout pout face?" Mr. Music pushed out his bottom lip to mimic my supposed expression.

"I thought you were tired of that book?" The first day of school he talked non-stop about his toddler and how that was all he wanted to read, or I guessed all he wanted read to him, since he was two.

"Gah, I am." He dramatically pressed the back of his hand to his forehead and tipped his head back. "But when you come in with that pathetic face, looking like someone discovered your secret crush and plastered it all over the school... well, the pout pout fish comes to mind. Now stop spreading the dreary wearies all over the place."

His inane rambling pulled a chuckle from my chest as I skirted around him.

"Who's talking about secret crushes? I love a good dish."

Ryan, a very flamboyant boy, strutted into the room.

"Astrid. We were discussing her secret crushes." Mr. Music hopped up onto his desk.

"Oh really." Ryan passed by his usual table and took a seat across from me. "You're new here. I was meaning to come talk to you before, you know give you the SRHS welcome. You looked prickly, so I was waiting for a good opportunity. Talk of secret crushes, *bam*. Here's my opportunity." He grinned, flashing the whitest teeth I'd ever seen.

"There are no secret crushes." I smirked and tucked a chunk of hair behind my ear. Ryan was the first person to actually talk to me since the first day of school. I wasn't about to screw this up by scaring him away with a flippant comment.

It was now Thursday. Almost four days of not speaking to another human at school, outside of answering attendance. Or the welcoming committee this morning, but that didn't count of my list of actual human encounters.

Part of me wanted to be the prickly bitch he thought I was. The other part of me, the lonely part, was excited to have a conversation.

"Okay, sure. You haven't had time to properly scope out the meat selection. I can help you with that." He nodded his head succinctly.

I kind of loved his personality already. I could tell he was going to bring lots of laughs and frustration. At least, the fun kind of frustration only your friends could give you.

I laughed. "Not really in the market for any kind of meat right now."

"Tacos? There's a fine selection of fish here too, girl." Ryan shrugged like it wasn't a big deal to him either way.

"Uh... no. I definitely prefer the meat, but I'm new and boyfriends aren't something I need to be focusing on." Not to mention my parents would kill me if I told them I had a girl crush. I could already feel their hypothetical disappointment and condemnation.

He squinted at me. "You're one of those girls? Everybody needs love. You just leave it up to Ryan and I'll get you sorted right out. What's your type?"

"I don't have a type. And really. This is my senior year. What I need to be focused on is getting a plan together after graduation."

Mr. Music clapped his hands, drawing my attention to the front of the room. "All right, how many of you crazy kids have a college plan?"

What a coincidence. Exactly what I planned to get into with Ryan.

A few kids raised their hands, but not many. I guess I wasn't the only slacker in the place.

"That's sad. Aren't most of you all juniors and seniors?"

There were a few grumbles and more raised hands throughout the room. I hadn't done either, instead just listened as a silent participant.

Mr. Music jumped down. "Okay, that's a discussion for another day. Today, I have news. I just hung up with my contact at the university and they have a new scholarship available. One of their alumni has made it big and is generously offering this opportunity. So, here's the deal. There's going to be a competition showcasing top talent. Each school in the state is allowed to send two portfolios, meaning winners. The school and benefactor will choose one talented winner to receive a full ride." He paused, letting that sink in.

I straighten in my chair and paid more attention. A full ride.

"Mr. Music, does that include the dorm and food?" There was probably a better way to ask that, but my mind was spinning with ideas.

He pointed a charcoal stained finger toward my face. "Yes! It covers everything one hundred percent. Even with a living stipend. The stipulation is that you maintain a B grade average, and any work on display would be at the benefactor's gallery."

"The guy paying for the scholarship owns a gallery?" A squeaky girl across the room piped in.

"Woman. Way to play into the male dominated society, Jess."

The conversation faded to the background as my mind wandered. Hope and excitement warred in my chest as I mentally picked over his words, looking for anything that would ban me from entering. It sounded like anyone with an interest in art was welcome to enter.

This could be the flipping chance I'd been waiting for. That shiny delicious carrot dangled in my face, leading me down a golden path to freedom. I only needed to out create pretty much everyone in the entire school, and then somehow take the winning spot.

With that thought, my good mood deflated. I could barely shade an apple properly. The whole reason for taking art was because I loved it, not because I was awesome at it. My sketchbook was sitting on the corner of the table, so I pulled it closer, flipping through some of my previous work.

A drawing of a mannequin that was decidedly lopsided. The cliché fruit bowl with defined pencil shading that looked like a four-year-old couldn't stay inside the lines. Next was a perspective drawing that was decent, but I used a ruler and a heavy-duty eraser to clean it up. Something told me this wasn't the quality work they were looking for.

Ryan nudged my foot, and when I glanced up, he pushed the corners of his lips into a smile. I shook my head, not feeling indulgent of his friendly personality anymore. His eyes narrowed, bouncing back and forth between my own before he rolled his and turned back to Mr. Music.

The rest of the day passed in a haze of assignments and lectures. For the most part, I had a fairly decent workload. Economics, honors English, and biology II were my main core classes. Then with art, Strength I–which was a fancy name for basic gym–and a free period, it balanced out nicely.

By the time I got home, I was in desperate need of a nap and a good look at my life choices. My backpack hit the ground as I slipped my shoes off and slid them under the bench in the mudroom.

Sharp clicking of heels moved closer and I braced myself for conversation.

"There you are. Your father's bringing over a few work associates for dinner. I laid a dress out for you, with some accessories. Be back downstairs in an hour." Mother finished clipping in her earrings and walked away.

My day was great. We had a pep rally and it was amaze-balls. There's a scholarship I want to apply for, but I don't think I can. All the things I would say to a nurturing mother passed through my head. I heaved a weighted sigh, we would never have that kind of relationship. We never had.

The next hour seemed like only minutes. Ready for the dinner, I was dressed like the perfect little Stepford daughter, complete with fake pearl earrings and matching necklace. I didn't want to go down, I'd much rather stay in my room. Weak light from the sunset stretched past my window, highlighting the cute bay window seat. It was time to head downstairs, but I prolonged it by walking to my window.

There was a great view of the street from here. The little girl was there, riding her bike in circles right in the center of the road. It was a pretty peaceful street with little traffic. Only one car passed by, but it slowed until it stopped completely, right in front of our mailbox. The doors didn't open, and it was dark enough that I couldn't see who was inside.

Damn, it was time to go down. If I wasn't there and part of the greeting committee, I'd lose the few privileges I had.

The Mary Jane pumps my mother left out for me thumped on each stair. My parents were already in the small foyer when I reached the bottom of the steps. Mother was straightening her skirt, while Dad was smoothing his tie.

A weird feeling coasted down my arms, my fingers curling into loose fists. Tonight was different from the other nights. Whoever was outside must be a big deal for my dad. Maybe some elder of the church, or someone with deep pockets. There was no telling really.

The doorbell rang and it was the most ridiculous thing I'd ever experienced. Our front door had a huge frosted pane of glass right in the center. They might not have been able to see us clearly, but these people had to see our silhouettes standing right *here*. I could see them and our porch light wasn't even on.

Dad opened the door with a jolly smile, arms out in a welcoming gesture.

"Stan. Barb. It's nice you both could come. Dinner's about ready, I think you'll really love Trina's cooking."

Not only was he acting like Mr. Cleaver, I suddenly felt like I was in the *Twilight Zone*. A distinguished older man stepped through in a sleek suit, followed by a Botox addicted woman with raven black hair. Dyed, for sure, based on her fair complexion and the almost white roots poking through.

It was who followed behind them that flipped everything sideways. Ragnar, in gray slacks and a white button-down shirt appeared and the moment we made eye contact, I scowled. Then there was curly.

Maybe I was being an angsty teen, but I felt like the world was getting back at me for some horrible deed I unknowingly committed.

Curly snickered when he noticed me standing here. It was very clear they both recognized me.

Fuck them.

Chapter
4

A sharp pinch to my side startled the grumpy look right off my face. Mom had caught the looks between us and was apparently not happy.

"We're excited, and thank you again for inviting us over." The man shook hands with Dad and there was a slight awkward pause.

"This is my wife, Trina, and my daughter Astrid. She just started at Silver Ranch High."

Attention swung to me and I tried really, really hard not to roll my eyes at the fake small talk that no one really cared about. The last thing these strangers would find interesting would be the high school I was enrolled in.

Now the two guys, they cared—but only because I hadn't jumped on the opportunity to get some. Or give them some, however they wanted to look at it. It wouldn't surprise me if girls tossed themselves at their feet for a chance to jump on their dicks. That kind of attention inflated egos until they couldn't tell a girl who wanted them, from a girl who didn't. Well, this girl definitely doesn't want any of what they're offering.

The dad and mom—because I assumed this was a family unit—shook our hands and gushed about how great it was to finally meet us. And by finally, they meant they waited a few weeks. School had only been in for one week and we got here shortly before that.

"Stan, and this is Barb," Stan placed a hand on Barb's back as she shuffled forward. "And this here is our son Rhys, and my nephew, Trey."

Rhys, the Viking from school, pressed his lips together in a tight smile and extended his hand to my father, then mother, finally coming to me. His hand was calloused, his grip firm.

Up close, he was a fine specimen with blue gray eyes framed by thick brown lashes. His cheekbones were chiseled like some kind of Greek god. My heart pounded under his gaze.

"Nice to meet you," His voice was smooth and cultured. Way more than I had expected of a high schooler.

Ah, we were pretending we hadn't met that morning. I could do that.

"Nice to meet you, too."

I relaxed when he turned away and went to his dad's side. My gaze kept drawing back to him, studying him as he found something very interesting in the corner of the room. Couldn't be dust bunnies. Mother Dearest would never stand for that.

Trey followed the line of handshakes and when he got to me, hatred flashed in his eyes.

It was safe to say, I hadn't made a fan in him. But to be fair, he hadn't won any brownie points either. I had a feeling the only reason he hated anyone was because they refused to fall in line with what he wanted. Typical rich kid.

"A pleasure," Trey lifted my hand to his mouth, kissing my knuckles.

Disgust coated my skin and I tugged my hand. He had a

death grip on my fingers, and short of making a scene, I couldn't do anything about it.

"Likewise," I snarked.

Luckily, the parentals were already chatting and moving toward the living room.

Our house was much bigger than the house we came from in Tennessee. That house was cute but modest. It was provided by the church, which hadn't had a lot of money. Dad's new church has much more affluent members in the congregation. Hence, this place that was at least double the size. Although, we probably had one of the smallest houses in the neighborhood.

"Astrid, why don't you come help me in the kitchen and then you can help set the table?" My mother smiled perfectly.

"Yes, ma'am," I was happy to escape what was going to be a bad night for even a few minutes.

As soon as I was in the kitchen, Mom gripped my arm and yanked me into her. Fine wrinkles fanning her eyes became more prominent as she squinted at me.

"Listen here, I don't know if you know those boys from school or not, but tonight, they are your best friends." She emphasized best through smiling, clenched teeth. It was like she was afraid someone would walk in so she had to keep smiling no matter what.

"You're hurting me," I whispered. "Who are these people? They don't look like Dad's normal church associates." Dad's normal dinner guests were old, pudgy men who wore ill fitting clothes and make lame Bible jokes.

Like, *how long did Cain hate his brother? As long as he was Abel.* They would laugh harder than anyone else, even Dad.

"It doesn't matter who they are. What is important is

you don't screw this up." Her breath fanned over my cheek as she gave me another shake.

"Got it," I pulled out of her hold and went directly to the cabinet, pulling out the nice dishes. If this evening was so important, she would want nothing but the best on display.

Dinner was tense and awkward. At least for me. While the adults conversed about church and local politics, Rhys and Trey both stared at me while they ate.

Mother kicked me two times under the table, so I made half-assed attempts at conversation.

"So, I saw you both during the pep rally. That was some dance." I dabbed my mouth with the corner of my napkin to hide my smirk.

Heavy blond brows slammed down. "Coach makes us do that. We're a club so the more support we have the better chance we have of getting better gear. Admissions is a big driver for the clubs."

"Where did you all learn those dance moves?" See, I could be nice when I had to.

Rhys' eyes briefly flicked to his dad, "Dad pays for a choreographer to come in and teach us the routine."

Caddy corner to me, Trey adopted the sleaziest car salesman smile I'd ever seen. Something about him just didn't give me good vibes. I directed my attention back to Rhys and pretended he wasn't there. If I didn't acknowledge him, maybe he would disappear in a poof of smoke.

"That's cool. I never learned how to dance. I prefer to stay in the background." Truth, I hated being in front of people. I locked up and shut down. Politician, news anchor, WWE wrestler, all jobs I could mark off my potential future plan.

Silence fell over the kiddy side of the table after that.

The weight of Rhys' stare sent tingles down the back of the neck, but I refused to acknowledge him. The green beans were much more interesting, especially after I used my fork to cut them all down the seams.

After dinner, the adults shuffled to the living room and us kids went to the basement.

This was new. Probably because none of the previous business associates had kids. I was usually excused to go to my room after dinner, rather than entertaining two strange boys by myself. Over the last month or so, my already modest mother had declared war on sexuality. My father must be the driver of this particular add to the evening because Mother would have never agreed to it.

Once we were downstairs with the door shut, I fiddled with the TV, putting *Avatar* on to play. With my back to the guys, I said, "Listen, I don't want either of you here anymore than you want to be here. We'll watch this movie from very far ends of the couch, and when it's time for you to go home, we'll act like we had a great time. Capiche?"

I turned around once the intro started playing. Rhys nodded and took up one corner, sprawling out with a frown. Trey sneered but took a spot next to Rhys.

I blew out a breath and sat on the other end. Thank God we had a sectional. It made it easy to be far, far way.

The whole event was honestly a bit anticlimactic. With the way Trey showed his dickness in the hallway, I would have thought he'd have tried to make the night hell. Not that I was complaining. I totally wasn't. Anytime I could have less drama in my immediate life, the better.

Photographing other people's drama? Now that I loved.

Thirty minutes into the movie, Mother called down to collect the boys. I allowed them to go first like a good little host, smiled politely at the door and flipped them off in my head as soon as they were gone.

Both of my parents walked away, so I too escaped upstairs to the comfort of my new bedroom. It was bigger, and draftier, but I'd already put a mark on it with my decorations. In this new town, and new house, it was my sanctuary.

Stace had perfect timing because as soon as I shut the door, my cell rang.

With a small smile, I greeted, "What's up, beyotch?"

"Nothing homie. Missing your face." Her voice was sullen. I bet if I could see her, her lower lip would be sticking out past her nose.

"I'm missing you too. Anything crazy happen? You've been in school at least two weeks so I know you have the latest details." I curled up in my bay window watching the outside.

"Actually, you wouldn't believe what happened." Stace perked right up at the chance to share some scandalous gossip. "Renee is pregnant."

I gasped. "Nuh-uh." The car in front of our drive did a U-turn, and then crawled down the street.

"Yes! Matt's family is flipping out."

I listened to her ramble while staring at the car. It was weird, going maybe five miles per hour. Once it passed the stop sign it turned into a house on the opposite side of the street.

"What the heck?" I muttered to myself.

"Huh?" Stace interrupted my thoughts.

"Nothing, I was watching something on the street." The glass was slightly warm on my fingers as I leaned into the window.

She picked back up where she left off, and I watched the garage door open. The car disappeared.

It was the largest and most elaborate house on the block. They could live there. Totally, with their sleek clothes and arrogant attitudes.

If they were that close, why not walk?

They did have a pretentious air about them, so I could see that they'd want to drive. Not to mention, not get their clothes sweaty in the ninety-degree weather.

Now only half invested in the conversation, I let Stace finish her story and then made some lame excuse to get off the phone.

As I lay in bed that night, my thoughts wandered to Rhys and his family. I tried not to think about dick face Trey, though. The question of how Dad knew them crossed my mind more than a few times. Especially since I hadn't seen them at church.

———

THE NEXT TWO weeks were monotonous and lonely, except for my time in art with Ryan. He definitely spiced things up, but not in the way I might have thought.

"Astrid, sit here." Ryan called as I came through the door of the art room.

He had a look about him that said he had all the dirt, and he was ready to serve it up on a nice hot platter. One day, when I was completely in the zone flipping through my pictures, he walked up behind me. Ryan oohed and ahhed over the shot as he abducted my phone, scrolling through all my pictures. Somehow, he weaseled my secret out of me and now he was directing me to the people that pissed him off.

Not that he had to work hard at it. It was ridiculously easy to pinpoint the bullies of the school and all of his targets were people I already captured or would have.

"What's the hot item of the day?" I spread my sketchbook out on the table. Our table was off to the side so the kids in class generally left us alone. Not that I put out a welcoming air, either.

"Juicy, juicy, juicy. I've had an angry hard on for this guy in my math class. I bet if you followed him you could get all sorts of blackmail worthy information." He laughed like we were going to send this guy to prison or something.

"And just what did he do to you? Hmm?" I had come to really like Ryan. He wasn't as close to me as Stace was, but it had only been two weeks. Something about his weaseling ways was getting right under my anti-people wall.

But even in that time, what hurt him, hurt me too. It could also be my need to latch onto someone. Yeah, better to not examine that particular thought too closely. He looked out for me so I colluded with him in these little revenge games. And that was enough for me.

He understood I would never share the pictures. Anything I found was just for us to laugh over.

"This guy is low key homophobic, and it drives me crazy. He doesn't come right out and say anything, but it's all over his face anytime I walk too close to him or happen to talk to someone sitting with him." He grinds his teeth. "You are like a thief in the night the way you can get pictures. It's a gift. I'm dying to know what you can find out about this guy."

"That sucks, Ry. But you still haven't told me who it is. Kind of hard to do what I do if I don't know who I'm going after."

Ryan drummed his fingers on the table and glanced

around the room one more time. He was really paranoid about whoever hit his hot button today.

"His name is Trey. He's a douche."

No wonder, if it was who I was thinking of. "Trey Bennet?"

He nodded solemnly.

Nope. No way was I following that guy. He already hated my guts. There was nothing that Ryan could tell me that would change my mind.

"I don't think he's an option for my little hobby. He's bad news bears." I broke eye contact and I wasn't even sure why.

Trey had dutifully stayed away from me just like the other guys in their group. Rhys had the same lunch I did, but other than a few pensive stares, he pretended I didn't exist.

"What? Your skills are top notch. It's practically poetic the way you are able to get your shots. And don't even get me started on the actual compositions."

My heart warms at his words. Taking pictures had always been something that I'd kept close to the vest, because people are judgy. And honestly, if Ryan hadn't found out by accident, then he never would have known.

But he does know, and he's the type of person to tell the ugly truth even if it hurt my feelings. So that he had this type of confidence and respect in my abilities made me happy.

"That's sweet of you, but I get a bad vibe around that guy. It's not a good idea."

Just when Ryan opened his mouth, Mr. Music slammed the door, signaling the start of another wonderful lesson.

"Kids, today is a work day. You all have your still life assignment in the center of the room. I will be meeting with all the Juniors and Seniors in the class that are interested in the scholarship." He jabbed his finger at his desk where a sheet of paper was taped down. "Write your name down here if you want to chat. I'm happy to look over your portfolio if you have it uploaded. Now, chop chop." He clapped twice to magically throw us into productive mode.

Low murmuring twisted around the room as chairs were scooted into position. Ryan tried to catch my eye but I was on a mission.

"I'll be right back."

About the best thing that could have happened in the move was uploading my previous artwork onto the school's portal. I could easily show Mr. Music what I was working with. I cringed for him on the inside. Who knew what he would say when he reviewed my stuff. Chances were, he wouldn't shoot me down right out. He seemed more of the type to gently let me down, then direct me toward something like math. It didn't require the kind of skill and patience art did, and when he saw my elementary school worthy portfolio, he'd know right away I wasn't talented in art.

Skirting around the table, I speed walked to the teacher's desk so I could beat the masses. Only, when I turned around, apparently I was the only one that was interested.

What was wrong with these people? Did they have such perfect lives with perfect families, they had no desire to get a shot at a full ride?

That's straight. The less competition for me. An advantage I needed.

Ryan craned his neck around, watching me walk back to the table. My fingers twitched at my sides and I glanced away. He was my friend, but he still made me uncomfortable when he stared at me. It didn't matter who it was, if I couldn't immediately decipher what was working behind their eyes I got nervous.

"Interested in majoring in art? I hadn't realized you wanted to go that route, but it makes sense."

"What do you mean?" My chair scraped against the scuffed white speckled tiles.

"Come on. I mean your photos. You could totally work on a portfolio of photography and rock it. You definitely aren't going to make it anywhere on your sketches." He flipped the top of my sketchpad open and let it fall shut.

"I'm trying really hard not to be offended by that back-handed compliment, because you're genius, Ryan!" The spark of excitement that ignited in my tummy died off quickly. "That's not going to work. I don't have any of that type of artwork in my portfolio."

"Astrid," Mr. Music called from the front. "Do you have a laptop or do you want to use mine?"

Heat stained my cheeks as I pushed away from the table. Now everyone knew I didn't have my own laptop for school. Not that I needed to have one, most kids carried one because they had to have as many electronics on their person as possible.

Being from a "nice" Christian family, they felt that screen time was addictive and not a good behavior conducive to loving Jesus. Hypocritical really, considering how my parents treated others.

I should have just stayed at the front so it wasn't broad-casted across the classroom.

"Yours."

We tucked ourselves away behind the desk, and his monitor gave at least a little illusion of privacy. I made sure to position myself where the screen and Mr. Music were the only things in my line of sight.

"So, you want to major in art?" Mr. Music said absently as he scrolled through my portfolio once I pulled it up.

"Um... I do. I would like to, if you think it's possible." Please say it's possible. It would crush my spirit if he laughed or sent me back to my table.

"Where's the confidence?" Mr. Music shifted around in his chair and pushed his glasses on top of his head.

I studied his eyes for any hint he was mocking me, but he appeared innocently curious.

"Come on. You can see for yourself that I can't draw my way to the bathroom on most days." I threw my hands up defeat.

I hadn't known why I even bothered. The competition for a full ride was going to be steep regardless of the motivation I had backing my interest to shoot for it.

Seconds away from heading back to my desk, Mr. Music gurgled in the back of his throat.

Weird.

"I see what you mean. Usually lines are straight, but your squiggly lines are all over the place. You might have a career in abstract art. Can you give me some deep insight and emotion behind random splotches on the page?"

He gestured to a thumbnail of a painting I attempted last year of a flower arrangement, fit for my grandmother's funeral.

Mr. Music was a great guy and one of my favorite teachers at this school. But right now, I couldn't tell if he was mocking me or genuinely offering a way for me to have a shot.

"Sure, I could make lots of things up to explain that hot

mess. I somehow don't think that's going to win the scholarship though." I deadpanned.

He swiveled in his chair until he faced me fully, staring too hard for my comfort.

"Tell me why you want this scholarship, Astrid." He demanded.

Caught off guard, I had no idea how to answer this question. The honest way? That I needed a shot at surviving life on my own terms. The suck up way? That I'd always dreamed of being an artist.

"I enjoy art. I want to immerse myself in something that I appreciate, instead of selling out to the idea my parents want me to be."

Ha! That was a little bit of both.

Mr. Music smooshed his lips to the side as if he was weighing my words.

"Talk to me about art. What medium is your go to?"

"I haven't really had a go to. I've always taken art classes and done the assignments, but you have my portfolio right there. It's not life changing by any stretch of the imagination." I pointed to the screen.

Ryan popped his head next to mine as he pulled a chair up beside me, screeching all the way.

"I don't mean to intrude on your appointment here, but I couldn't help but overhear the conversation." He was the picture of innocence and I snickered at his wide-eyed expression.

"By all means Ryan. You have the floor." Mr. Music grinned at Ryan like he expected this type of behavior.

"I was trying to tell Astrid before she left our table, there is an alternative option for her to enter the competition, without embarrassing herself with her chicken scratch." He sounded so formal, until the last bit. That made me want to put gorilla glue in his face lotion.

I slapped his arm. "Real nice, Ry. I thought we were friends."

"We are. That's why I hijacked your chat. Give me your phone." He reached for the baby blue phone in my lap, but I snatched it up and out of his reach.

"I don't think so. There's classified information on this device."

"Like you're getting any. Give me the damned phone." I was so shocked, he pulled the phone right out of my hand without any fight on my part. The bastard knew how to catch me off guard.

"Secrets my ass. If you have such dangerous stuff, your password should not be one-one-one-one." He bent over my phone, looking for my camera app.

"This is all highly amusing, but there is one other student in this class that would also like to chat about the scholarship."

When I glanced up, Mr. Music seemed like he didn't care at all. He was amused but attempting to play the hard ass teacher part.

"Here." Ryan shoved the phone in Mr. Music's face. "This is a picture that Astrid took at the mechanic shop in town."

A deep line separated Mr. Music's eyebrows as he reached for the phone. There was no tell whatsoever on his face that gave away his thoughts.

I waited for him to laugh, or for pity to enter his eyes. It's what my parents would have done before telling me that art would have no future. I didn't even need to mention the possibility of the art scholarship to know their reactions. A patronizing gleam would take over my dad's eyes as he lectured me on how starving artists were a drain on society and no daughter of his would live that life.

My mother, on the other hand, would raise her voice and shake the sharp green vegetable knife in my direction, as she reminded me of my uselessness and how without them, I wouldn't be able to tie my shoes.

"You took this picture?" Mr. Music's voice crackled like a warm fire.

He startled me right out of my thoughts and into the present.

"Yes?"

"You're not sure?" Now he was looking at me like I was a few rhinestones short of a bedazzled phone case.

"No, I did take it. I just don't know if that's a good thing or not."

His dull brown eyes drilled into me, small wrinkles crinkling at the corners. I sucked in a breath at his expression.

"This is nothing short of amazing, Astrid. Especially, or maybe precisely because it was taken on an old android."

Ryan nudged my ribs with a sharp elbow, but my brain didn't quite get the memo that it should have hurt. It sounded suspiciously like Mr. Music thought my picture was good. Like artistic good.

"You mean that?" The surprise and disbelief practically took on a solid form between us.

"Yes. I do." He spun around and started scrolling through my portfolio again. "Why isn't there any photography in your portfolio?"

"The only pieces in there are assignments I've done. I haven't really had any photography assignments." I shrugged.

"Okay, truth time kid. How serious are you about

studying art? Is this scholarship something you really want to pursue?"

The feverish tone of Mr. Music's voice jazzed me right up, making it hard to sit still.

Did this mean he thought I had a shot? The end of the school year started to look like a bright pinprick of light at the end of a long tunnel, instead of the electric chair waiting to shock the life from me.

"Yes. Absolutely. I love art. I'm not great at everything like drawing, but I can take a decent photo." My nodding didn't begin to even hit the tip of my conviction.

"Show me a few more pictures." He demanded and handed the phone back to me.

When I opened the phone, the picture I'd taken of Beck lit the screen. Warm sepia colors blended across the phone, highlighting the veins in his hand and forearm as he used the cloth to wipe the headlight.

Swiping right, I stopped on a picture of the neighbor girl squatting over a crack in the sidewalk. Her pigtails blew in the wind with wasps of sweaty hair stuck to her forehead.

"This one." I flashed the phone long enough to get a nod, and then found a side profile of my father with a drink in his hand at our old house. He stared at the desk like it offended him for having the audacity to simply be, and his knuckles were nearly white from gripping the glass so hard.

It was the last night before we started packing to move here, to Colorado.

"And this one."

"That's... that picture right there is a great shot." He tapped the screen with his forefinger. "You guys go sit back down and I'll talk to you before you leave."

Less than five minutes was all it took to look at my port-folio and weigh my worth. Was my work really that bad, or was my photography that good? He didn't seem like the kind of guy to cave if I pestered him for his thoughts, so I opted to follow his instructions instead.

Feeling antsy and out of sorts, I was out of the chair before he finished speaking.

Ryan toddled after me, squinting at me as if he didn't recognize me anymore.

"Why are you being weird?" He leaned back in his chair.

"I'm not. Okay, maybe I am. It's just strange getting this kind of attention for something I know my parents wouldn't approve of. It makes me nervous."

And it did. Most days, I would plan and dream of ways to defy them and finally get out from under their roof. It had been my dream since about thirteen when the blinders fell away, revealing what hypocrites they really were.

But putting an actual plan into motion? That took a whole different set of balls I still wasn't used to. I'd get there. But the feeling was alien.

"Your parents, gotcha. You don't need to say anymore. I know all about disapproving parents."

The door to the classroom creaked as it opened and a head stuck in.

"Mr. Music?"

Jonah. The nerd I slammed into the day of the pep rally stood in the door. His hair was artfully disheveled like he ran his hands through it recently, and he kept the majority of his body out in the hallway. Clearly he had other places to be.

"Yes, Mr. Perez?" Mr. Music seemed unusually distracted now. He was always present, always ready with a weird dad joke or strange quip.

"The principal is requesting you in the office." Jonah's voice didn't match his appearance at all.

That day in the library I was too self-absorbed to really notice. And his voice over the microphone was so distant and impersonal, it hadn't hit me until just then.

He had this deep baritone, and a bit of a bite in his words. Almost like he thought he was better than everyone else. As the reigning student body president, I was sure he did. Then there was his meek and nonthreatening appearance. Up close, I could see how attractive he really was, but for some reason it almost seemed like he wanted to tone it down.

Mr. Music sighed and pushed away from the desk. "All right. Class, Mr. Perez is the man in charge while I'm called to the principal's office. Don't get any funny ideas." He wagged his finger at everyone before bustling out of the classroom.

Jonah stepped in and shoved his glasses further up his nose as the door slammed shut. A hush fell over the usually chatty class.

I mean, this crowd wasn't rowdy per se, but Mr. Music was cool and didn't care if people talked while working on their drawing.

A few lone claps echoed through the room, as a guy in the back corner stood up. I twisted in my seat to get a look at what he was doing but Ryan put a hand to my arm and shook his head.

Ignoring him, I rotated until I had a good view of the guy. This was the one class where I paid more attention to the assignments than the students, so I really only knew the people at the table closest to us. His name escaped me but he was definitely in the rough crowd. Black rimmed eyes and spiked hair seemed to suck in the light as he glowered.

Then there was Jonah, standing inside the door but not attempting to make conversation with anyone. He must take orders seriously to stay here while that kid looked at him as if he used the last of his eyeliner and pissed on his hair gel.

"You should leave. You don't want a repeat of what happened last time you were left alone with me." Goth guy pushed himself to a standing position, bracing on his fists that were firmly planted on the table.

Jonah shoved his hands in his khaki pants and rocked back on his feet.

"I don't believe we're alone." He made an exaggerated point of surveying the room. His eyes briefly caught on mine before he looked back to the guy.

"You think you're so smart. Is that it? You think you're better than me?"

Wow. This guy was really getting worked up and Jonah hadn't even done anything, other than remain cool under fire.

"Mike, I don't need to think I'm smarter than you. I know it."

My mouth popped open as Mike's face turned the same color as my mother's violet pansies. That was a slam if I ever heard one. And Jonah had delivered it as if he stated a silly fact like the mountains were closer to the sun.

Mike dodged the edge of the table as he stomped toward Jonah.

There was a lot of anger on Mike's end. Too much for him to be upset over something trivial or superficial. These guys had some kind of history. They were probably childhood best friends or something, but whatever was in the past, Mike had a bully boner for Jonah.

A tick in Jonah's jaw was the only outward sign Mike's temper affected him.

As someone who hated being the center of attention, I hadn't wanted to play into this scene that Jonah would remember for days to come. Everyone staring, whispering and laughing behind his back. I wouldn't wish that horrendous torture on my worst enemy. But I couldn't pull my gaze away even if my mother was beating me over the head with her beloved crystal bowl.

Mike closed the distance. Five feet, two, and then toe to toe with Jonah. His hands connected with his chest and I swore the room vibrated with the force of his crash into the wall.

Jonah winced but didn't make any attempts to defend himself. He merely held his hands up in surrender and dipped his head in submission. It hurt to see him so bowed over when he obviously wasn't even trying to protect himself.

"Mike, there's no need for this. I didn't mean it."

This was wrong. Something was off with this situation, but I couldn't quite figure out exactly how it rang false.

Scooping up my phone, I discreetly angled the camera so I caught Jonah's expression over the bunching of Mike's shoulders.

I slid the phone in my back pocket so no one would suspect I had just created evidence of the attack. It shouldn't have bothered me anyway because half the people in the class were recording. Before the end of the period it would be trending on all social media platforms and circling in private group chats. Jonah was an ass, but now I didn't see him in such a black and white light.

Mike fisted his hands in Jonah's shirt and slammed him against the wall. "When are you gonna give it up?"

This had gone too far. Normally I was the last person to wade into a confrontation, especially with hotheaded, hormone ridden guys, but guilt tugged at the edges of my conscience.

I was the reason that Jonah bumbled his way through his speech at the pep rally. I'd bet my phone that the papers that flew all over the place were his notes.

Regret didn't sit well with me and if I could rectify it, even in a small way, I would. Ryan tried to stop me, but I was small and fast. No way he could have actually detained me without making a scene of our own.

I snuck up on Mike like a panty thief in a sorority house, and ducked under his arm.

This guy really rubbed me the wrong way so I leaned as far away from him as I could while I shoved him away from Jonah.

What I hadn't expected was the hard body of Jonah behind me. Was he some kind of geeky superman? Undercover as the chess geek?

I wasn't distracted for long, because as soon as Mike regained his balance he lunged for me.

Oh fuck.

I hadn't thought this far into it. My pitifully sheltered life flashed before my eyes as the tattooed fist sped toward me.

Ryan barged between us at the last second and ushered him away.

"You need to calm down, man. I know you weren't about to hit my girl. Go sit down."

The sound of Ryan's voice seemed to shake Mike out of his little episode. He cast one lingering look over Jonah that was full of the purest hatred I had ever witnessed before he readjusted his shirt and headed back to his chair.

"Yeah, whatever. You need to teach your girl that

getting between two dudes is fucking dumb." He grumbled the whole way.

Fingers lightly gripped my hips as I was pried away from Jonah. I was still pressed against him, smooshing him between me and the wall. And everyone was staring at us. Me.

Great. Fucking great.

Ryan took my shaking hand and led me to the table. I glanced at Jonah over my shoulder to see if he was all right, but he was already gone.

Chapter 5

"Where'd Jonah go?" Mr. Music slipped into the classroom, heading straight for his desk.

"He, uh, left right before you got here." A timid girl by the door spoke up.

The lingering tension clouding the room must have been all in my head, because the teacher didn't blink an eye. He busied himself as low whispers crept back to normal levels.

Someone was sharpening a pencil at the old metal sharpener bolted to the wall. The sound momentarily blocking out the rest of the students.

"Astrid. What the hell was that?" Ryan bent close, and I could almost see steam rolling out of his nostrils.

If I had a red cape, he'd probably charge.

"Damn right, what the hell was that!" I whispered. "That poor guy didn't do anything. Why did he get attacked like that?"

Some of the fight leaked out of Ryan as he sat back and scrubbed his hand over his face. His lips twisted in a grimace before scooting forward again.

It was almost like he debated on what to tell me. Which meant there was something to tell. And according to the budding friendship I was building with Ryan, he would tell me. If not right now, then by the end of the day.

It became very obvious early on, that Ryan physically couldn't hold his tongue where gossip was concerned. At least not with those he considered a friend.

"You aren't going to believe me, but I have no idea."

Yeah, right. Ryan had a direct line in to every click. It would be an empty night at a Panic concert before Ryan didn't know the dirt. I had no idea why he hung out with me so much.

"Put your eyebrows away. They're distracting me." He covered my eyes with his hand.

Okay. Whatever that meant.

"Seriously. Even if you don't know everything, what do you know?"

My vision brightened when his hand lifted from my eyes.

"I'm telling you, it's paltry crumbs compared to what I normally have. So Mike and Jonah only started going to school here in ninth grade when the district lines were rearranged—"

"What does that mean?" I flicked my gaze over the closest table to make sure no one was paying attention.

They weren't, thankfully. But everyone was working on their project and if we didn't at least pretend to be doing the same then Mr. Music might not be as inclined to help me.

Flipping open to the last page in my sketchbook, I nodded at Ryan to do the same as I arranged my pencils before starting on the drawing.

A small lag in conversation wedged between us as Ryan followed my lead. Then he cleared his throat and focused on his paper as he kept talking.

"I keep forgetting you came from an even smaller town

than Silver Ranch. It's just that we aren't that small because of the city close by. Anyway, the suburbs grow when the city grows. And Denver's been growing for a long time. A few years ago they rearranged the lines so more kids went here and another school was built in Crystal Springs to capture the overflow of students."

Ryan's voice took on a lulling quality as he explained the ins and outs of how they decided who went where. But bottom line, more students came here when the economy started booming.

"Back to Jonah and Mike," I muttered.

"Fine. You're like my little sister after a glitter bomb. You don't give up." He tapped his pencil on the paper and looked up at me.

He paused for dramatic effect and I couldn't stop myself from leaning closer. If he didn't spit it out soon I'd give him his very own septum piercing.

"They started here at the beginning of freshman year and there's always been this sort of bad blood between them. No one that came with them talks about it, but they must have been best friends or something at their old school."

He stopped speaking and started legit drawing on his still life. That speck of information was useless. It didn't give me any insight into Jonah or help me understand why I wanted to stand up for him.

I shook my head to clear my thoughts. This wasn't the time to analyze myself, not when there was a chance I could submit a portfolio for the scholarship. That more important.

"Now, tell me why you felt the need to channel your inner cat woman."

He said that as if it was unheard of for people to stand

up against bullies here. The elite of the school definitely ran in cliques and treated the other students as less than, and there was definitely more powerful cliques than others. But I was sure there were decent people here willing to stand up for others. Right?

"Remember the day of the pep rally?"

"Of course. That was the same day I first talked to you, wasn't it?"

"Yes. Well, I ran into Jonah in the library and I'm pretty sure I made him drop all of his notes. I mean, he could have avoided me too, but I still feel bad. Ya know?"

Ryan's face screwed up in disbelief. "You're telling me, that you had an accidental—I'm assuming this was accidental—run in with Jonah. And now you're all gung-ho for saving him from someone he clearly has history with?"

The way he said that made me sound like I had a savior complex. Which I didn't, at all. In fact, I'd surprised myself by stepping between them, breaking one of my cardinal rules. I didn't ever put myself in a position where people noticed me. On purpose anyway.

I tipped my head back. "It was a spur of the moment decision. I won't suffer from the same sickness twice."

"Good. Because we have some real assholes at this school. Like Trey. Who you should totally take blackmail pictures of."

And just like that we came full circle. Ryan distracted himself with thoughts of one-sided revenge and I let the other conversation drop. The rest of the class was uneventful as we actually worked on our assignment.

I put a little extra work into mine just in case I had a hidden talent that was waiting for the right moment to spring free. Sadly, this wasn't the moment and my flower arrangement resembled a vase of tiny baby fists more than a graceful bundle of fake lilies.

Disgusted with myself, I flung my pencil across the table. It rolled over the side and bounced on the floor, stopping under one of Mr. Music's grungy old man loafers.

"Astrid, if you're giving up this quick, are you sure you want to try for the scholarship?" A smile teased the corners of his mouth, but doubt slithered around my body.

I wanted to do this. But what happened if I wasn't strong enough to hack it? Nope, stop that self-doubt in its tracks. That was what my mother wanted me to think, but I was not who she was molding me to be.

If it wasn't for the Sunday school teacher at my old church, I would without a doubt be reviewing potential bachelors to target in college Bible study. Ms. Cantrell never came out and said my parents were bad in so many words. But what she did say encouraged me to want more for myself than my parents led me to believe I was worthy of.

"Astrid, your life is yours and yours alone. It's okay to live it for yourself. Everyone has a passion, and you just have to find yours, doll. Try lots of things until you find it, but when you do, don't let anyone stop you from pursuing your own path."

Such simple words. Funny how common, everyday words had the power to change your outlook on life and yourself.

"Of course, I want to go for it."

He grinned and pulled up a spare chair. "Perfect! All right. So question. Do you have a camera?"

"No," I drew out the vowel because I could see where this was going and it wasn't going the direction I wanted it to. I didn't have a job so I couldn't afford a camera.

"Okay, not a big deal. I actually have a contact at the DU that'd be willing to help out. He was my roommate when we were in college, so he owes me a few favors."

Mr. Music laughed like we were all in on this secret joke, but I had no idea what the joke was.

I also didn't know what to say. So I stared at him.

"Next question, do you have a car?"

This one I could answer.

"Yes." See, that was easy.

"Cool, cool. What I want you to do, is go over to the university tomorrow between the hours of five and seven. Those are his office hours. We don't have a photography class here and he can get you suited up with everything you need to know. I did some quick checking and I don't see any reason why you couldn't enter with a photography portfolio." He slid a sheet of paper over with a name and address written in large block letters.

Dan Brown

1001 Smith Hall, Room 201

Denver, CO

THE PAPER BLURRED as my freaking tear ducts stopped working. Fuck these teenage hormones! I didn't even know why this affected me so strongly. He didn't promise me the scholarship—not that he could—and he didn't even say I'd have a good shot.

Mr. Music was literally only giving me the means to take the opportunity in my own hands. And that... that meant a lot to me.

"I'll go as soon as school's over." My voice wavered over the last few words and Ryan awkwardly patted me on the back.

"If you take his advice to heart and work hard, you might just be able to make it as one of the two finalists of SRHS. That's the best I can do for you at this point. But I'm willing to help you as much as I can along the way."

I glanced up and Mr. Music's kind eyes. They reminded me so much of Ms. Cantrell. The bell rang and with purposely measured movements, I gathered my things and left the classroom with Ryan. He didn't say anything about the interaction with the teacher, so I didn't either. Sometimes the best friends understood when you didn't need to talk about it.

The next twenty-four hours were the slowest of my life. I managed to avoid the parentals for the most part. It was Wednesday night, so my dad was at a Bible study for the elders and my mother was with the women's committee, planning the next fellowship dinner.

For the first time in my life, the youth program didn't have a Wednesday study group. Hallelujah! Dad always made me go and give lessons, like I was going to follow in his footsteps someday. I wasn't.

I kept waiting for my dad to announce we were starting one and I was the trailblazer to get other kids to join. If luck was in my favor, he wouldn't have this bright idea until after I graduated.

Eight months. A little over eight months and I would be legally free to leave this house behind.

Exhilaration and worry waged war in my thoughts. I couldn't decide if I was more excited the end was near, or afraid I wouldn't have a plan, and I'd have to stay here anyway.

That would be the worst, to stay here knowing if I'd done something differently, then I could have left on my own.

At school, concentration was fleeting, and I was a poor conversation partner for Ryan. He understood, though. He babbled on about his newest secret crush to fill the silence.

We sat under one of the only trees that actually resembled a tree at lunch. Ninety percent of trees here were evergreens and didn't provide a whole lot of shade from the burning sun.

"Did you hear what I just said?" Ryan nudged my foot with his.

"Yes. Pat gave you googly eyes and now he's in love with you forever. What kind of name is Pat? The only other one I know is an elder at church, and he resembles flubber more than a sexy beast of a teenager." I ribbed him for his choice of crush. I really didn't care, but it was fun to rile him.

He scowled. "Like he chose his name. He's Irish and it's short for Patrick. Attraction isn't in the name, but the personality."

I laughed and crossed my ankles. "Very philosophical of you. Will you tell me the ones that are the hardest to love are the ones that need it the most? I beg to differ there. My mother needs no extra love."

Across the courtyard, Rhys leaned against the faded brick wall with one of the dance girls pressed against him. Her fingers trailed up his chest as she said something to him, but he wasn't looking at her.

He was staring after Trey who was jogging toward the parking lot. Those guys were suspicious as fuck. I didn't know what Trey was up to, but I swore he was a criminal in the making.

A balled-up paper towel whacked me in the forehead.

"Nice." I batted it away.

"You weren't listening to me. Everybody needs love.

Including Pat. But anyway. Are you going to the university today?"

The sun was crazy hot today with its insistent rays of sunshine. I grabbed the floppy hat off my backpack and plopped it on my head. No one else here had any kind of head protection on, so I looked like a unicorn. That was okay, I was an incognito unicorn, since the hat hid some of my features.

"I was planning on it."

"Want me to ride with?" Ryan sounded a little too excited. Probably looking for an excuse to ogle hot college guys.

"Nah, I feel like this is a journey I need to take alone. It will just make me nervous if you go with me."

My sunglasses went on right before I leaned back on my hands, completing my *I don't give a fuck* unicorn persona. The courtyard was an interesting place for congregating, with lots of open green space and benches. My last school didn't have this type of freedom and it was fascinating to watch all the students play court in the sunshine.

Without even realizing it, Rhys was the focal point of many jealous and lustful stares. Even though he wasn't the star of a school sport, he was a big deal.

Then there were the little cliques that rotated zones around the grass. They all seemed to center on the jocks, but each held their own court. Jonah was out here too, sitting with a group of students that had textbooks laid out around them. Jonah was clearly the leader of that group, sitting higher above the rest and shaking a pencil at everyone.

"All right, fine. But you meet me in the art room before school. I want to know exactly what happened. Maybe you'll meet the man of your dreams tonight. I need to make sure I'm there for you every step of the way." Ryan tilted his head down and his sunglasses slid to the tip of his nose.

I didn't respond as I took a bite of my apple and continued people watching. Why couldn't I make a living doing this? I'd be freaking amazing at it.

Well, I guess there was the pap, but I didn't want to be one of those creepos spreading celebs secrets like STDs all over the internet.

The bell rang and Ryan picked my bag up as we headed into the school. I couldn't tell you what happened through the last two blocks of the day. My mind fluttered all over the place as my fingers kept curling around the folded piece of paper in my pocket.

Jonah passed me in the hallway when I was on my way out to the parking lot, and even though we hadn't touched he did send a nice hate filled glare my way.

You're welcome buddy. That showed me for trying to be on the right side of good Samaritan.

Sliding on my sunglasses, I pretended to look right over him as I skated around a pimply couple swapping saliva right in the center of the hall. I had better things to do than worry about Jonah's volatile moods.

Outside, the warm breeze and fresh air pumped me up to the point I thought I could float right over to the university. Excitement buzzed at my fingers and toes as I raced to Freda. In just a short drive and mini waiting period I'd have a better sense of how I could create a portfolio.

"Don't get kidnapped!" Ryan yelled from across the parking lot.

I flipped him the bird and a death scowl for making people look my way and slammed my door shut. But even that couldn't distract me from my mission.

Traffic was light right before rush hour so I managed to

make it there an hour early. Hip restaurants around campus taunted me with delicious smells, but my stomach was too tied up to satisfy my hunger.

This would be me next year. I would be like these girls that were taking their destiny in their own hands. Said girls passed by me as they laughed and bumped into each other. Going to class, a restaurant, anywhere they wanted with no one who cared if they had lives outside of church.

I see you, wonderfully independent college experiences, and I'm coming for you.

People were piling out of the Smith building as I reached the door. They were oblivious to me, so I had to wait on the side until a gap appeared. Sliding right through, the hall was strangely quiet and my steps echoed off the walls. Everyone had fled the building, leaving only one or two stragglers behind.

I didn't know what I expected, but I thought there'd be more people lurking about and doing college things. I know they held night classes here. Posters and artwork hung on the walls reminding me of a much more sophisticated elementary school, giving credit to their students and fluffing them up with the warm and fuzzies.

I stopped at the end of the hall and pulled the folded piece of paper from my pocket to check the room number. It was more of an unconscious movement than anything else. Since about three minutes into my possession, the name and address was seared into my brain. Room 201.

The second floor was completely empty and it was still at least thirty minutes before the time Mr. Music gave me. National park stickers plastered the face of door 201, giving a little insight into the guy that was Mr. Music's old room-mate. From outward appearances, he seemed like he could be a cool person.

People who hiked and visited national parks as a hobby would be cool, right? I bet he loved photography too, and living in the moment. That's how I imagined outdoorsy people to be.

Not that I would know. The most I knew about untamed nature were the church retreats, where we studied the word of God in the great outdoors. One time I did get to go kayaking, but that was about as adventurous as it got. It was a lake with lots of long, wooden docks, and an abundance of buoys roping off no go areas, so take it for what it was worth.

The door was halfway open, and the lights were on inside. Maybe he was here early.

My pulse thumped so hard, I could feel it in my wrists. Swallowing down my excitement, I stepped through the door.

The room was completely empty, with only a little scuffling coming from the closet.

Ha! He was here. I eased forward, not sure if I was ready to alert Mr. Brown to my presence just yet.

Hello was on the tip of my tongue when I peeked around the door.

A regular storage closet, similar to what we had in Mr. Music's room, was the first thing I registered.

The second, was a guy with his pants open and a girl on her knees in front of him. He moaned when she must have done something extraordinary with her tongue.

Fuck. This turned me on and mortified me all at the same time.

A soft gasp escaped me as heat flooded my cheeks.

His eyes snapped open and I flushed even deeper. This guy's eyes were the perfect mix of yellow gold and vibrant green. And the fact that his attention was locked on me short-circuited my brain.

It was only seconds of that heated gaze until his eyes widened. I guessed the haze of passion muddled his mind. Not that I could relate, since you know, still virgin here, but I could imagine.

"Oh fuck!" He shoved the girl away and she released his dick with a pop.

"Eek!" I screamed and spun away. As soon as the girl fell back on her butt, his angry erect dick bobbed hello.

And. It. Was. Pierced.

"Fuckin hell. Who are you and why didn't you knock?" Anger whipped through the small enclosed space.

"I, um... I'm sorry. I'm here to see Mr. Brown. I was told he'd be here after five."

"Yeah, well. It's not even four-thirty so it might have been a good idea to knock. Don't you think?" His voice has lost some of its heat and was now a nice level of irritated.

I couldn't blame him. Although, dude probably shouldn't be getting a blowjob in a school closet. That opened up risks he wouldn't have had in his dorm room.

"Thatch, call me later and we can finish up where we left off." A wet smack signaled a kiss goodbye, and the girl breezed past me without a second glance.

I'd love to have that kind of confidence, where I didn't care about people catching me doing something sinfully illicit.

Hands on my shoulders propelled me out of the doorway and into the room. I was almost afraid to turn around, not wanting to see what his eyes looked like now that I'd pretty much ruined any chance of friendship.

"Astrid, right?"

All right. It was time. I spun on my heel and stared right

at him as he shuffled stuff around on the desk. Amazingly, I didn't burst into flames.

"Yes. But you're not Mr. Brown?" I hadn't meant it as a question but he clearly wasn't more than twenty or twenty-one.

"Nope. I'm his assistant. He's out sick today but he sent me an email of what to gather for you. I'm Thatcher by the way."

He turned around and leaned on the desk, extending his hand to me.

His eyes were warm, the yellow almost nonexistent now. That was too bad. It was a good look for him. He jerked his head to the side to move his hair out of his face.

Charcoal stained his fingers and small paint splatters specked the back of his hand. Thatcher shook his hand again to get my attention and I jumped, thrusting my hand into his. Only after I grabbed his hand did it dawn on me. He was touching his junk seconds ago and he didn't wash his hands. Oh well, too late now.

"Sorry. It's been a weird day."

"I bet," A shimmer of amusement rolled over his eyes and I instinctively knew he was referring to my cock-blocking moment.

I flicked my eyes down to his zipper but he had definitely lost the stiffness in his... posture.

I cleared my throat. "So, what did Mr. Brown leave for me?"

"Here," he reached behind him and grabbed the box. Setting it on the table beside me he started taking out different items and arranging them on the table.

A few old text books on photography, the art of light and composition. It was the next thing that came out that brightened my world in the sweetest way.

He held a black camera case in his hand and his fingers all but mesmerized me as they opened the buckle, revealing a slightly beat up but beautiful camera.

"Nikon N2000. Here, you can hold it."

I gingerly took it from his hands and turned it over in mine, tracing my finger along the lens.

I'd never had my own camera, other than my Android, and the experience of holding one for my own personal use was a thrill I hadn't experienced before. Did Thatcher realize this was such a profound moment for me?

He probably wouldn't care if he did. Not some cool art major. And especially not over the dorky high school, cock-blocking student.

"Is there a manual with this thing?" I glanced up and met his stare.

"Sure is. But I can show you the basics. My emphasis isn't photography, but I've taken a few beginner classes."

He took the camera back and ran through the different settings, basic functionality and information on the lens.

I'm sure if I were a cartoon, I'd have pounding hearts circling my head. This was heaven for sure.

"So what is Dan giving you all this stuff for?" A note of curiosity threaded through his words as he leaned back on the desk, putting a couple feet of space between us.

"There's a scholarship opportunity I really want to try for. I would love to say I'm a real photographic genius, but really, I suck at all other mediums. Photography is something I've enjoyed as a phone hobby, and the only real chance I have to make it as one of the school finalists." Self-deprecation soaked my voice.

"Yeah, I heard about that. That's got to be pretty exciting. I know I'd loved to have had an opportunity like that when I was in school."

"You aren't here on scholarship?"

I cringed as soon as the words left my mouth. Thatcher had an artsy sort of grunge going on. With a threadbare red flannel, opened over a black T-shirt, paired with ripped jeans, he wasn't exactly winning any fashion awards. But he didn't strike me as poor either, and that's what I just implied. "I didn't mean it like that."

He chuckled under his breath. "Don't worry about it. And yes, I *am* here on scholarships, and a work-study program, but I also have my fair share of student loans. So an opportunity to get a full ride, that'd be golden."

I loved that he wasn't trying to make this whole situation more awkward than it had to be.

"Well, that's if I can get one of the finalist spots from our school, but then I'd have to win the whole thing. I'm cutting it a little short since this is my senior year." Damn, the bitterness was strong.

"If you don't mind, can I see some of your work? I might be able to offer some suggestions." He seemed genuinely interested.

"Yeah, sure." I pulled up the same pictures that I showed to Mr. Music. Biting my lip, I waited until he had looked his fill. These people, man, they had great poker faces. Their expressions didn't give a clue on if they thought I was the next Henri-Cartier Bresson, or if I was just another wannabe with no talent.

Thatcher whistled under his breath. "These are actually really good."

"Gee thanks," I couldn't hold back on the snark. His surprise offended me a little.

"No, listen. I didn't know what I was meeting you here for, but you definitely have an eye. What's your plan? When do you have to have a portfolio by?" He glanced up and a buzzing raced along my spine when we locked eyes.

I also blanked on any answer. Fuck. I wanted to be an adult and get away, so I better start getting my stuff together.

"I need to figure out how to use the camera first and then see what inspires me. I haven't been given the deadline yet." Lies. I totally had, but it completely escaped my poor addled brain.

"Were you supposed to study with Dan or anything like that? Or just pick up this stuff?" He packed everything back in the box.

"Just pick this stuff up." The box was heavier than I thought when I took it from him. It was the weight of opportunity in my hands. I gripped the box a little tighter at this symbolic moment.

Thatcher hummed softly under his breath while he watched me. "I'll tell you what. Let's exchange numbers and I can help you with photography. Any help is an advantage for you at this point."

What the flipping flip?

"You want to help me? Why? You don't even know me." I wanted to accept his offer but there had to be a catch. He must be angling for more backroom blowjobs.

He sighed. "Listen. I don't know what has you so determined to get this scholarship, but you practically have hope and desperation written all over you. Consider this my good deed."

Who the fuck did this guy think he was? I bristled and lifted my lip in a sneer. Thatcher's brows drew together as if he didn't quite understand why I was getting angry.

First Beck, offering me his one good deed of the year.

Now Thatcher, wanting to take me under his wing because he felt sorry for me.

No, I'd show them. I didn't need anyone's pity to get ahead in life. I was strong. I was smart. And I would do it on my own.

No, that wasn't quite right. I was going to accept the help of these guys that thought I needed it, but not in the way they wanted to help.

They wouldn't even know they contributed to success.

Chapter 6

"That's okay. I don't need your pity or your help. Thanks for meeting me with this stuff." I lifted the box in a salute and turned my back to him.

"If you change your mind, my name is Thatcher Reed. And I don't pity you. I admire you actually." He called after me.

I ignored his words and marched out to my car with a new fire in my heart.

As soon as I got strapped in, I dialed Ryan on the Bluetooth. A deliciously intriguing idea popped in my head and if I could pull it off, it would be epic.

"Hey girl! It's not even five yet. You got the goods?" He asked like I went for some kind of drug deal.

Rolling my eyes, I eased out of the parking lot to head toward home.

"I did. An instruction manual, some textbooks and a camera. A real life freaking camera to create art with, Ry." I nearly squealed.

"It must be good shit because you sound like a basket of sunshine in a snowstorm. Want to grab dinner and we can look over the stuff and do some test shots?" Loud clanking came down the line, so he must have been out somewhere already.

"No, I'm going home to get started on some research. But I was calling for another reason. I had an idea on what I can do for my portfolio submission. I'm reconsidering following Trey. There are a few people I'd like to follow. I could expose their lies in a glorious display of art. Without anyone actually knowing it was them, of course." I was rambling but my excitement was getting the better of me.

"Whoa, whoa, whoa. There's a lot there. Why the sudden change and how'd you come up with this idea?" Ryan sounded confused but not against it. There was definitely no disapproval in his voice.

Ryan, always up for some good snooping and gossip.

I didn't want to tell him about the storeroom or the revelation I had come to in the last thirty minutes. That would be too much embarrassment for one day. And knowing Ryan, he would never let me forget it. He thrived on stuff like that.

"I've been wracking my brain trying to figure out what I could do that would be worth anything. The only thing I'm really good at is candid shots when people don't know I'm watching."

"You mean stalking." He interrupted.

"Shut up. I mean watching. Anyway. If that's what got Mr. Music to take a chance on me and get a loan from his friend, then that's the line that I'm going to follow." I pulled out of the college, leaving endless dreams and potential roads of success behind me.

"Ooh. The possibilities are endless on the dirt you can get on these guys. I mean the art you could make." He cleared his throat and then busted up laughing.

"But there are rules, Ryan. I won't take any pictures that

will get me into trouble. And no shots of faces. I want the pictures to be abstract enough that I can use them and they won't be identifiable. And any juicy info we learn, stays between us. Can you promise that, Ryan? I can't let you in on this if you can't keep secrets."

He scoffed like he was highly offended. "Girl, I'm gay. I just came out of the closet at the end of last year. If there's anyone that can keep a secret, it's me. Don't worry. Your scholarship is more important than me trying to get Trey his comeuppance. You have my word, Ass."

I sputtered. "Ass?!"

"Sorry! It seemed like a good nickname in the moment. I didn't think about As-strid starting with ass. It was a mistake, I swear." Rolling laughter filled the speakers of my sweet Freda.

"Whatever. Don't do it again."

"Sure, sure." He sounded like he was crying now.

"That's all I wanted to say." And then we descended into awkward territory. My ability to make small talk ranked right up there with my ability to draw.

Ryan didn't let the conversation lag, though. That's one of the things I loved about him. He could talk for days and I didn't have to do anything.

"This weekend, Remy Masters is having a party. Trey and his buddies will be there for sure, along with at least half the school. That's the perfect place for you to get some practice in. Everyone will be drinking so they won't even notice you have a camera in your hand."

I wished. Mother Dearest would never let me go to a party. I was lucky to have any freedom at all with Freda. And that was only because she worked so late here, she nor dad were hardly ever home anymore.

"I won't be able to go to a party. Remember my parents?

Parties are definitely not on the approved list of outings for their religious morals."

"Hmm. You just let me think on that. Old Ryan will come up with a way to get you out of the house." He murmured.

"Sure, if you can make it happen without my parents finding out, then I would love to go. No drinking though." I had to break myself into the freedom with carefully planned out baby steps. With alcohol, I was bound to do something stupid that screwed it all up.

"Got it. If you want to catch these guys in the act of something scandalous, then you best be sober anyway. I'll drink enough for the both of us."

I tapped my fingers on the steering wheel. "You do that. Let me know when you find a way for me to sneak out."

He groaned. "Is this your passive aggressive way of saying goodbye?"

A small chuckle escaped me but I didn't respond. It was true, I was ready to get off the phone.

"Then I guess I won't tell you about the laptop my mom wants to sell." His words ended on a question when he damn well knew I wanted a laptop.

"What? What kind? How old?" I jumped all over the opportunity to get my grubby hands on another tool to fuel my plans.

"An old Dell. Maybe two years old. My mom is horrible on technology, I could count on my hands the number of times I've seen her on it." Static fills the line like he's rolling around in bed.

"How much?" I winced at how high my voice raised. Hopefully I didn't deafen him with my banshee impersonation.

"Two hundred even. I already got it for you, and she

said if you don't have it, you can make payments." The bastard was smug, knowing exactly what he was doing for me by snagging his mom's laptop.

"I have it! I'll have crisp twenties for you tomorrow. Thank you!" This was the most excitement I'd ever heard in my voice and if this wasn't such a big deal, I'd be concerned.

"Awesome. I'll catch you at school tomorrow, Ass." He drew out the last word.

"Bye." I flipped the bird at the stereo like he could see me and disconnected.

My street was empty except for a few cars parked on the road as I rolled down it. I was ashamed to admit that my eyes were pulled to Rhys' house more than once as I passed by. As the most imposing house on the block, the yard was immaculate with groomed shrubs and beautiful, bright flowers, and the white, wicker porch furniture that looked like it was fresh off of the showroom floor.

Which was odd, wasn't it? The Colorado sunshine was harsh and unforgiving. After a few days in the sun, the fabric would have faded at least a little bit.

When I pulled into the driveway I hopped out with my box. If luck were on my side I'd be able to get the box upstairs without any questions. Balancing the box in one arm, I reached out to open the front door, only to have it whisked out of my reach.

Startled, I stumbled backward and glanced up as Stan Bennett stepped out onto the porch. His graying hair was swept away from his face and he had a slightly ruddy complexion that hadn't been there the other night.

"Astrid," his voice was jolly as he steadied me with a hand on my shoulder. "What a pleasant surprise."

"Mr. Bennett. Nice to see you." The sharp smell of his cologne assaulted my nose. Wow, he needed to lay off the scent. No one must have told him about the two squirt rule.

I looked past him, half expecting and dreading Rhys or Trey to follow him, but the hall was empty. Was it crushing disappointment for elated relief that blanketed me? Maybe a bit of both, for different reasons. Now was not the time to examine those feelings too closely.

"We'll have to have you over for dinner one night, dear. Trey has spoken so highly of you." He tightened his tie and his fingers readjusted the clip. He looked like the kind of man that liked to be perfectly put together.

Um, no. I'd rather not. I'm pretty sure a Brazilian wax by fire would be less painful than dinner with Trey and his family.

"That would be delightful." I smiled, trying not to gag.

Although, if I wanted to watch them, then what better way than to enter their home on invitation. Just think of all the juicy information I could gain. There would be no picture taking. It wasn't like I could hide the camera in my hair.

"Great. I'll have Barb set it up with your mother. They're becoming thick as thieves already." He chuckled under his breath as he leaned over me, like he was sharing a dirty secret.

Instead of staying to indulge him, I sailed right past him into the house. "I'm looking forward to it. Have a nice day, Mr. Bennett."

I didn't wait for the door to shut as I jogged up the stairs. The house was quiet, so Mother Dearest must still be at work. Dad was probably in the study, doing whatever it was he did in there. It's always been a huge mystery, but I hadn't cared enough to actually investigate.

This was perfect. Neither parental ever came to my

room and checked up on me, so I'd have a little bit of time to myself. I might actually be able to keep this stuff without them seeing the extent of it.

At my window seat, I set out the books and camera, then slid the box in my closet. The next two hours, I poured over the textbooks, soaking in as much information as I could. I was so invigorated with all of this knowledge, there was enough energy coursing through my body to power the suburb.

"Astrid!"

Oh joy. Mother Dearest was home.

I stretched when I stood and headed out to the hall.

"Coming." Taking the steps two at a time, it only took a few seconds to reach the bottom. My mother was sitting at the kitchen table, pulling off her clunky pumps and rubbing her feet. As a pharmacy tech at the local pharmacy, her job required lots of standing. I didn't feel any pity for her though. She chose that career and she had to live with the good and the bad.

"Yes, Mom?"

She looked up at me and her bloodshot eyes gave her a harsh and haggard appearance.

"Where are your applications for college? I spoke to the counselor this morning and they said that early admission has already passed." Her mouth dipped down at the corner.

My eyes widened as I tried to think of a good response. I knew early admission had already passed, but I also didn't want to apply to the colleges that she wanted me to.

"I was actually at the university about scholarship opportunities tonight."

"The university? We already decided on the Colorado Christian University or the Bible College. Your father wants you to follow in his footsteps." Her tone brooked no argument. They decided where I should go. They'd decide what I would study, and who I would marry if they could.

"I was thinking I could go to the university. They have a lot of different programs for undergraduate degrees in case I want options." Of course I wanted options but I couldn't come right out and tell her that.

She sat back and pulled out the hair clip holding her bun in place. "If we're paying for your college, you don't get a choice. Anyway, your indecisiveness shows how much you don't know about the world. You'll do what's practical and won't be a waste of our money."

"You mean the church's money?" I covered my mouth with my palm.

Oh shiznit. That popped out before I knew I was even thinking it.

My mother slowly stood up, and stepped so close her warm breath fanned my face. Her hand flashed out, catching the hair at the base of my neck. I squeaked in pain as my head jerked back.

"What did you just say? I know you didn't put down your father's job and spit on the fact the church takes care of us." She yanked harder and I bent back to lessen the bite of pain.

This was new for her. She'd never laid hands on me before, and for some insane reason, this seemed like the real her. Like the mother I'd been living with all of these years was a lie, and the shell she wanted everyone to see had slowly cracked and fell away, until it only left this version of herself.

"I didn't mean it like that. I only meant that if I could get a scholarship, then the church could put the money toward other things."

"Stupid girl. I better not hear you talk about the church

or their generosity that way again." She shoved me away from her and I stumbled into the wall. "Talk to the counselor tomorrow about the two colleges your father approved of. End of discussion."

"Yes, ma'am." I mumbled as I scurried out of the kitchen.

How could someone treat their child so coldly? If I ever had kids, I'd be a damn good mother. I had the perfect example of how not to be. The corners of my eyes burned with unshed tears, but I refused to let them fall. A deep, steady breath helped to calm my emotions, as I headed back to my room.

The door to the study was partly open and my dad's shadow darkened the desk. My mother hadn't been quiet. And I for sure hadn't been quiet when she had a hold of my hair. So my dad had just ignored it all. Sitting there in his study like it hadn't even mattered. He was never mean or abusive to me. No, the only one that offered me that particular joy was my mother. But sometimes, when he refused to step in like this, I hated him just as much. For such Godly people, their sense of right and wrong was a warped and distorted compass that I doubted would ever point them true.

Maybe I'd snag some photos of my parents too. I'd never dream about using them for the portfolio, but something about having photo evidence of their truth empowered me.

Even if I never did anything with it, it would be priceless to me.

THE NEXT FEW days passed fairly uneventful. Mr. Music worked with me on the side to master using the camera. He gave me a pass on the regular assignments to work on my portfolio. That was a major boon I would be forever grateful for.

I was happy to say that I'd make some pretty great photos with the play on light in the back of the class. Every time I played with the light and the placement of the random object of the day, I learned a little more. Understood the art a little better.

Friday at lunch was another sunny day where I looked like the despondent vampire with a sun allergy, all wrapped up in my floppy hat and sunglasses. It was especially ridiculous when everyone around me was soaking up as much vitamin D as they could. They might as well have been laying naked and horizontal to get the maximum amount of rays.

"Astrid, did you know that Trey and Rhys will be there at the party this weekend?" Ryan nudged my leg with his bright red Nikes.

"Isn't that the point of going to the party? To have an opportunity to see them in their natural habitat, when they would be most likely to have their guard down?"

"Are you wearing a barbed thong or something? You're acting like you have spurs up your ass." Ryan crossed his arms and openly lusted after Pat, who was standing in attendance with the in crowd. Right next to Rhys actually, but who was watching? Not me.

"Sorry, Ry. My mother made me fill out college applications last night to the colleges they approved of."

"No apology required." He shrugged.

"What were you saying? Trey and Rhys will be at the party?" I prompted and attempted to look at least a little remorseful. Ryan shouldn't have to put up with my poor attitude.

"Trey and Rhys are going to be at the party. Didn't you say their dad is an associate of your dad's?"

My gaze connected with Rhys' for a fleeting second before I broke contact and turned my attention to the parking lot instead.

"Yeah, but I don't hang out with them, so I can't tag along and be like 'oh hey guys, can I come and take pictures of you without your permission?'" I plucked a piece of lush green grass and tossed it Ryan's way.

He snorted and wiped the grass off his lap. "Of course not. But your parent's don't know that. I say you tell your mom you're going to hang out with Rhys. That's the more believable of the two options anyway. No way your mom would think you would really hang out with a prick like Trey."

That was debatable. I almost felt like mom and Trey were cut from the same cloth, because they were certainly both stitched together with self-entitlement and a touch of cruelty.

"Trey hasn't showed that side of himself to my parents. He's all manners and smiles."

He immediately shifted back to the important conversation. "Your parents sound like real schmoozers. If your mom thinks you're going to hang out with the son of your dad's work associate, she'll be too busy planning your wedding to worry about where you are." Ryan widened his eyes like he had single handedly earned my acceptance into college with his mere suggestion.

"I don't know. My mom's weird about that kind of stuff." And she was. I wouldn't admit it to him, but this was actually pretty brilliant, and she could totally take the bait. Then again, she could see right through me and call Rhys' mom to confirm.

"Humor me. If she doesn't go for it, I'll sneak you out and she'll never know."

At this point in my life, so close to freedom, I was starting to feel reckless. If I didn't start testing the boundaries now, then I'd be stuck until graduation and that would hinder all of my plans. The last thing I wanted was to tether myself to them for longer than absolutely necessary.

"I'll try it. If it backfires, you have to give me all the juicy gossip."

"Girl, like keeping my lips sealed was even an option. Of course I'd give the gossip." He patted my knee.

The bell rang, and the throng of students started to pile inside the doors. How could they be so eager to rush back inside? All that waited for us were heartaches and pop quizzes.

"I'll catch you later, Astrid. Pat is calling my name." Ryan touched my arm.

Scrunching up my nose, I twisted around to see Pat talking to Rhys in the corner.

"Not literally. You're so crazy sometimes." He rolled his eyes and loped off toward where Pat stood by the front doors.

I took the path less traveled and entered from the side. English was my next class so I had to stop and switch my books. Two more hours, and then I'd put Ryan's idea to the test.

By the time I finally got to my car, I'd taken two quizzes and read two chapters from the textbooks I'd gotten from the university. Using all my downtime was becoming a very efficient way to learn as much as I could.

"Astrid." Ryan jogged up to me, beaming from ear to ear.

I smiled in return. "What are you so happy about?"

"You'll never guess what! Hey, can you drop me off at home? I'll tell you on the way." He ran around the car, nearly knocking over a freshman walking by.

The kid flipped us the bird and kept on walking.

"Sure, I'd love to give you a ride." I answered, even though he wasn't really asking.

He fingered the magpie card hanging from the rearview mirror, as I shut the door and turned on the ignition.

"What's this?"

I left the car in park as I turned the card over so he could see the lyric. The Avett Brothers were one of my favorites that I rotated on the regular.

Head Full of Doubt/Road Full of Promise was possibly one of the most meaningful songs for me. Other teenagers went to vapid parties and dreamed of boys who only wanted empty one-night stands. But me? I wanted something more significant. Something that couldn't be taken from me. And I found some of that in the Avett Brothers lyrics.

"Decide what to be and go be it. What's that from?"

"Only one of the best songs ever." Shifting into drive, I navigated out of the pit of hormones and despair. In other words, the high school parking lot.

"Any way. I have a date to the party Saturday night." He bounced in his seat, pretending to wipe a tear from his eye.

"Ryan, I thought the whole point was to go incognito so I could get some great shots of bad decisions."

"Don't worry, there will be plenty of those. But that isn't even the best part!"

He was starting to scare me. If there was one thing I learned about Ryan, it was to be afraid of anything that excited him. Wow, there were so many places I could take that, but I wasn't going to. Nope.

"And that is..."

"Rhys was there when I walked up to Pat, all cool and nonchalant. You know what he asked? He asked if you were coming to the party with me."

"What?" I screeched.

The red light barely caught my attention as I slammed on the brakes and shoved a finger in my ear for a good wiggle. I had to have heard him wrong. I was bottom of the rung, low end of the food chain, practically invisible. Yeah, he had dinner at my house and we had our little tiff, but in no parallel universe did Rhys care if I went to a party or not.

"Rhys? The king of the school?" That might be a stretch but everywhere I saw that guy, girls were falling over him and guys were trying to be his friend. I'm pretty sure the new choir teacher swooned when he passed by her the other day in the hall.

"Yes! He is the top tier for sure. I may hate Trey, but Rhys is a whole other bag of cookies. Completely edible, white chocolate macadamia nut cookies." He hummed in appreciation.

"He's pretentious and he doesn't police Trey at all. If he's such a big deal at school, shouldn't he take responsibility and do something about his asshole behavior?" He seemed like an okay guy, but if he wasn't willing to correct the wrongs of his cousin, he couldn't be *that* great. And I wasn't talking about a random punch in the hallway. I'd seen Trey around school and he was the same douche every day. If Rhys cared to do anything about it, he would... I don't know, but it would be nice if he could at least appear to make an effort.

Ryan laid his hand over mine at the steering wheel,

where my knuckles had whitened from my grip.

"Easy there, killer. He's not so bad. I don't know what the deal is with him and his cousin, but he's always been nice to me. Even when other people were trying to make me feel less than the candy wrapper on the sidewalk. That makes him okay in my book." Some of the sassiness left his voice. He really did believe Rhys was a good guy.

I still wasn't convinced.

A small pang dinged around in my chest. Ryan was openly gay and thriving now, but it hadn't started out that way. It made me wish I could have been here to be his friend when he really needed one.

"I'm sorry you had to go through that. I'm glad he wasn't a jerk to you."

He blew a harsh breath from between his teeth and fell back onto the seat.

"Man, I was all excited because he was asking about you, thinking maybe he'd be good for you. I didn't realize you had such a hate on for him."

I sputtered and laughter escaped. "What are you talking about?"

"You got all worked up there. You don't think there could be anything between the two of you? He was very curious. You don't want to know what else he said about you?" He taunted in a singsong voice.

I was speechless. Utterly speechless. These types of conversations where we talked about boys I liked or boys that liked me were completely foreign. At the same time, a gnawing curiosity was tearing away at my self-control, and a small smile slipped onto my face.

"Aha. You do want to know. I can tell from your secretive little smile, that regardless of what you think about him as a person, you want to jump his bones. Or bone."

"Ryan! I do not." He snorted. "Okay, I'd have to be dying of a deadly, pus-oozing disease and I'd still have to admit he's hot." My mouth formed awkwardly around the admission, but what the hell. I spoke truth.

"I'll have to take you to watch a hockey practice sometime. And all that aggression is really good for the soul. I mean our greedy little souls, not theirs."

We laughed and it felt really good. Normal. I had a normal friend. There was no way I could stop the glowing smile that spread across my face. Too bad Ryan took it as my love of Rhys.

"I told him, why yes, you would be there with me every step of the way. He then proceeded to tell me that maybe he would see us there. Isn't that awesome?" His excitement was too loud for the small enclosure of Freda.

I almost lost an eardrum from the strength of his yell.

"That's the whole conversation? He asked if I was going and that he might see us there? I don't get it. It sounds like just a regular conversation." Ryan had some kind of super-power to read his mind if he pulled more from his words other than friendly small talk.

"Ugh. What are we going to do with you? Don't you know that in hot guy speak, he practically proclaimed his undying love and asked you out all at once?" His hands flailed with each word.

We pulled up outside of his house and I put the car into park.

"I love you, Ryan. You are the best, and only friend I have at this school. But I don't know what that means. And I'm not convinced that's accurate. And I'm going to work on my portfolio anyway, so I won't have time for him." I leaned my head on the headrest and turned toward him. From his expression, he hadn't liked what I said.

"You're hopeless. Absolutely hopeless. I want that for

you. To get a kickass portfolio and get a sweet ride to college. But I also want you to experience crushes and be crushed on. I'm already too cynical. Let me live vicariously through you." He pouted like that was going to sway me.

And honestly, it kind of did.

I sighed. "We'll see how it plays out. It's not like you don't have Pat for your puppy love infatuation."

"That works for me. And did you hear me say I'm too cynical? You're this innocent dove flapping through your teenage years, untouched by the hard truths of love. I want to experience that first blush with you... Call me later and tell me if your mom bought the story. And just in case you didn't put it together until now. Rhys said he'd see you there, so it's technically not a lie now." Ryan slammed the door and waved over his shoulder as he strutted up the sidewalk.

Shaking my head in both exasperation and happiness, I pulled away and drove home. His misconceptions of my life were sad and insanely inaccurate, but I'd let him keep them. I had other things to do anyway. It was time to see how much Mother Dearest really thought of dad's work associates.

Chapter 7

For once, both of my parents were home at the same time. It always seems like one was working or the other was out at some kind of church event. Which, it looked like they were on their way out somewhere classy. Dad was straightening out his tie in the hall mirror, and Mother Dearest was putting her earrings on as she stomped down the hallway.

Yeesh. Maybe now wasn't the best time to bring up the party. It was tomorrow night anyway, so there was time. Seeing the steam practically rise out of her ears was not conducive to a calm and reasonable conversation.

Dad's head jerked up as soon as the door closed behind me.

"Hey there, Astrid. What are you up to tonight?" He smiled like he was the loving father everyone at church believed him to be. Like the father I wished he was.

"Not much, I'm going to study tonight." And I was. Just not what he thought I was going to study.

"That's fantastic. You're really doing your old man proud." He walked over and grabbed my shoulders in an affectionate squeeze.

It shouldn't have felt good, hearing this little bit of

praise from him. Not when so many other times he'd shown with his actions that I was an accessory, a living puppet for them to control. But it did. It warmed my chest to hear him say he was proud of me. And how fucked up was that? He was proud over something that wasn't even true. Over a lie. And this time, I was the liar.

"Thanks, Dad." I mumbled and dropped my gaze. If I made eye contact too long, would he see my lie?

"I'll be proud when you get into one of the colleges we're shooting for. It will be a miracle for you to get a scholarship to those places with your math grades. You make that happen and it will actually mean something." My mother sneered.

That warm feeling in my chest twisted into something ugly. I hated how she thought I was stupid. How she wanted me to know it. How she reveled in my miserable existence. But most of all, I hated her. And that feeling of self-preservation I clung to so often, disappeared in the wake of my fury. Reckless was my new name now. Risk taker. And I was going to push her to get my way.

"I'll try my best, Mom. Hey, tomorrow night I'd like to hang out with Rhys. Would that be okay?" I peeked at my dad through my lashes to gauge his reaction. Mother Dearest was clearly not pleased, her lips pressing into a tight thin line. There was a completely different reaction from Dad. He stood a little straighter and the skin around his eyes crinkled in satisfaction.

"I don't think that's a good idea, Astrid. You can invite him over here if you want to see him." She checked herself out in the mirror, swiping away mascara under her eye.

"I could, he just wanted to introduce me to some people at school since I don't really know anyone." I shrugged like I could go either way.

My dad pulled me into his side with his arm around my shoulders. The smell of his aftershave was comforting and foreign all at the same time. He hadn't hugged me since the end of last year at least.

"Now, now, Trina. What's wrong with her hanging out with Stan's kid? I'm sure he's raising good boys."

The twitch under her left eye was the only outward sign that she was not fucking down with what he had to say.

"You really think that's smart? Letting Astrid hang out with random boys we don't know very well. Who knows what she'll get up to without us there."

Fuck you too, Mom. In my head I was flipping her the bird. Actually, I was flipping both birds with my hands going circles like bike pedals.

"Nonsense. She'll be fine. Next time I talk to Stan, I'll let him know how important Astrid and her safety is. He'll make sure the boys understand." Dad decreed. He settled the conversation with mom like they often did with me.

Oh snap, crackle, pop. I hadn't seen that coming. Hopefully he would forget about this conversation and go back to ignoring me. If Mr. Bennett did mention this to his sons, I'd be found out for sure.

Mother Dearest speared me with a look that said *don't embarrass us*, more than *stay safe*.

"I won't do anything stupid, I promise." I tried to reassure her, but it didn't matter. I could hold a unicorn in my palm and she still wouldn't believe me.

"We're going to be late." She breezed right past us and out the door without another word. The arm around my shoulders fell away awkwardly.

"We'll be home later, don't wait up." He laughed uncomfortably.

"Have fun," I finger waved like a weirdo and locked the door behind him.

So many times I had wondered why those two were still married. It was obvious they weren't madly in love anymore, if they ever were. Maybe they both thrived on causing misery in each other's lives.

IT WAS six in the evening on Saturday, and I was starting to get antsy. My day had consisted of morning chores and then outside walks with my camera, taking pictures of anything and everything. I didn't want to brag, but I was getting really good at this photo business.

Everything was my subject, and nothing was excluded. Dancing light, filtering down through the trees. Sassy squirrels with fluffy, luxurious tails. Even the weathered, sun spotted hands of one beautifully old couple sitting on a bench. For that particular shot, I used a long lens that Thatcher had packed for me. What a godsend. I was yards away, but the zoom quality was top notch. I never would have assumed the photographer was more than a few feet away.

Then came time to get ready. This was a bit harder. I'd never really been let out on the weekends or had friends that invited me anywhere, to care about dressing up. I'd only ever been to one dance and it was the worst experience ever.

Mother Dearest set me up with a boy from the church that had enough grease in his hair to fry pork chops and smelled like he moonlighted as a pizza delivery boy. Not that there was anything wrong with pizza. I loved pizza. I just didn't find the smell arousing. If anything, I was hungry all night.

I'd gone through every possible combination in my closet and nothing said party. Nothing even said incognito. Every article of clothing that I owned was bright and cheery, like the boho girl I was at heart. I settled on dark wash skinny jeans and a flowy blouse. At least I'd be comfortable.

I'd tried to call Ryan at five, but he promptly schooled me that none of the cool kids emerged from their house until after eight at the earliest, then hung up on me.

Two long hours before Ryan showed up to get me, I did what any girl would do, and I went downstairs to grab a snack and watch a rerun of the old Sabrina.

I shouldn't have worried about my parents, because neither was here tonight. They let me know earlier there was some kind of Bible retreat for the ladies and elders they were hosting in Idaho Springs. Hindsight and all that, but at least I knew when Mother Dearest would cave. And it was when Dad vouched for me. Only, I didn't know how often that would be.

A loud banging on the front door jolted me out of a light sleep. The knocking continued as I swung up into a sitting position and grabbed my chest, trying to slow down the frantic pounding. I hated that feeling of being disoriented and the way my heart was making a bid to leave my chest.

"Astrid! Open up. It's eight-thirty and it's time to partay." Ryan sang through the door.

A nap had been a good way to pass two hours. Probably the best way, since I wasn't sitting around worrying over all the ways tonight could go sour. But now I was groggy and out of sorts. Not really in a party mood anymore.

"I'm coming." I yelled through a stretch before unlocking the door.

"Damn, girl. Did you get in a fight with the mascara

brush or what? And for the record, it won." Ryan pushed me backward as he came inside.

Lovely. I had racoon eyes from my little siesta.

"I was sleeping. Give me a sec and I'll be ready to go." Ryan went off to study the family pictures in the living room as I went to the guest bathroom.

It wasn't as bad as he'd made it out to be. Just a little smudge here or here. Once I was all sex goddess and untouchable siren again, I rejoined him.

"Let's go." I snagged my camera bag off the table in the foyer that had my different connecting lenses and pulled it over my shoulder like a purse.

"Yas! Let's go. Popping your party cherry is the high-light of my week." Ryan smirked and followed me out of the house.

"Just a week? I'm slightly offended by that. This is a big milestone." I locked the door and looped my arm through his as we went to his car.

He was driving tonight, but if he had too much to drink, I was the designated driver back to my place. That was my idea. I was too young and close to my mass exodus to die now. Next to me, Ryan grinned the whole way to his car. He had an extra bounce in his step like he expected big things from tonight.

Me, though? I had a different kind of thrill coursing through my blood. Tonight, I was going to officially start working on my portfolio. I wasn't sure if I'd use any of the shots since this was my first test run, but the reality was finally here. I was really going for it.

"I told Pat we'd meet him by the pool. He knows we're on our way. Maybe even Rhys will be there waiting on us." Ryan nudged me in the ribs.

I grunted noncommittally. I'd be a liar if I didn't admit

that a small piece of my heart was excited at the prospect of passing such an important milestone. Meeting a boy at a party. Then to have a chance to see past the distant and cool façade Rhys had going on. When Ryan glanced my way, his eyes were warm.

"Come on. You want to talk to Rhys. I can see it in your eyes."

"Maybe. Maybe not. But I am apprehensive about whether or not Trey will be with him. I really don't like him. And who knows what he'd do if he caught me spying on him." There, I admitted it. I was slightly afraid of the level of cruelty I suspected Trey had inside him.

"Astrid. I get it. Trey isn't really the kind of person we want you practicing on. Maybe when I'm confident in your stealth abilities we can find the dirt on him. I'd love to have some kind of leverage to hold over his head. It could make him less of an asshole." He smirked.

I punched his arm for his insult. "I'm stealthy. I've always been stealthy."

He laughed and tapped his fingers on the steering wheel to the beat of the Troye Sivan song playing on his Pandora station. "Okay, so in all seriousness, who are we targeting tonight?"

"I'd like to get some shots of Rhys. Outside of him, the only other person I've thought about is Jonah Perez."

Ryan's face contorted into an adorable look of confusion.

"Jonah? Why him. He's the king geek."

Didn't Ryan understand? I wanted the guys that had it all—at least for all outward appearances. Rhys was the popular boy. The one everyone envied and wanted to be close to. He had this good guy vibe, even though I knew he wasn't. If he was the good guy everyone thought he was, he wouldn't have let Trey get handsy with me in the hallway.

And Jonah, he was at the top of the class. Student body president. Straight A student. He was going places, while I'd be lucky to get a shot at this art scholarship. I definitely wouldn't be looked at for other types of scholarships. Not with my math grade.

"Because he's Rhys, only for academics. Both are so perfect they're practically untouchable. I've been thinking about how I want to work my portfolio and I think I want to show how they aren't so perfect. At least I'll know. I can't show their faces or anything." I pulled my leg up so I could turn into him a little bit.

"That's deep Astrid. And it sounds like it could backfire in your face a million different ways. You really want to pursue this type of project?" Worry coated his voice like a bad batch of hairspray.

"Yes. Positive." I nodded.

After a moment of pregnant silence, he sighed. "I guess I'll be your lookout. You'll need it. Maybe not for Jonah, but if Rhys finds out and by extension Trey, he could make life bad for you at school."

The mood in the car cooled significantly. I almost felt bad; I was bringing down Ryan's night. Almost. Then another part of me realized I needed help if I was going to pull this off.

"Well, I don't know if Jonah will be here tonight. Sometimes he comes to these parties and sometimes he doesn't. It's weird because it's totally not his scene, but he connects with people. I think that's how he's been student body president every year. Jonah is likable, but distant. He doesn't really have any close friends. Not like Rhys does. Now he should be here for sure." The corners of his lips started to curl. "I'll try to help you take pictures of him, but it might be kind of hard if he has you next to him. I got the feeling he wanted to hang out."

Ryan was a hopeless romantic, and it seemed clear he hoped we would be the next super couple. He might believe it, but I didn't think there was actually any truth behind his opinions. Honestly, it made me feel a little weird, he seemed so strongly invested, I barely existed in the same world as Rhys. If it hadn't been for that weird encounter the first week of school, and then dinner, I was positive he'd have no idea who I was.

"We'll see, okay. I don't think it's going to play out the way you think it is, but we'll see."

"Well, you're about to find out. We're here." He jerked his chin toward the windshield.

I leaned forward to get a good look at where we were. We were on some kind of long driveway with small elegant lanterns lighting the way. A closed gate slowed us down, but a man appeared out of the shadows with a clipboard. Ryan rolled down his window to greet the man.

What kind of place was this? Even Rhys' house, which was gorgeous and immaculate, wasn't anything like this. Our neighborhood was nice and all, but we didn't have cute fairy lanterns lining our private driveway, with a guard to keep the common people out. A shiver ran down my arms as the guard stepped closer. The whole scene made me nervous and the guard had no idea.

"Good night, sir. The code?" The guard bent and took a good look at me, too.

That was different. My eyes widened as our gazes locked, but he just nodded and stood back up. I guessed I passed his inspection.

No, sir, no serial killers in this car.

"Red yeti." Ryan said.

The guard waved us through as the gate started to open —how'd he do that? —and scribbled something down as we passed. Probably our license plate number in case we started trouble.

A mini-mansion sat catty corner to us, with a large circular drive in the front. Two three-car garages sat on either side of the house and there were tons of cars parked everywhere.

There were dozens of trees scattered throughout the yard, which was odd in Colorado. So many trees in one place had to be the work of a landscaper. The front door opened as we parked and three guys stumbled out with their arms around each other. Loud music poured through the doorway and bright neon lights flashed over the windows.

So much noise. So many people. I didn't want to do this anymore.

"Ryan, this isn't my scene. If I go in there, I'm afraid you're going to have to carry me out. Because I'm going to pass out from over stimulation." I spoke slow and even as I continued to stare through the suddenly foggy windshield.

Ryan belted out a deep laugh, and pushed my shoulder. "Come on, Astrid. There's nothing scary about this place. I've been to several of Remy's parties and while they can get rowdy, there's nothing to fear."

Two more girls spilled out and their nasal giggles were almost as sharp as the heels on their stilettos. I definitely missed the fashion memo, because skinny jeans and toms weren't even on the same cloud as party dresses and fancy heels.

"I'm also underdressed. Or overdressed depending on how you want to look at it." The anxiety wracking my body was surprising, but I'd always been a believer of listening to my gut. And my gut said this party was not for me.

"Don't be such a baby. You'll never get your chance at that scholarship if you don't take risks. And I've already floated around the rumor that you're trying to get on the yearbook staff. That's why your camera will be out and taking pictures. Genius, right?" He hit my arm with the back of his hand.

I took a deep breath and released it through my nose. He was right. If I wanted out of my current life, then I was going to have to step out of my comfort zone. Why was this so scary to me anyway? It was nothing different than going to a crazy pep rally at school and I did those just fine. This was a new experience for me. That was it. No one was going to care who I was or what I was doing here. If they even paid attention at all.

"You're right. That is genius. I'm ready." I glanced over and gave Ryan a large, pain filled smile. "Let's do this."

He whooped and slapped his hands on the dash. "That's what I'm talking about."

The music was so loud, it sounded like it was coming out of Ryan's speakers when he turned the car off. Not paying any attention to it, he jumped out and ran around to open my door. I had a brief thought of what it would be like on a date where the door was opened for me. There wasn't any time to dwell on it as he hauled me out of my safety bubble.

Hand in hand, we walked toward the entrance where we would hopefully find my targets for the night.

Ready or not, here I come.

Chapter 8

Sweaty bodies and cloying perfume clogged the foyer as soon as we stepped through. The music was so loud inside it seemed to be coming from every direction. Actually, that was probably some kind of surround sound set up going on.

"Ryan!" Pat was pushing his way through the gyrating crowd with a huge grin on his face.

I didn't think Ryan would have to work too hard to get another date with this guy. From the moon eyes Pat gave Ryan, the guy would probably end up asking Ryan out before the end of the evening.

Ryan released my shoulders to give Pat a hug and a kiss on the cheek. It momentarily distracted me from the chaotic flash of lights and bass. It was super adorable.

"Pat, where are you hanging out?" Ryan's voice dipped in alto as he stared dreamily into Pat's eyes.

A giggle lodged in my throat, but somehow, I managed to tamp it down and keep on my cool girl façade.

"I was waiting for you. Let's go out back. Remy has a fire pit going." Pat grabbed Ryan's hand and started leading him through the crowd while I was left there clutching my camera in my hand.

Ryan stopped and doubled back to snatch my hand. "Come on, crazy. You can't just stand in the doorway like a lunatic. These brats will think you're going to go Carrie on their asses." Ryan laughed and we traveled through the house like kids crossing the street, holding hands in a duck line.

I tried to absorb everything as we passed through the house, but it was just too much. I did recognize a few kids from school, but we were already gone before I had time to properly see who was here.

We passed through open double doors onto a huge, fancy patio. When Pat had mentioned fire pit, I pictured burning barrels in the yard, surrounded by kids in grunge hoodies. In reality, there was a swanky stone fireplace open on either side of the fire, with a dance floor set up on the far side of the patio.

The same club music and strobe lights were set up around the back yard, even classing the place up with a smoke machine. Could I call this a yard? I felt like it was more of an estate.

Even still a bit intimidated, I was really digging the scene. The place had so many people, it had that anonymous feel going on. I could totally get behind this kind of party.

Pat led us over to a group of couches around a smaller stone fire pit. There were a couple people lounging over the furniture that I recognized from their group at school, but no Rhys.

When I entered their orbit, several looked my way and my heart started to thump erratically. At least they weren't sneering at me. They had more of an uncaring indifference in their expressions.

"Hey guys. This is Ryan and his main chick Astrid.

Right? Astrid?" Pat sat down and with a tug, Ryan and I followed like dominos on the side loveseat.

"Um, yeah. Hi." I smiled and my eye twitched a little.

"'Sup guys." Ryan did the chin lift that instantly made him cooler.

Their conversations picked back up and I was left out, thank God. They chatted about shopping and ski trips. I'd have nothing to add to the conversation. I doubt they did bargain shopping like I did to stretch my budget.

I let my gaze casually roam over the people dancing and standing off to the side. Many of the more popular kids were out here but I didn't see either of my targets for the night.

"Where's Rhys?" Ryan whispered to Pat as he squeezed my hand.

I doubt anyone noticed but a flush still stained my cheeks. I was sure Pat thought he was asking for me—which he was, but not at my behest.

"He hasn't shown up here. Neither has Trey. They'll probably be here later." Pat eyed me thoughtfully and shrugged.

Yep. He totally knew Ryan was asking for me.

I pulled the camera bag over my shoulder and grabbed the short lens to keep my hands busy. The cool night air that kissed my skin was just the right temperature to keep from shivering. I scooted to the edge of my seat but the little bit of heat from the fire pit still eluded me.

Two of the girls on the couch to my right kept glancing at me curiously. Fuck, I needed to get out of here before someone actually tried to make asinine conversation with me.

"Ryan, I want to get some shots and work on my skills." I lifted the camera in my hand.

He looked at me as if I suddenly appeared out of a

cloud of glitter dust and rainbows. How nice. He forgot I was here in his love haze.

"Yeah, sure. I'll be right here." His eyes widened in his plea to stay put.

I sighed. I'd probably be less noticeable if I were alone anyway.

"I'll come back when I'm done." I stood up when Pat spoke.

"What are you taking photos for?" A hint of suspicion entered his eyes. Of course he'd have thought it was weird to take pictures. He probably thought I wanted blackmail material.

He wasn't *that* far off.

"She wants to get on the yearbook committee. I told her to start documenting big events that the seniors would want to see and then present it to the committee. This is a great place to start. Remy's parties are epic." Ryan replied smoothly.

"Oh, got it. You know, Astrid, I'm on the yearbook committee. Show me what you have on Monday. We definitely want the yearbook to be epic this year." He smiled kindly.

"Sure thing." I smiled and dipped out of their little seating area. Pat would be awesome for Ryan, with a genuine heart. It kind of burned my soul to outright lie to him. I had no intention of meeting him on Monday.

Strolling around the back, I took some random shots of people on the dance floor. Nothing too scandalous, but I needed to have something to show on Monday in case Pat pushed the issue.

Surprisingly, people didn't really pay attention to me with a camera in my hand. They were so absorbed into themselves and each other, I wasn't even a blip on their radar. It probably helped that I stayed on the edges.

So far, I'd witnessed three couples making out, two girls and a guy trying a three-way kiss, an argument over cheating, and Bella dancing with her boyfriend but making eyes at the basketball star she favored so much. I really didn't understand that one. He clearly had no stamina.

I was ready to head inside to see if I could find Rhys or Jonah when movement through the trees caught my eye.

That was odd. I assumed there wasn't anything past the trees, but this was obviously a huge property. From what I could tell, there were at least two or three people past the light and all male. Curiosity was going to be my downfall, damn it.

The light didn't stretch very far, and after a few steps it was basically pitch dark. The new moon didn't help either. I made it to the copse of trademark Colorado trees, walking through the Christmas tree grouping, and carefully tiptoed to avoid making any extra noise. The bumping music was distant and the silence was overtaking the open space.

Well, silence was subjective because the murmuring of the people out here still trickled through.

I moved closer and soon I could see three guys standing behind the garage. A motion sensor light was on but too far away to show their features clearly.

Whatever they were talking about wasn't pleasant. In fact, from their body language it seemed like two guys were ganging up on the third. The third guy turned more in profile and I gasped.

Was that... That was Jonah. And one of the other guys was Mike from art class.

"I'm done with all that. You would be too if you knew

what was good for you." Jonah gritted as he bunched up his fists by his thighs.

Mike shook his head, but all the anger he'd had in class was absent. His posture screamed weary and beat down. "You don't get it. You don't ever get done with them. It's not an option."

This was a good shot. Caught in the shadows, confrontation in the night. I flipped the on switch of my camera and inched closer. The shot would be all light and shadows but it would be beautiful. Exactly what I was looking for.

"No, I'm doing everything I can to get out of there. I'm set to be valedictorian and I've already been accepted into several universities with scholarship options. I'm done." Jonah crossed his arms and braced his legs apart. His stance was intimidating, so at odds with the Mr. Academic vibe he gave off at school.

I lifted the camera to my eyes to line up the shot.

"You're going to end up dead!" Mike rushed Jonah and pulled on his shirt.

Click.

The flash went off. The flash went off illuminating the guys!

Fuckity, fuck, fuck, fuck. This was a fuck situation.

I spun around and crouched, hiding in a small ball. There was no way I'd be able to run. Even if he didn't catch me, he'd see who I was as soon as I entered the light.

"What the hell? Who's there?" Mike stepped away from Jonah with panic written all over his voice.

"Run. I'll see who's here." Jonah said as he started jogging my way.

It was probably the worst thing I could have done but I curled up tighter, hugging my knees to my chest.

I'd learned a lot about myself since I moved to Silver Ranch. And what I knew was, between this situation and walking in on Thatcher, I possessed neither fight nor take flight. Nope, I froze like a damn petrified statue. Footsteps passed me and then doubled back. I shook so hard from fear of getting caught, I was going to pass out at any minute.

Damn it. That would be bad.

The footsteps circled me before they stopped. I peeked through my hair to see him swinging his phone around, using his flashlight app to find me.

I was looking at him when his light landed on me. I couldn't see his face but he paused.

"You? Are you following me?" He sounded outraged.

I was outraged too. Outraged I didn't make sure the auto flash setting was off.

"Um... no."

I guessed it was time to stand up and stop looking at this guy through my hair like the girl from the ring. When I got to my feet, I tucked my hair behind my ears and bit my lip. If I acted like he was crazy and imagined it all, would he believe it? No, that was a lame idea.

"No. So you weren't just stalking me through the trees, and you didn't just take a picture of me?" His flashlight app was still shining in my eyes and I couldn't see past the insanely bright light.

"Do you mind turning that thing off?" I shielded my eyes. "No, I wasn't following you." Only a tiny lie. I wasn't following him at that particular point. "And I did take a picture. But it wasn't of you necessarily. I like taking pictures of people. The light was very dramatic and I was trying to capture the mood. I didn't realize the flash was on." I sniffed.

He dropped his hand and the sudden darkness invaded my vision. I could see his silhouette, but that was about it.

He sighed and stepped so close he was touching my side. My arm tingled where his hard stomach pressed into me and I almost stepped back, but I wanted to know what he was doing. Not to mention, he smelled good, and it was playing havoc on my senses with raging adrenaline coursing through my body.

"Let's see it."

Ah, that was the only reason he was close to me.

Begrudgingly, I turned on the camera and selected the pictures option. The last picture I took of Jonah and Mike came into view. It was a great composition with lots of movement and action. Their expressions were a mixture of aggression and indignation. He was going to ask me to delete it, damn it, and I couldn't think of a way to keep it. Mike was stretching Jonah's shirt to the side and... I squinted to see what was peeking out and then decided to zoom in. A tattoo curled over his collarbone in reds and blacks.

"Okay, that's enough of that. Please delete it now." Jonah blocked the picture with a hand over the screen.

Ugh. There it was.

"I really like the picture. I swear I won't use it for anything." I glanced up and his features were slightly outlined by the light slipping through his fingers.

His face truly was a work of art. Straight lines and firm lips set into a deep frown. His glasses definitely added a bit of mystery in the dark.

"Please," I whispered, tilting my face up to his.

He looked toward the building behind me, then he grabbed my hand and led me toward the front yard, not unlike Pat led Ryan.

"What are you doing?" I tried to tug my hand out of his grip, but he tightened his hold.

He stopped at the corner of the building where the front was visible but we were still hidden in the shadows. Athletic guys stood in circles, high fiving and horsing around while watching beautiful, giggling girls stumble over each other as they strutted toward the house.

"Do you see them?" Jonah stepped behind me and whispered in my ear.

"Of course." My fingers tightened on the camera.

"Those people, they have it all. Good homes, trust funds, bright futures. It's all laid out for them already. Their biggest worry is who they'll take to prom." He paused, letting it sink in like he was telling me some forgotten secret.

"I'm not like them. My family and this town are trying to pull me under and keep me chained to a life of misery. I have to fight for everything I get, and I'm fighting to get out of here. I refuse to let anything stand in my way. I'm the only one that gives enough of a shit to change my future. Do you understand?" His lips moved against my ear and his hand dug into my hip.

"Yes." Because I was the same. I was stuck and I knew the only way out was to create my own path. No one else cared to help me, so I had to help myself.

"Then you understand why you can't keep that picture." Jonah dipped his head and pulled my hand so I stepped closer to him.

My heart went out to Jonah. He was going places, and he was going to *be* something. But he wasn't there yet. He was still fighting to get out of his nightmare, and I wouldn't do anything to jeopardize his path. I'd still take my pictures. But I'd do it another way.

"I—"

"Astrid! Is that you?" I jumped and we both spun around to see who had called out to me.

At first, I didn't recognize the guy. He had on tight jeans with holes at the knees and a delicate silver chain dangling from his jeans. A black T-Shirt with LOVE ME written in white block letters molded to his muscles as he reached us.

Oh my gawd. This guy was sexy in a *you'd have no regrets over the dirty things I could do to you* way.

"Do I know you?" I wanted to know him.

"I'm wounded. After all I've done for you." He smirked and pressed both hands to his heart. "You really don't remember me, jail bait?"

"Beck!" I gasped. I greedily perused his body as I stepped away from Jonah. He grunted but released me. My guess, he was not pleased to be interrupted. "And I'm eighteen, so I can't be jail bait."

Was that me flirting? I didn't recognize my own voice, but I kind of liked this side of me.

Beck smirked and shoved his hands in the pockets of his washed-out jeans. "Everything okay over here? It looked intense." He eyed Jonah with a hint of distrust.

"Fine." I piped up. "What are you doing here at this jail bait party? It doesn't seem like a place you'd hang out." I smiled.

"I was just picking up Andy, my drummer. We have a gig tonight over at the Iron Horse." He glanced over his shoulder and I followed his line of sight. A similarly dressed guy was standing by a sweet vintage mustang. When he turned around he shot Jonah an indecipherable look. "Why don't you come with? You can watch me play." There was no question in any of his words.

"I don't know." I cringed.

I wanted to go. I wanted to go almost as bad as I wanted to move out. Almost.

This was a dream experience I was sorely lacking. Go to a concert with a hot guy in the band? I was a live wire trying to justify leaving Ryan here.

"I'd make sure you get home safe. Scout's honor." He held up a hand with his two middle fingers separated. That was a vulgar gesture wasn't it?

"Fuck, I'm not going to hurt her. Who do you think I am?" Jonah snapped and pressed against my back.

Beck held up his hands and smirked. "I didn't say you'd hurt her. I know her. I also know these parties. Are you saying that you're going to watch her the entire time and make sure she gets home safe?"

Jonah wasn't responsible for me and I didn't expect him to be, but I wanted to see his reaction.

He looked like he was in pain, and didn't know what the right answer was here. That was probably a blow to his ego. He seemed like the kind of uptight guy who had all the answers, and had a strategy ten steps ahead of everyone else.

"I can't stay here. I have somewhere to be." Jonah finally answered and he looked at me in apology. For what, I wasn't sure.

"Perfect. Then you can come with me." Beck beamed triumphantly.

You know what, I would text Ryan. He wouldn't care as long as I was safe. Maybe I could get him to bring Pat to the show.

"I'd love to." I turned on my camera and deleted the last picture. I held it up so Jonah could see it was gone. While he studied the screen, my eyes lingered on his collarbone and shoulder, where the tattoo was. I'd be lying if I said I wasn't curious about his ink. Would it be some kind of mathematic art to symbolize his love of academia, or something masculine and meaningful to remind himself he wouldn't always be in his current life?

"Thank you." He whispered and reached out to catch my hand for a quick squeeze. As soon as it happened, the brief touch of fingers was over and he was walking back the way he came.

Jonah had a lot more layers than I thought he had. He was still the chess champ, the perfect guy I knew he was. But he was a little bit more than that, and I was going to find out exactly who he was.

Beck stepped closer and nodded toward Andy. "Ready?"

"Yeah, hold on just a second." I pulled out my phone and typed a quick text to Ryan. The message said delivered but as I waited, he didn't open it. If I took Beck over to their spot on the patio there was a chance he would talk me out of going. And right now, I wanted nothing more than to go and forget who I was for a little while. My parents were gone tonight and wouldn't be home until lunchtime tomorrow, so I didn't want to waste my time as Ryan's third wheel.

Shoving the phone back in my pocket, I look at Beck with a grin. "Let's go."

The silence as we walked over to the mustang was a little uncomfortable, but I hadn't known how to fill it. That's why my friendship with Ryan worked so well. He filled it for me, and I was only the listening participant eighty percent of the time.

"Astrid, this is my drummer, Andrew. Andrew, this is Astrid. She's new around here." Beck placed a gentle hand on my shoulder.

Andrew smiled, showing off a dimple and held out his

hand. I had to shuffle my camera around to take it because it was still out. "Nice to meet you. You go to SRHS?"

"I do. Senior this year." Beck motioned to the car and we took the hint, climbing in before continuing our conversation.

Andrew got in the back without asking so I could have the front seat. "That's cool. Me too. I go to the community college part time so I'm only there for two classes in the morning. And one's a teacher's aide, so I don't think that counts."

This guy was adorable. He kind of reminded me of a puppy with his friendliness and open expression. He wasn't closed off or guarded like Rhys or Jonah. Or even like Beck.

"So what kind of music do you play?" I snapped my seatbelt as Beck pulled away from the curve.

"Alternative. I guess you could say we also have a touch of emo. We mainly play love songs. The chicks eat it up." Beck winked at me.

Andrew snorted. "Yeah, Beck loves to write the sappy stuff."

My ears perked up at that. He wrote their music? Now I was even more pumped to not only know the band, but listen to their own original music.

"That's really cool." I nodded to both of them, twisting in my seat a little so I didn't have to keep craning my neck to talk to Andrew.

There was that damned silence again. Only this time we had Radiohead playing softly in the background. A few minutes passed before Beck spoke up.

"So how do you know Jonah?" There was a strange tone in his voice, but I couldn't quite decide what it meant.

"School. We bumped into each other—literally—on the first day." Vague was the way to go. While I might have opened up a little more to Beck, or maybe not, I definitely wasn't going to spill my secrets with Andrew.

"It's not any of my business, but you might want to steer clear of him. And those parties." He glanced at me with a stern expression.

Hold up. First, it wasn't any of his business. And second, he did an amazingly nice thing for me, regardless of why. Although, it still chafed to think that he felt sorry for me. But he was barely even an acquaintance with absolutely zero clout to tout his opinions.

"You're right. It's *my* business." I crossed my arms and turned back to stare out the front windshield. It felt like a lecture was coming on and I was in no mood to hear it.

He sighed. "Okay, I know that came off wrong, and I swear I'm not an ass. You just seem like a nice girl and I want to look out for you."

I sneered. "You're not helping." So he basically saw me as a little kid.

"Fuck, all right. I'll just lay this out, and you can do with it what you will. I won't mention it again. Deal?" He scrubbed a hand down his face.

I glanced over my shoulder to get a look at Andrew's expression, but he was wide-eyed and straight faced. Clearly uncomfortable. He probably hadn't thought the conversation would turn so quickly when we'd just met.

"Fine." I twirled my hand in the air for him to continue.

"First, those parties. Remy has only started having parties recently, but they've been getting wild. Part of the reason why I came to collect Andrew tonight," his voice dropped in pitch as he stared at the drummer via the rearview mirror.

Andrew coughed but otherwise stayed quiet.

"I was at the party. It was harmless. No one bothered

me." Until I snapped that picture, but Beck didn't need to know that.

"It's early. Barely nine-thirty. After ten or so, drugs come out and it gets wild. Fights, hookups, any number of things happen. Go if you want, but at least you know what to expect." He took a deep breath. "And Jonah. Did you know he was in another school district until a few years ago?"

I nodded and then realized he couldn't hear that. "Yes, I knew that."

"I went to that school. It was a rough lot. There were a few nice kids, but... you know the term wrong side of the tracks? That was the majority of the families in that district. There's a lot of motorcycle gangs and druggies. A lot of the kids try to get out, but most never do. And Jonah, he's from one of the worst families. They're mixed up in bad stuff. And I don't want to see you get pulled down with them."

He paused, and I soaked it up. Wow. That was so much information, and while a small part of me could appreciate his concern, I felt a lot of it was unfounded. You couldn't judge someone from what you thought you knew about their family. Look at mine. I was the perfect example of how opposite someone could be from their parents.

"Thank you for telling me and trying to look out for me," I said softly. "But, you're wrong about Jonah. I've seen him at school and he's going to make it out. If anyone does, it will be him."

And I believed that. With my whole, beating heart. Only a small part of me was bitter that it was so clearly going to happen for someone else.

He sighed. "That was my soapbox. Are you ready to have some fun tonight? I did promise you a good time. I'll give you the full Beck treatment." A mischievous glint entered his eyes.

Andrew cackled in the backseat, and the tense vibe evaporated as if it had never existed in our small, enclosed space.

I checked my phone and there was a text from Ryan saying to enjoy myself and text him when I got home. Now he could have a fun night without trying to babysit me.

Relaxing into the soft leather seat, I made a promise to myself. Tonight, I would put aside my big ideas of getting out for a normal night as a teenager. I deserved it.

"I can't wait." I laughed.

ABOUT TEN MINUTES LATER, we pulled into the parking lot of the Iron Horse and Beck parked in the back. Honestly, it was scarily dark and ominous back here. It was not someplace I would park without these guys.

"What's your band's name?" I unsnapped my seatbelt and climbed out of the skateboard he called a car.

"Midnight Marionette." Andrew said as he climbed out of the back. Good thing he was about my size or else he wouldn't have fit back there.

I thought about the name. "So, midnight puppets. Because you perform at night?" That didn't really make any sense.

"Maybe someday I'll tell you," Beck winked, and butter-flies erupted in my stomach.

I rolled my eyes and stopped at the trunk as he got his guitar out. "Need help with anything?"

"Nah, the rest of the guys have everything else. I just

don't trust anyone with my baby." He hugged his guitar to his chest.

My camera bag was still strapped over my shoulder and an idea hit me. "Do you mind if I snap some pictures when you guys are on stage? I'm trying to work on my photography skills." I lifted the bag at my side.

A beautiful smile broke over his face. "Go ahead. You can say you were the first to ever capture our magic while performing."

Beck had a magnetism about him and I leaned closer as if I was a lonely planet in his orbit. I stopped myself and wiped the goofy grin off my face. He already thought I was helpless and naïve. No reason to add lovesick puppy to that too.

"If any turn out decent, I'll make sure to print them for you." I tucked a loose strand of hair behind my ear. What was I doing? Was I... gasp... flirting?

He dipped his head and I could feel the warm fan of his breath over my lips. The minty smell of his gum washed over me. This guy was potent and if I didn't control myself, my eyes were going to roll back in my head.

"Thanks, pretty girl." He whispered.

"Let's go guys. We're going to be late." Andrew called from the back door.

I jumped, but Beck just chuckled.

"Come on, jail bait." He placed a hand on my lower back as he walked me to the back entrance of the Iron Horse.

"I like pretty girl much better than jail bait." I grumbled to myself.

Beside me, Beck smirked but didn't turn back my way. I knew because I was watching him out of the corner of my eye like a love-starved lunatic.

Andrew tugged the door open, and the yellow light falling through did little to hide the grunge caked on the door. This place was dirty and smoky, but it held a special kind of charm.

We walked down a long hallway, passing stagehands in T-Shirts and giggling girls dressed in miniskirts and band tanks. Beck got more than a few sultry hellos, and he smiled and nodded back.

Another band must have been performing as their music was loud but faded backstage.

A thrill of anticipation shot down my spine as I followed Andrew. Already this was an experience like no other, and I hadn't even done anything except walk inside the building. Soon, we entered a room where there were two more guys standing with beers in their hands, and a chick on each arm.

My first instinct was to sneer at the cliché scene, but I choked it down. I was the damn cliché tonight with Beck. Oh, that burned to think about, but not nearly enough for me to regret coming here.

I was going to live it up, damn it.

"Hey guys," Andrew chirped as he went to the corner, and started rummaging through a few boxes.

"Rhett, Will, I have a friend along tonight." Beck gave me an extra push so I was within reaching distance of these new guys.

I smiled as they turned my way. Both were dressed a little more rock band than either Beck or Andrew, with spiked hair and leather collars. Both were a few inches taller than me and seemed friendly enough.

"She your date for the night?" The one closest to me smirked and suddenly I didn't think they were so friendly anymore.

"Nah, man. She's a friend. I promised her a good show and then I'd get her home safe." Beck threw an arm around my shoulders.

That stung. I mean, it was true. But I felt like the hot band guy friend zoned me.

"Your fans aren't going to like seeing her here. They'll think you're off the market." The same guy laughed.

Great, Beck was a heartthrob. I kind of knew that already after seeing him tonight. He gave off that *bad boy I want to take home to mom and dad* vibe. Hopefully, I wouldn't have to fight off hordes of horny women tonight.

"Nice to meet you. Will." The other guy said and held out a hand, dislodging a groupie.

I shook once. "Astrid."

"Rhett," the first guy and followed suit.

Again, I took his hand to be polite. "Nice to meet you."

Beck laid his guitar case down by a ratty old couch that looked like it had seen a threesome or ten, and came back to me, catching my hand and linking our fingers.

"I'm going to get Astrid settled. I'll be right back."

"Have fun, Astrid," Andrew waved at me as Beck pulled me out of the storage room? Band holding room? It hadn't been anything special, not like I would have thought a club would have supplied for the band.

"Is this a real club, like over eighteen, or is this just a coffee shop or something?" I asked to fill the space as we walked down another dank corridor.

"That's right, you're not from here. This is technically a real club and has bouncers at the door. The lines are a little blurred for us since we're performing. You know, Andrew won't be eighteen for two more months. The rest of us are legal." Beck stopped us at a door. The music was so intense,

I could practically feel the vibrations through our joined hands as he pushed it open.

"Like I said at the party, I'm eighteen and I have my ID with me. You won't have to worry. And I won't drink. Scout's honor." I yelled as we entered the area between the stage.

Crowds of women gathered by the fence roping off the stage, screaming, dancing, and shaking around sloshing, red cups. They were pressed so tight to the chain-linked fence, it looked like it might fall over at any minute.

Beck put pressure on the small of my back when I stopped moving forward.

"What's wrong?" He dipped his head next to mine.

"This is really intense, Beck. I don't think I can be in that crowd by myself." I shook my head and tried to take a step back, but he caught me with hands to my hips. My breath momentarily sped up, and my skin tingled where his fingers molded to my body.

"Good thing you aren't going in that crowd, now isn't it?" With that, I had the courage to move forward and see where he led me.

Women started to recognize him, screaming "Beck! Beck!" over and over again, until he acknowledged the crowd with a lifted hand and a fuck me dirty smirk.

My head spun from soaking in this new reality. The mechanic, the guy with the druggie mom and a kind heart, was a small celebrity here in the club. Or heartthrob based on the amount of horny women throwing themselves at the fence, trying to touch any part of his delectable body.

He pushed me against the stage as we moved across, seeming to stay far away from the crowds as possible. I did not blame him one bit. A pair of panties landed in front of us, stopping me in my tracks.

What. The. Hell.

Should I be worried that Beck was in danger of being kidnapped by one of these randy mom squad members? Because, looking out at the women, very few were my age. Most looked to be in their late twenties, early thirties.

"Here." He stopped me just off center where about five metal chairs was sitting, facing the stage. "These are for the press or security guards. Since we aren't that big, we don't ever have press, and only half the security guards. There are usually a few extra chairs between the whole line anyway, so you should be good."

"Should, huh." I was glad he was so confident.

"You'll be fine," He shouted over the music.

I nodded my head and fingered the buckle on my camera bag. "How long before you go on?"

He checked his phone and leaned close to my ear and shouted, "In about fifteen. I'll just collect you at the end of the show and you can walk off with us."

The music cut off before his last couple words, and he nearly busted my eardrums from his close proximity. *Ouch.*

"Well, well, well. What do we have here? Beckham White. And who is this pretty thing, hmm? Are you finally off the market?" A throaty, dry voice purred over the speakers.

This had to be a bad dream with all of the bad luck I had tonight. First getting caught by Jonah, now being called out at a concert. *No Bueno.*

Beck had pulled back just enough I could see all of his features in the magenta and neon blue glow of the ever-moving stage light. As we held eye contact, a decadent smile slowly crept across his face. That twinkle of mischief entered his eyes again, but I lost it as he twisted toward the stage.

"Red, you're not really trying to break hearts tonight, are you?"

The front and center guy removed the mic from the stand and strutted over to us. He had blood red hair so deep, for a second I questioned if he had a head wound or not. But then it clicked. Red. Red head. With dark kohl lining his eyes, he looked like the epitome of jaded, emo rocker. His eyes were done so well, I contemplated asking for tips. It didn't matter now though, Mother Dearest would kill me if she saw me like that.

"It's not something I relish, but this isn't your normal gig." He waved a tatted hand in our direction.

"Then if you must know, yes. I'm now spoken for, and my girl here is about to have my love child. Since she's now such an important part of my life, I figured she deserved a little special treatment for the show." Beck wrapped a muscular arm around my shoulders and pressed so tight to my side, there wasn't an inch of space between us.

He said love child. Please don't let me have to go to the bathroom during the concert. These women would shred me for killing their fantasy.

Red's eyes widened comically before his face morphed into a confused grin. He seemed to be mulling over if Beck was serious or not. He flicked his eyes to me, but I was blank faced. Whenever I was the center of attention or in an uncomfortable situation, I tended to freeze and my face lost all emotion.

"You heard this ladies. Beckham is no longer available for any late night romps going forward." Red addressed the masses.

Groans and boos rose up through the crowd until I was afraid they were going to tsunami our asses where we stood.

"Finish your set, Red. My girl's waiting to see me in action."

"Fine, fine. Whatever you say." He strolled back to the stand and placed the mic back in. "Tell your girl goodbye so you stop distracting my fans. They can't enjoy my lyrical genius with your hot bod standing there."

Beck chuckled and it was warm and delicious, sending a sinful shiver over my full body. He turned his head toward mine and I took the chance to smell him. He smelled amazingly like trouble.

"Be good, pretty girl." He winked and leaned in slowly, giving me time to move. I didn't know what I would move from until his lips touched mine in a soft caress. It was barely there, but boy had I noticed.

I touched my lips as he separated us. His eyes laughed at me as he backed up. "See you soon, babe. Grab lots of pictures for me to frame in our house." The volume of his words carried over the crowd.

He turned away and retreated through the side door.

I can't believe it. My first kiss. My first kiss was epic, and memorable, and a fucking joke.

Chapter 9

Once he was out of sight the women behind me settled down. The band on stage started playing again, announcing it would be his last song. As soft, soothing tunes circled the room, I pulled the dented metal chair away from the fence, but still leaving room to see the stage.

Two big burly men ambled down the space, taking up standing positions facing the crowd on either side of the platform. Man, Beck and his band must be a big deal around here. If that was the case, what was he doing working as a mechanic? Surely he could make just as much doing this.

"That's it for us folks! Thanks for coming out, and let's send a giant fucking welcome to the Midnight Marionettes!" The band raised their guitars as they jogged off stage.

The small reprieve from the crazy, lust-ridden women was gone. Wolf whistles and screams almost deafened me. I bent around in my chair to get a look at the crowd and the lusty women pushing each other to get closer. I had never been this excited over anything in my life.

Yes, ladies, I know. Beck is like a chocolate drizzled lava cake, tempting you off the diet you didn't want to be on anyway.

The energy from the crowd getting pumped over Beck's band seeped into my own blood stream, pumping me up.

Another five minutes went by, then one of the guys ran out. It was either Rhett or Will. I hadn't paid enough attention to them to really pick apart. Their matching outfits didn't help either. Andrew was next, then the other band member. Each picked up their instruments, or in Andrew's case, drum sticks, and started to play a generic beat. Or maybe this was the opening to one of their songs?

The screaming got louder and the women chanted 'Beck' over and over again. He really knew how to hype up a crowd and I was no exception. I stood and whistled with the best of them. A blue light circled the stage and I lifted the camera to my eyes. This was a moment I wanted to catch. The moment where Beck was onstage but the show hadn't started. When their fans were on their tip toes, holding their breath and waiting to see what the first song of the night would be.

This time, I made sure the flash was off. The flash would take away from the vibe and that would ruin the beauty.

Beck jogged out with a devilish smirk and waved. Not a dorky wave, but a wave that said he was about to rock our world. Right as I snapped the picture, the spotlight landed on him. Perfect. I spun on my chair, taking a picture of the crowd. Sometimes, the audience was just as powerful as the performer. Because their enthusiasm made the show, and this was one I didn't want to miss.

"How's everybody doing tonight?" Beck's molten voice whispered over the crowd. The collective sigh almost made me snicker. Almost. Because I sighed too.

Cheers erupted and feet stomped.

"The Midnight Marionettes want to thank you for coming out. We hope you'll enjoy the show." He picked up a bright blue guitar and pulled the strap over his head. He strummed a note without even missing a beat, in constant motion. As soon as that note sang, the rest of the band joined in.

The show was beautiful, poetic, and soul moving. I took so many pictures, of both the band and the crowd. I climbed in the chair and got all angles of the packed room. Sometimes it wasn't about the performer, but how moved the crowd was. And something told me that Beck might appreciate some of these pictures, immortalizing his influence over so many that enjoyed his lovesick songs.

The next tune to come on was slow, and sensual, leaving no doubt that sex was on Beck's mind when he wrote it. He prowled over, with his instrument slung over his back and crouched down, directly in front of me. His voice was sex and sin wrapping around me as he sang. I couldn't keep the cheesy grin off my face when he winked. I wanted to remember this moment forever, so without bringing it to my face, I tipped my camera toward Beck and snapped a quick picture. I hoped with all of my snarky arty heart that it caught his expression.

The last song ended and the band left the stage, leaving every one of us bereft of their soul touching beauty. Unsure of what to do, I pushed past the security guard toward the exit. The music had shut off and the loud conversations seemed out of place. Like when you go skating and then you take the skates off, but your body keeps trying to roll around. That was what it felt like. I heard the remnants of the music and it was severely lacking.

Right before I ducked out from the main floor, a familiar voice stopped me in my tracks. That couldn't be...

Standing at the end of the metal fence was Thatcher Reed, chatting with a few people. My heart turned into a kick drum on steroids as I stared at him. He looked the same as that day in the classroom with a grunge shirt and ripped jeans. Carelessly casual, and right at home in the throng of Beck's adoring fans.

"Thatcher?" It slipped out before I could seal my stupid lips shut. I should have left already, but I must be a glutton for punishment. Especially since he was about two feet from me with no doubt he heard me.

He twisted his head to see who called his name. His lips parted in surprise as if this was last place he thought he'd see me. I was the innocent, cock-blocking schoolgirl. This was definitely the last place he'd see me, if not for Beck's interference.

"Astrid? What are you doing here?" A smile bloomed on his face and flat out shocked me.

He was happy to see me? How odd.

Thatcher turned to face me fully, giving his back to the group he was with. One girl sneered at him before turning it to me. She was a keeper.

"To see the show. I assume the same for you?" I cringed. I sounded like a lame librarian.

He laughed under his breath as he leaned on the bar. "Yeah, you get any pictures?" He nodded to the camera clutched in my hands.

I grinned. Even without looking at them, I knew I had to have gotten some amazing shots. "Yes. I did."

"Can I see?" Thatcher held out his hand expectantly.

Still on a high from the experience, I slid next to him and pulled the pictures up on the screen. The neon lighting created such an ethereal background with the smoke cutting in and out of the light. The first picture was Beck crouched down and I was ecstatic to see I captured him perfectly. He was a little off center, but nothing that wasn't easily edited in photoshop. At least with a few Lynda.com tutorials. Beck looked like every broken heart he left in his wake was worth it. For the women, not for him. Although, he probably enjoyed the ride too.

Thatcher whistled and pushed his head so our cheeks were nearly touching.

"That's something else. Maybe you don't need my help after all."

I turned my head and my breath caught with how close he was. Even in this cesspool of scents, he smelled good, like spicy sandalwood.

Clearing my throat, I looked back down to my camera. It was hard not to preen at his praise, but I managed. "I did do good, didn't I?"

I clicked through the other pictures and he hemmed and hawed, letting me know which ones he liked best. He seemed to favor the same ones I did, and that boosted my confidence even more.

"You definitely have an artistic eye. Seriously, I'd love to help you. Even if it's just to watch you grow as an artist." His voice dipped, sending a shiver from my neck and blanketing my shoulders.

I wasn't angry today, like I was at the end of our brief conversation before. Genuine interest filled his eyes and melted my resolve a little bit. A different perspective was never a bad thing.

"Astrid. I thought you would have come backstage already." Beck poked his head out of the door with a wide grin on his face. He was definitely riding a high too, only a different kind.

I straightened and stepped away from Thatcher when Beck's gaze switched to him.

"Thatcher, man. How's it going?" He came out but still stuck close to the door.

I didn't blame him. He'd get swarmed if too many people noticed him.

"Beck, great show as always." They shook hands.

Luckily, most of the crowd had dispersed and no one seemed to notice Beck except for the group Thatcher was with. Two of the girls came up on either side of Thatcher, smiling seductively at Beck.

"That was awesome tonight, Beck." The girl next to me spoke in a husky voice, pulling strands of honey blonde hair away from her face. Her perfume was sickly sweet and not in a good way.

My nose twitched, but I stayed in the same spot.

"Where are you going tonight? Want a buddy to join you?" The other girl giggled.

The urge to gag was strong, but that would have been immature and hanging out in an older crowd that was the last thing I wanted to be. Neither guy seemed to notice my struggle, of course.

"I can't tonight ladies. I have a date already, right Astrid?" A dimple popped out as his gaze landed on me.

My cheeks flamed instantly and Thatcher's head snapped my way. He totally hadn't been expecting that. Even though Beck came out to get me, he still hadn't expected it.

"Uh, yeah." What was he thinking? I knew he was messing with me, but my awkwardness was reaching a new level with all of this attention.

He reached out and snagged my hand, pulling me close to him as he draped a heavy arm around my shoulders. He was sweaty and about twenty degrees warmer than where I was standing a second ago. Beck could double as a heat lamp and sell out faster than the mom club could swipe their credit cards.

Thatcher had an unreadable expression on his face as he studied me in all my gawky glory.

"You gonna be around tomorrow, Thatch? We can grab a beer or something while I work on your car. Didn't you say it needed some maintenance done?" Beck said casually.

Thatcher's gaze lingered on me for a few more seconds before he switched to Beck. "Yeah, that'd be great. I'm open all day tomorrow. I can meet you at your place around noon?"

"Sounds great. I'll catch you later." Beck stepped away to give Thatcher a man hug before turning to me. "Ready?"

"Yeah." I was broken, only stringing together one or two words at a time.

The stage lights shut off, leaving the florescent lights to beat down on all of us. Beck waited for me to go in front of him but I stood there, staring at him. Awkwardly.

"Yo, jail bait. You ready or what?" Beck stepped closer.

"I told you to stop calling me that." I snapped.

He laughed and put a hand to the small of my back. "Then let's go."

I looked over my shoulder as he lightly shoved me forward. Thatcher was watching us and waved when our gazes met. I sent him a pathetic half smile and then he was gone.

Beck led the way once we were in the hallway with an extra spring in his step. He was super riled from performing. It showed in the way he moved and how his eyes darted all over the place, taking in the moment as if he was never going to experience this type of fame again.

"How do you know Thatcher?" I caught up to him, but speed walking was not my thing. Almost immediately, I started to huff.

Beck slowed down when he looked at me. I don't know what he saw, but my red face and heavy breathing was probably a clear sign that I couldn't keep up. He hooked his arm around me again, but this time his hand landed on my hip.

Ho boy. His attitude was infectious and so was his free hugging. The casual way he touched me was a turn on I'd never experienced before. My poor body was about to erupt into flames, and he didn't even know it. Or maybe he did. His smile brightened exponentially when the heat licked up my face and down my neck. Oh God. I bet I looked like a tomato got in a fight with the ketchup. And not a sexy, blooded vampire fight. More like a toddler throwing their lunch away during a tantrum.

His touch was more frequent and personal now that the show was over. It was almost like he was more touchy feely when he was jazzed.

"He brings his car into Tacky's for oil changes and small maintenance stuff. He's a cool guy so we started hanging out, and now I do his stuff at my house. We can drink beer and shoot the shit while I take care of his car." We passed the band room and I peeked in, then quickly averted my eyes.

"Beck, there's a mini orgy going on in that room." Will and Rhett were on the couch with two half naked girls on the laps, making out. The girls were making out.

He cackled and squeezed me tighter to him. "That happens."

"You don't have to take me home. Thatcher could have

given me a ride." I was talking out of my ass. I didn't even know why I said that, I was just uncomfortable witnessing a scene like that with someone with me. Now if I was alone, it wouldn't have bothered me. I would have even documented it.

Actually, strike that. I would have felt like I was making porn. I would only have taken artistic shots with no boobage.

"He likes you. Which is odd, I've never seen him with anyone before." Beck opened the back door, shrugging off two more girls trying to get his attention.

"He definitely gets the girls." I blurted. This whole night had me all scrambled, saying things I shouldn't.

"That sounds like there's a story behind it." He trailed off expectantly as he opened the passenger door for me. I climbed in, hoping he'd forget about it as he walked around the car. He did not.

"Well, out with it."

I sighed. Did I want to tell him this story? He knew Thatcher so he wasn't some anonymous person who couldn't put a face to the story. The light from the back floodlight twinkled in his eyes, begging me to share all my hidden secrets.

I sighed. "Let's just say when I met him, he had a friend with him. You can ask him for the rest if you want." That was sufficiently vague; I mentally patted myself on the back.

"So, how did you meet Thatch?" He pulled out gum, handing me a piece.

"There's a scholarship I'm trying to go for, and unfortunately, I suck at all art except for picture taking. My art teacher set it up so I could borrow a camera from one of his friends at the university. When I went to pick it up, Thatcher was the one waiting. I've only met him one other time from tonight." I watched him as he drove, feeling calmer because he couldn't stare back.

"Huh. I'll definitely have to ask him for the details then." He popped his gum and smirked at me.

The drive to my house didn't take that long and it was over before I was ready to leave him. We listened to music for most of the ride but even that was fun. My house was dark and lonely as he pulled into the driveway, taunting me with the lifestyle my parents were determined I follow. I wasn't ready for this night to end.

"Beck?" I said.

"Yeah, Astrid?" The smile in his voice colored his words.

"Do you want to come in and see the pictures?" I cringed when I heard the hope sprinkled through my voice. I did not want to seem like one of the groupies at the bar.

"I don't know," he sounded weary, "I don't mix that well with parents."

I brightened. "That's completely fine. Mine are out of town until tomorrow."

He was quiet for a moment and then nodded. "Yeah, why not."

Excited, I started to open my door, but hesitated. "Just for pictures and to hang out. There'll be none of what was going on in that room."

"Sex?" He smirked. Smart ass.

"Yes, sex. Nothing like that." I didn't believe he was coming in for that, but I wanted to draw the line very clearly. I liked Beck. He was fun, hot, and talented, but I wasn't ready for one-night stands.

"That was never a thought in my mind." He crossed his heart.

"Good." I blew out a breath. "Pull in the garage after I open it, that way no one will notice your car. Just in case."

"Ah, man. You're taking me back to my high school days of sneaking through windows to see girls." He laughed.

"Ha ha." I fake laughed. And just like that, I snuck my first boy into the house.

Chapter 10

He followed behind me as we entered the house. I turned the light on over the island in the kitchen, looking around trying to see what it might look like to a stranger. He'd notice the immaculate way the stainless-steel refrigerator and faucet would shine. The smell of apple pie from the bath and body works plug in would assault him. Would he notice the lack of personal touches? The only form of family my mother liked to display were the pictures in the hallway and then a few staple family photos in the living room.

"So, this is it." I spun, sticking my fingers in the back of my jeans.

Beck looked just as uncomfortable as I felt as he hovered in the doorway. For some reason, it made me want to laugh. Where was the Casanova from the bar?

"Nice house." He grinned and crossed his arms and taking on a Mr. Clean stance.

"Thanks... Let's go in my room. We can put the pictures on my laptop." I turned to head toward the stairs before I hesitated. My room? Why did I say that? Now he was going to think I was trying to seduce him on the sly. I couldn't go back on it now, so I kept going.

His footsteps on the stairs behind me gave me this strange urge to go faster. I jogged the rest of the way, keeping my hand on the camera bag to prevent any unnecessary jostling. It might not be mine, but it was my ticket out of here. No harm would come to this beautiful contraption on my watch.

In my room, Beck walked over to the window.

After I connected the camera to the laptop, I joined him while the pictures were transferring. The view was the perfect American suburbia stereotype. Cookie cutter houses, except for the Bennets', neat and trimmed landscapes, and haloed streetlights. A beautiful prison.

"Nice street." He said and I busted up laughing.

"You've been a regular ladies man and expert conversationalist all evening, and now it's nice house, nice street." I wiped the amused tears from my eyes.

He grinned ruefully. "Yeah, when I calm down after a performing high, I tend to lose my charming quality. Sorry about that. I'll try harder until I leave."

"Sit down here, I'll grab the laptop." The bay window was the perfect viewing spot. It was surreal to entertain someone here, but I loved it.

Crossing my legs underneath me, I balanced the cool laptop on my legs. Beck scooted closer as I pulled the first picture up, the one of him crouched down in front of me. I stared at his profile, eating up the awed expression on his face.

This kind of appreciation made art worth it. I bet that was how he felt with hundreds of fans singing along to his songs.

"Astrid, that's... Can you send that to me?" His arm went behind me as he bent closer.

"Of course. Look at some of these other ones." I cleared

my throat. We flipped through each picture, stopping longer on the ones he seemed to love. It was probably a weak way to spend the time with a boy in my bedroom, but it was the perfect ending to the perfect night. Almost perfect night, outside of getting caught by Jonah.

"What's your email address?" I dropped all of the pictures he wanted into an email.

"I'll type it." He nudged the laptop away from me and started tapping the keys.

I leaned over his shoulder out of sheer curiosity.

beckfandom@gmail.com

Snickering, I inched back in the corner against my favorite pillow and look out the window.

"Don't laugh, I needed an email for when I make it big." He laughed at himself and slid the computer back my way.

The email was gone and the picture of the crowd screaming their love was left on the screen. A small smile tugged at the corner of my lips. He really was going to make it big someday. It seemed everyone had something that could catapult them into adulthood in style.

"That crowd was completely crazy for you. You'll make it before too long." I tipped my head back against the wall.

"Yeah, maybe." He let loose a tired sigh. "I'm always a hit in the local places and some people are even starting to sing along to our songs. It's the greater population that's hard to reach. A few hundred people aren't going to support me though."

That sounded awfully pessimistic. I sort of wanted to punch him for not being more grateful for his talent. Especially when it was so obvious as tonight with people chanting his name.

"Why the frown?"

Beck reached out and touched my knee, then retreated as if he'd never closed the two-foot gap.

"Whining doesn't suit you. Where's the cocky guy from the Iron Horse?" I feathered my fingers over soft denim on my thigh.

He straightened up and bent toward me.

"Whining?" His voice went high in his surprise.

Ah, he hadn't expected me to be so blunt. His brows slammed together, and he looked like he wasn't so pleased to be here right now. Yikes, I totally offended him.

Cringing, I started to reach out, but decided against it and dropped my hand. "Look, I didn't mean that. Actually I did mean that, but I didn't have to just say it. You have an amazing gift and you're going to get out of this town one day. It's just a matter of when. And it's kind of a turnoff to downplay it, and say you aren't good enough."

His jaw had slowly dropped, highlighting the slight honey blond stubble. Then he snapped his mouth shut and grinned crookedly.

"I was turning you on?" His voice dipped into sensual baby making mode.

"What? No. What?" I replayed my words in my head. Damn. I said it was a turn off and his twelve-year-old brain translated that as I was previously aroused. "Nice jump there. The gap in that logic is so wide I'm surprised you aren't a splatter on my floor."

He laughed, bending over with his arms wrapped around his middle. The happy, carefree sound warmed my body so quick, goosebumps popped up on my arms. I tried not to stare, but he was gorgeous like this.

"You're pretty witty, Astrid." He said as he wiped tears from his eyes. "And honest. I like that."

The look in his eyes heated me for a different reason.

Bright green specks in his hazel eyes drew me in, until I couldn't hold his stare anymore. Dang, he was intense.

I shrugged awkwardly and stared out the window again.

"You're a senior and eighteen, but the way you react sometimes... you're not like the girls I knew in high school. Those girls were vultures. How are you so innocent?"

I mulled over his question as I traced a pattern on the window. Was I innocent? I didn't think I was. I knew things, watched things. Maybe I was lacking in experience because I had the parents from hell, but I wasn't innocent. I'd like to believe I was more socially awkward than anything.

"My dad is one of the pastors at Bright Horizon. So let's just say, I've probably had a different high school experience than you."

"Aw man. You're a preacher's daughter? I should probably leave. I'm surprised I haven't caught fire being in your bedroom." He sounded amused and only about half serious.

"I'm more than just a preacher's daughter. Like you're more than just a mechanic." I snottily replied, my gaze darting back to him.

"I'm joking, I'm joking. So how did you all come to be here. In sunny Colorado? Small minded Silver Ranch?"

"Job opportunity. They are also willing to pay for my college. Dad worked it out as part of his salary, but he had to take a pay cut."

"Wow, they must love you a lot."

"Yeah..." I didn't want to get into that particular conversation right now. And as much as I actually liked him, he didn't get that part of my life. He fixed my headlight because he felt sorry for me. What would he do if he knew the whole story? Even Ryan didn't know everything.

"How old are you?" I changed the subject and honestly, I was curious.

"Twenty-one. Two months ago." He said proudly.

Wow. He really was an adult. And I was barely out of jail bait range.

"Why do you work as a mechanic? You should be making music all the time."

"I love you for that. But unfortunately, the money we get from gigs has to be split four ways. We barely get a couple hundred and we can only play on the weekends. Hardly enough to pay the bills."

I nodded. That was kind of sad. "You didn't want to go to college?" After the words fell from my mouth, I regretted it. I didn't know if he didn't and I was making assumptions. I was an ass. Perfect nickname Ryan gave me.

"Nah. I never liked school. I didn't have the grades or money for it either." He shrugged like it wasn't even an issue.

I desperately wanted to ask about his mom, but if I wasn't willing to talk about mine, I wouldn't ask him about his.

Across the street, the garage door opened and a car reversed hard out of the driveway and sped away. I jumped up, mainly because of what house it was. The car that drove away was the same one Mr. Bennet drove here the night of the dinner. And whoever it was, they weren't happy.

"What's wrong?" Beck stood beside me, gazing in the same direction that held my attention.

"I know the people that live in that house. Did you see that car?" I nearly touched the glass trying to get a better look.

"I didn't see it, but I heard it. Definitely a luxury car. I could tell that even through the sound of squealing tires."

"What do you think happened? It's after midnight." I said like the time made a difference. But it didn't. Anytime a car left like that it meant something not good had happened in that house.

"The dad was caught cheating, or found the wife with drugs." His voice was nonchalant, like that kind of thing happened all the time. "There's no telling really."

"Let's go find out."

"What?" Beck nearly shouted, spinning me around with a hand on my elbow. "You can't be serious."

Oh, I was serious. I had this insane urge to see why Rhys never made it to the party.

"I know the guy that lives there." Not really. Or not well. And Trey didn't count. "He was supposed to be at the party tonight and never showed up. I want to check on him."

"You can't do that in the middle of the night. You can call tomorrow. What is that guy, your boyfriend or something?" He pressed his lips together.

I wanted to believe there was a bit of jealousy there, but I was sure it was all in my head.

"No, and I'm going now. With my camera. You can come or you can go home. Your choice." I unplugged the camera form my laptop and slung the strap over my head. The cool plastic was already a familiar weight in my hands. I'd miss it when I had to turn it back in. Maybe by then I'd have a job with enough money to buy my own.

Beck made a strangely sexy sound in the back of his throat that said both *you're insane* and *I'm a sultry stud muffin*. A laugh bubbled up and he looked at me like he should take me to the mental ward instead of across the street.

"All right," he sighed. "I'll go with you to make sure you don't get the cops called on you."

Yes! I officially had a partner in crime.

"Thanks, Beck!" I smiled brightly and patted him on the arm.

He didn't look as amused as I was, more like resigned to his dreaded fate of an eternal life in a *High School Musical*. That was okay, there were worse fates than spending an eternity with Zac Efron.

"Yeah, yeah. But no going in. Only looking through windows." He scratched his head.

"Done. I wasn't planning on going in anyway." Adrenaline rushed through my body in anticipation of what we were about to do.

This was forbidden, dangerous. And yes, it was more dangerous than anything I'd done because if we got caught, it would be trespassing. But that wasn't enough for me to turn around. I needed to know what was going on over there. Rhys Bennet was a mystery I wanted to solve, especially considering how night and day he and his cousin were.

Beck followed me as I ran down the stairs and out the back door. If we were going to be super sleuths, I had to make sure no one witnessed us leaving the house. This way we could travel through the shadows on the side of the yard. The way the streetlights were scattered over the neighborhood, there was a pocket of darkness we could slip right through. A light breeze rustling through the trees and the distant rumbling of cars on the highway were the only sounds.

No, that wasn't the only sound. Muffled thumping sounded like it was coming from Rhys' house. I motioned to Beck to hurry up and broke into a light jog. Once we were on the edge of their property, a gate on the side of their house came into view. I slowed down, studying their place.

It was completely dark in the front, except for little solar lights lining the walkway. If I hadn't witnessed the getaway car, I would have thought everyone was asleep in their perfect house with their perfect dreams. Another crash jolted me from my musings, and I hustled to make it to the gate. Luckily, it was a standard gate that wasn't locked. They probably didn't expect to have creepers stalking their yard at night.

The back yard lacked the solar lights of the front, and with hardly any moonlight it was hard to see two feet in front of my face. A huge window was close to the corner of the house, hopefully they didn't have any curtains back here. I mean, they did have a six-foot brick wall surrounding their yard. No need for privacy. Well, unless they had crazy people walking around their house. Like me.

Beck tapped me on the shoulder, and I jumped a foot in the air. Fuck, it was like he was the scary cucumber coming to get me.

"Over there." He whispered in my ear, pointing to a cottage looking thing in the corner.

There weren't any lights on facing us, but the far wall glowed as if there might be lights on the other side of the cottage. That was it. That had to be where all the commotion was coming from. If it had been in the house, they had already gone to bed.

I kept to the wall as I edged around the yard. Ten steps in, Beck placed his hand on my waist, as if he wanted to make sure I didn't run away from him. With every step I took, his hand slid a little further down, until his fingers were flirting with the hem of my shirt at my hip. My breath caught and I almost stumbled. Almost. It was so innocent, but the touch was blaringly loud in the dark of night.

Muted voices knocked me back to reality and I kept walking until I was between the house and wall. Bright light shone through a window on the far end. Shadows passed over it and the voices got louder as we moved closer. I ducked under the window to avoid being seen. The bottom of the window was about shoulder high, thank God. It was easier than trying to convince Beck to let me climb him like a tree.

I let out a slow breath as I tried to control my nerves. My heart beat so loud, it throbbed in my ears. I glanced at Beck and he was staring at me, missing all the signs of skittish excitement I was throwing left and right. He winked and motioned for me to look in the window. I should have moved, but I kept ogling him. He rolled his eyes and pressed his face into my neck.

"Astrid, look in the window and satisfy your curiosity. We need to go." His hand on my hip squeezed once and he stepped back, leaving me a puddle of hormones at his feet. Okay, not really, but it was pretty close.

I counted to three and stuck my head high enough to see inside, and gasped. It was some kind of living room and it was *wrecked*. A cabinet lay on its side, furniture was randomly scattered around the room, and it even looked like broken porcelain or some kind of dishes littered the floor. Rhys had his back to the window as he knelt, probably cleaning up the mess.

"You got another bag ready yet?" Trey hollered right before he appeared in the doorway.

"No." Rhys' answer was clipped and angry.

Trey pinched the bridge of his nose and clenched his eyes. "This is your fault. You know that, right?"

That was cold. And I didn't even know what happened. It also didn't sound like a smart thing to say. Rhys must have agreed with me because his shoulders tensed, right before his head whipped around to face Trey.

"What the fuck, man? You're going to pin this on me? Some fucking cousin you are." Rhys practically shouted at Trey.

"What does cousins have to do with this? It. Was. Your. Fault. You shouldn't have stuck your nose in business that wasn't yours. I'd be pissed at you too." Trey kicked an antique looking wooden chair.

"Fuck off. You're just like him. I can't stand either of you. Why are you still here?" Rhys growled.

"Like I have anywhere to go, dickhead." Trey snorted, but it was an ugly sound.

"Not to live. I mean here right now, right this second in my breathing space. Go in the house. Get away from me." Rhys tossed a handful of something that clinked in the bag.

"Whatever, I was trying to help you. You can do it your own damn self." Trey started to walk our way and I crouched down.

That was close. His shadow darkened the window but after a few minutes, a door slammed on the other side of the cottage, followed by the door of the main house. I let two whole, torturous minutes pass before I was confident enough to peek inside again.

Rhys was in a different spot now, his shoulders hunched in on himself. Every arrogant and mean thought I'd ever had toward Rhys suddenly seemed sour in my stomach. Since the day of the pep rally, I'd been secretly envious of this perfect guy. He was the popular boy. The one everyone wanted. With hockey and his family money, he'd be able to go to any school he wanted. It never occurred to me that he would be in a similar prison. It softened the heart I had been trying so hard to harden.

My eyes widened when he turned his head. He had a shiner from hell. Already. And that was assuming it just happened. He hadn't had it at school yesterday, anyway.

"It's time to go," Beck whispered in my hair.

I shook my head no. How could I leave right now? He looked devastated. Even if he didn't know I was here, he wouldn't be alone. Sometimes that was what I hated the most. Being alone when I was upset or hurting from things my parents did or said.

I raised my camera to capture this heartbreaking moment of the star hockey player beaten and broken on the floor, cleaning up the mess of his parent. Several clicks later, Beck poked me again and gave me big eyes.

Ugh. I didn't want to go. I wanted to stay and see what Rhys would do, maybe get a few more pictures. Beck had a point though. We were trespassing, and we could be in a lot of trouble if we were caught. Maybe not me, since they knew my dad, but Beck could be. And the self-righteous air his dad gave off, he would totally take it out on Beck. I couldn't let that happen to him.

Beck stared at me expectantly and I nodded, I just wanted to get one more glimpse of Rhys. When I turned around, Rhys was standing at the window staring down at me. A sneer on his face and fury in his eyes.

Damn. Tonight wasn't my night. At. All.

Chapter
11

Should I run for it?

Beck looked athletic, I was sure he could keep up. And at the moment, I was insanely happy there was a glass pane between us. It gave us more of a head start. He'd have to go through the little cottage—granted it wasn't big—before he'd be outside to really chase us. We could hide in a neighbor's yard until then.

I reached out and caught Beck's hand and squeezed, letting him know I had a plan.

"Don't even think about it." Rhys braced his hands on the windowsill and bent down. Surprisingly, he was more intimidating up close and personal. "I know where you live, Astrid." It hadn't bothered me before, but now that he was talking to me, he sounded muffled, like he was underwater.

Beck laughed humorlessly. "He's right, Astrid. We're caught, like I was afraid of."

This had to be the worst end to my perfect night. Damn me, and my peeping Tom tendencies.

As the seconds ticked by, I ping ponged between Beck and Rhys. They both stood completely still, waiting for me. Resigned to my fate I tried to smile at Rhys, but I was pretty sure I looked like Trey tried to shake my hand with his dick.

"Come around to the front and come in." He left the window to probably unlock the door. I sent a silent prayer up to the heavens that I hadn't just blackballed myself at school.

We didn't bother with stealth mode as we made our way around the house. There was no need now.

The door was already open with a no-nonsense Rhys in the way. If he ever looked like an angry Ragnor, it was now. His light blond hair glowed from the light behind him, also casting his face in shadows. I definitely wouldn't want to meet him in a dark alley, or a little cottage in the middle of the night.

Beck gave me a little push, so I went in first. The entry was just as trashed as the living room, and standing inside it was like entering a battle zone after a gruesome fight. What happened here?

Rhys walked ahead of us after he locked the door and motioned for us to sit on the couch. It was out of place, because it was pulled away from the wall, but we did as he wanted anyway. He flipped over a chair in front of us and took his own seat.

I decided I wasn't going to speak until I had to, so I studied the room instead. Actually, it was more like I didn't want to look Rhys in the eye after getting caught spying on him. The place smelled nice, like some kind of warm citrusy scent. They probably had lemon plug ins around here some-where. The end table closest to me seemed like a good place to stare. It was one of those really nice mahogany tables, all sleek with chrome handles. Modern. There were also deep grooves etched into the top like something had landed on it and slid off.

I'd never been in a place so soon after a fight like this and seeing all the damage, it scared me.

"So... I was waiting for you to start, but it's clear you aren't going to. Why are you here?" He leaned his elbows on his knees and focused all of his intense Ragnor self on me.

Not Beck. It was like he didn't even acknowledge Beck was with me. I glanced to the side to make sure Beck had followed me in. Shew. He had. I would have kicked his butt if he tried to leave me.

My brain said stall, but I had no idea how to do that. I could flash him. If I showed him boobs would he forget about me hanging out under his window? I squinted at him, trying to read his vibes. No, I didn't think he'd fall for the boobage.

He seemed much too in control of his horny teenage desires for that. I might as well tell the truth. At least enough so he doesn't flip out.

"We were in my bedroom and we saw your dad's car race out of the driveway. It worried me so we came over to check it out." I still had that cringe on my face but at least my voice sounded normal.

"Uh huh." He looked at Beck. "And who are you?" He did his own bit of squinting, only it looked sexy and intimidating on him. "You look familiar. Do I know you?"

Beck scratched the back of his head again. That had to be his thing. I'd seen him do it several times even in the short time I'd known him. "I work at Tacky's in town. You might have dropped your dad's car off for an oil change before."

He conveniently left out he was in a band. But maybe that was to seem less important than what he was? Or he might not identify as a musician, seeing himself as a poser.

"Yeah, I've done that before. I'd almost believe your story, except for the camera you're holding in your hand.

Why were you taking pictures of me?" His voice turned deadly and the hair stood up on the back of my neck.

I didn't believe he would actually hurt me, but sitting in a destroyed house, staring at a guy with a pretty bad black eye, was not helping to calm me down.

"She takes pictures. That's her thing." Beck supplied as he turned to me. "I thought you said you knew this guy? That you were supposed to meet him at the party?"

Eeep. Rhys would know this was a lie, regardless if he asked about me or not. And it also made me out to be a crazy desperate chick, lying about the extent of my nonexistent relationship with Rhys. Those kinds of girls were psycho, and I resented it, but I put myself in this position.

Rhys' eyebrows shot up and then furrowed again. Who knew what he was thinking? I knew what I *was* and that was bad enough.

"I may have said you were supposed to be at the party earlier. I don't think I said we were meeting. It was really so Beck would want to come with me." Now it looked like I lied to Beck to get what I wanted, when really, it was more of an offhand half-true comment. I was really winning tonight.

He threw his hands up in the air. "I would have come with you no matter what. I wouldn't allow you to get arrested."

I wanted to slide down in the deep cushions since I felt about two inches tall.

Choosing to avoid that whole topic, Rhys went somewhere else equally as horrifying for me.

"Do you make a habit of creeping around people's houses at night? Taking pictures when they're unaware?" He quirked a blond eyebrow.

I blew a raspberry and adjusted in my seat to get more

comfortable. If I had to answer this, I was going to explain and hopefully make him think I was less of a weirdo.

"You're making it sound like I stalk people to capture them in compromising positions. That's not it at all, okay? It's a... a hobby I guess, to take pictures. And yes, I like people the most, and I've also gotten some crazy pictures." I shouldn't have admitted that. "But it's all things I've stumbled on. I like photography." I shrugged, fingering the on and off button of the camera.

Rhys nodded, then traced one of his brows with an index finger. I watched the movement, mesmerized by the sensuality of the action. Now would be a perfect time to take a picture, but I was pretty sure he would frown on that.

"Then why were you taking pictures of me?" He repeated.

Damn. I was hoping he would forget about that and we could quietly slip into the night.

"Would you believe it was an artistic shot?" I arranged my face into a pained smile.

"No. It's an invasion of privacy." He leaned back and spread his legs while crossing his arms. He was the picture of vibrant masculinity. The real one, not the posers from the pep rally.

Where's a fan when I needed one? It was suddenly a hundred degrees in here.

"So maybe that wasn't my most shining moment. I'm a sucker for candid emotional scenes."

A curtain of anger descended over his face as he glared at me.

I get it, emotion isn't your thing.

"Let's see them." He bit out.

I turned on the camera and took a quick look through the few pictures I was able to capture. He wasn't quite in profile, but it wasn't his back either. He was hunched, defeated. Sitting in the center of domestic destruction, possibly wondering why it all had to come to this. At least, that was what the picture said to me. When I glanced up, he was watching me, his right eye almost completely swollen shut.

I got up and moved to his side, kneeling by his legs. Beck moved like he was going to get up, but in the end stayed sitting on the crooked couch. Rhys' leg was warm against my side. His gaze burned into the side of my head as I turned away from him so we could both look at the pictures the same time. There were three in total. All virtually the same, except for little nuances here and there in the twist of his shoulder and the tilt of his head. I loved them, even knowing I shouldn't have taken them.

"I'll delete them." I sighed. I barely touched the delete button when he stopped me with his hand on my wrist.

Goosebumps erupted along the arm he was touching and when I glanced up, our faces inches apart. Good grief, he was gorgeous. His nose was slightly crooked, probably from some outrageous hockey fight. Intense ice blue eyes that looked like they held the secrets to the universe. And slightly disheveled hair that begged me to run my fingers through it.

"That's a great moment you two are having." Beck commented.

I couldn't pull my gaze away to see what he was doing, though.

"You don't have to delete them. My face isn't visible, and only someone who really knew me would be able to recognize me in that picture." He let his fingers slip from my arm.

"Really?" I beamed. I didn't believe that was true. He

was a stud in SRHS, and I'd wager my... no, not my camera — my good grades that at least half the school would take one look at this and know immediately it was Rhys.

He traced my mouth with his gaze and smiled. "Yeah. Don't say I never did anything nice for you."

That killed my rising good mood. Why did these guys have to keep reminding me they were doing me favors? It was really starting to get on my last art loving nerve.

"Thanks." I deadpanned.

Feeling weird sitting at his feet, I moved back to the couch next to Beck. He sent me a questioning look, but I ignored it. He could ask me whatever it was when we left.

We all stared at each other for a few minutes. I wasn't quite sure where the conversation was going to take us at this point. He clearly wasn't going to call the cops. Or his parents. He hadn't made me delete the photos. Short of asking him what happened here, which I would never do, there was nothing left.

"Aren't you going to ask?" Rhys moved back into his sexy pose.

I blinked. Was he opening this door?

"Are you offering?" I countered.

"That depends. How long were you at the window?" A small amount of tension slithered into his voice.

"We were only there for about five minutes tops, man." Beck reentered the conversation, sliding an arm around the back of the couch. Rhys watched it but didn't comment.

I was sitting forward, so he wasn't actually touching me, but something about the move seemed territorial.

"So, you heard?" He prompted.

He was going to make us say it. Repeat what we heard. I mean, I guessed I'd want to know too, but it didn't make it any less comfortable.

"Only Trey saying that it was your fault. That was really about it." I mumbled, staring past him to the glossy antique china cabinet laying on its side.

When there wasn't a response, I looked back at Rhys.

"So... what happened?" I broke my own rule, but I started it by cracking the proverbial door and feeding my curiosity.

"Let's just say, I found out my dad isn't as faithful as I always thought. And I confronted him about it." He left no room for any other comments so I merely nodded.

Beck and I made eye contact, and quickly diverted our gazes. It would be really shitty of us if Rhys thought we were judging him or his family. Little did he know, between my overbearing Bible thumpers, and Beck's drunk mom, we weren't in any position to throw stones.

"I think it's time I got Astrid back home." Beck stood, stretching his arms over his head.

Out of the corner of my eye, I caught a strip of tan flesh below his shirt, but I kept my gaze locked on Rhys.

"Yeah, that's a good idea." Rhys got up and moved the formal sitting chair over to the corner of the room.

"Do you want help straightening this place up?" I offered sheepishly. The set of his shoulders said he wanted to pretend we were standing in the school hallway instead of in the destroyed living room of their guest cottage, but I couldn't leave without making the offer. The manners beat into me from birth wouldn't allow it.

"No. I got myself into this mess, I'll clean it up. That's why Trey said it was my fault. Because I confronted him. Trey would have been happy to ignore it for the rest of his life. Hell, he'll happily follow in my father's footsteps." He spat bitterly.

"You did what you thought was right. There's nothing

wrong with that, and you shouldn't be punished for speaking your truth." I stepped closer to him, my voice low. Beck could hear everything, but it gave the illusion of more privacy this way.

"No one wants the truth. The world is all about the lies." His words hit me square in the chest.

They reverberated around inside my rib cage until they settled over my heart, branding me with their verity.

My truth, his truth, that wasn't going to get us anywhere. If we wanted to make it out of this life unscathed, it was all about the lies.

12
Beck

Fuck, the sun was singeing the hair off the back of my neck. Good thing Thatcher brought the good beer.

"So, Astrid. How do you know her?" Thatcher leaned a hip against the side of his shitty Corolla. It had definitely seen better days. He might be in a good place now, and he never talked about it, but Thatcher's childhood wasn't so different than mine. I could sense it, which was probably why I liked him so much.

He thought he was being all slick, acting like I hadn't seen him looking down Astrid's top last night.

"I helped her with some car trouble. You?" My voice bounced off the engine as I checked the brake fluid.

Out of the corner of my eye, he shrugged, taking his time to answer. I'd bet he wanted to keep that little tidbit to himself, but that wouldn't fly.

You better answer dickbag, or I'll put detergent in your windshield fluid.

"At the college." His voice was too light, and even if Astrid hadn't alluded to a damn juicy story, I'd know he was lying out his ass.

"And?" I straightened, wiping my hands on an oily rag. A cocky smirk teased my lips and he scowled back at me.

"She's trying to get a scholarship. Dan asked me to meet her to pass over some stuff. She seems like a nice kid." His eyes narrowed, daring me to question him.

"You have no idea what kind of girl she is. And don't for a second believe that's all I think happened. I know you well enough now to know it's not." I laughed and went back to checking everything over. If nothing else, Thatcher took care of his car. I wished everyone stayed on top of their maintenance like this.

"What's that supposed to mean?" He was actually confused.

Last night, when I first saw them together, it seemed like they had a history, even if on the short side. But if he had to ask me that, then he didn't know her at all. Something about that was so deeply satisfying. I turned my head and grinned to myself.

"She's not as innocent as you think." I left it at that. If he thought there was some delicious secrets under the surface, he'd want to know. Maybe enough to tell me how they met. I was playing on his weaknesses, but I couldn't help it. I *needed* to know.

"Beck, what's wrong with you, being all cryptic and shit? Don't tell me she's one of your small-town groupies." The veins in his forearms popped as he gripped the side of the car.

"Nope. She's not a groupie at all. I offered to take her to my show to get her away from one of Remy's parties." I replied smoothly. "I'm done here. Let's grab a chair and we can catch up a bit before you head home."

He nodded but continued anyway. "Who's Remy?"

"Bad news. A kid at the high school who throws out of control parties." That was different. Since when had I started thinking about high schoolers as kids?

"What? I did not get the wild vibe from her." He adjusted in his seat and popped the lid on his craft beer.

"She isn't wild. I got the impression she was only there with a friend." A no-good friend from the wrong side of the tracks. Who knew how she would have ended the night with Jonah. He seemed like a decent guy on the surface, but that was all it was. A surface act, deflecting his true colors. Even if he was trying, his mom was so messed up in drugs and the local motorcycle gang that he'd eventually been removed from the home in seventh grade. His whole family were bad apples. Too bad he was already working for *them* then.

I'd cut off my left nut if he had somehow escaped their poisonous claws. Too many guys I knew ended up with that gang, either in prison or dead.

"Your turn."

Thatcher curled a lip as if in pain, but then sighed in defeat. "I wasn't expecting her for another hour or so. She caught me with Emily in the storage closet." He glanced away to hide the blush I had already seen.

I didn't know why it was such a big deal. He knew I played shows. Those fuckers turned into downright orgies sometimes. Not that I participated. All the time. I was more of a voyeur. It wasn't like I always turned away a good one-night stand, but Rhett and Will were man whores in the worst possible way. If they weren't spreading around STD's like hot butter on toast, it would be a miracle. I had a strict no sharing policy with them.

"So what, she caught you giving it good to her?" I chuckled. Where the hell did my sunglasses go?

"Not exactly like that. It was more of her giving it good to me." He coughed into his hand.

"No way!" I jerked forward, almost spilling my beer on

my lap. "She caught Em giving you head? Ha! That's classic. That might be worse. If she'd seen you banging her, it might have made her envious. But that, she sees you just as a taker." I snickered, extremely smug.

"What? No." He was clearly confused. He had a little sister he was tight with. How did he not know how women worked? Ridiculous.

"What are you confused about?"

"That wasn't how it was at all. She saw a few seconds at most. She didn't even leave the room, just spun around." A smile cracked for the first time since we started this conversation.

"That doesn't surprise me. She doesn't seem like the type to run." No, she wanted to stay in a situation as long as possible and court getting caught.

"Em didn't care. She'd blow someone in class if she was feeling it. I thought Astrid would be awkward and weird about it, but she wasn't. She didn't mention it again and neither did I." He shielded his eyes from the sun.

Where were his sunglasses?

"She was on a mission. I offered to help, and I thought she was going to accept it, but she changed her mind at the last minute."

"She doesn't need it. She's really good." I would know. I'd stared at the pictures she sent me every day for an unhealthy amount of time. Partly because they were awesome shots. Partly because of the depth required to take those kinds of pictures.

"I know, man. I saw her stuff last night. The pictures she took of you and the crowd..." He trailed off. "She should have no problem getting past the local high school round at least."

Wait, there was something more to this than just a hobby?

"Explain."

"A new scholarship was announced. Two winners from each high school, and then one winner total. That's why I had to meet her to give her the camera. I didn't really chat with Dan about it before then, because I didn't care, but he said her teacher thinks if she practices and works on honing her talent, she'd have a decent chance."

Good for her. She had people in her corner, willing to help her out. I was envious and a little sad. Would she want to hang out with me once she went to college? It was one thing to kind of be friends with Thatcher, but he sure didn't come around just for shits and giggles, only when he needed work on his car done.

"Hold that thought. I need to see if I have any sunglasses in the house. My eyes are getting sunburned." I hopped up and ran inside. Partly to look for sunglasses, but mostly to collect myself.

The door swung shut behind me, and my mom groaned from the couch. This was why I never let anyone inside. I never knew when she'd grace me with her presence or what state she'd be in. Hell, she'd tried to bring people over with her before.

Her brain cells had to be fried from too much crack by now, so she probably didn't remember she didn't live here. And never had. When I was two weeks out of graduation, she lost our trailer and Tacky's took pity on me. Helped me set this place up as long as I could make the rent on my own.

"Beck..." She slurred, tossing an arm over her eyes as she anxiously rubbed her legs together. "I need..."

"No, you don't need that." I bypassed her and pulled

out drawers in the kitchen. There were some old pairs in here somewhere.

"Beck," she said, right before rolling over and vomiting on the ugly shag carpet.

My neck tensed as I watched her. Fuck. I hated this. I hated *her* sometimes too, before the guilt started to pour into me. Ignoring the putrid smell, I lifted her off the couch and carried her to the spare bedroom, then grabbing a rag to clean her up. A giant, orange cracked bucket sat in the corner just for her. I moved it into position before going back to clear up her mess.

Looking down at the bile, with hardly any food, I almost lost my stomach too. I must have fucked up bad in my last life to deserve this. It was that, or know this was a random, undeserved punishment.

I couldn't think that way. That was just cruel.

Chapter 13

"Astrid, bitch. You better wake up!"

I screamed and flew off the bed like zombie church elders were on my heels. What the freak kind of dream was that?

"Oof!" I grunted and fell back on the bed after hitting a mostly hard body. Screaming again I opened my eyes, prepared to take as many zombies with me as I could, but it was Ryan. A non-gray, non-sightless guy. Not a zombie at all.

"Are you awake now?" Ryan was not amused.

"Yes," I rasped, my throat still dry from sleep.

My brain was fuzzy, requiring large amounts of concentration as I searched for what happened last night. I wasn't normally so slow, but staring at Ryan while he stared at me was making this awkward.

Then it all came back. All of my horrendously embarrassing moments. It was probably a good time to talk to Mother Dearest about convent school. It would be a Godly life with little chance of embarrassing myself. She would approve. I think.

"Why do you suddenly look constipated?" Ryan laughed.

Flipping him double birds, I sat up. "I was reflecting on my bad decisions. I don't think I want to stay here in this town anymore."

"What the hell happened last night, Astrid?" he flipped out in zero to sixty, like a fancy Maserati.

It kind of gave me the warm and fuzzies to have him so concerned. Needlessly, but the sentiment was still there.

"Nothing bad like you're thinking. Just embarrassing stuff. I got caught taking pictures. Twice." I cringed, and he answered it with a duck lip cringe. The face was hilarious and I laughed, glad he had leaned back. No one needed to know what Astrid breath smelled like in the morning.

"You didn't?" He gasped.

"Yes," I sighed.

I glanced at my clock, glad that it was only nine-thirty. There were still a couple hours before the parentals came home. Just enough time for me to straighten up, do a few chores, and head out before they arrived. I've been meaning to get a local library card anyway.

"Let me clean up. Then we can chat while I grab breakfast and do some stuff around the house."

"Okay," Ryan turned around and flopped backward onto the bed, bouncing me right off.

When I came back in, he was rummaging through the top drawer in my nightstand.

"What are you doing?" I fisted my hands on my hips. We were friends, and he was arguably becoming as close as Stace, but this was still an invasion of privacy.

"You're the first *girl* friend I've ever had. I was curious. I wanted to see if you were hiding lascivious secrets in a diary, or a little rabbit thing for when you read smut books." He didn't look up as he continued to see what was in the next drawer.

"What the hell? Not all girls are alike, just like all guys don't like vaginas. You'll find neither of those things there. Not to mention my dad's a pastor. That would get me landed in an all-girl school faster than I could say orgasm." I huffed, strutting over to slam the drawers shut. "Remind me to go through your closet when I visit your room for the first time. There's probably a half used jar of Vaseline and pictures of your mom's best friend. Or neighborhood cat lady."

"Gah! Don't say things like that. You're going to scare me right out of this friendship." We both dissolved into giggles, making an adorable puppy pile on the bed.

"Let's go down to the kitchen. You eat breakfast yet?" I popped him on the chest and started down the hall without him. Sun streamed through the windows, highlighting the immaculate kitchen my mother insisted on keeping. On the plus side, it made cleaning up after a meal for one incredibly easy.

He was quick to follow, perching on an island stool as I shuffled around the kitchen, heating up waffles.

"So, what happened?" He propped his chin in his palm.

Wanting to delay a little longer, I deflected. "You first. Mine will be longer. Probably." I stared down at the bright turquoise waffle maker, twisting the spatula in my hand.

"Girl, guess who has a date Friday night?" He squealed and danced in his seat.

"That's awesome! I'm so happy for you." I beamed at him. And I really was. He deserved a bit of happiness and Pat seemed really good for him.

"Okay, your turn." He sobered up so fast I nearly had whiplash.

"That's it?! Like seven words? I need more than that." To satisfy the appropriate level of information a friend needed to know about Saturday night shenanigans, and also to stall.

He quirked a perfectly shaped brow. What he didn't do, was say anything. We entered into this epic, tense stare down, where I gave him a *you'll never get the truth* look and he gave me an *I'll wait you out, honey* look. I wasn't willing to fold, he could get his happy ass out of my house if he kept it up. But apparently, my spine just wasn't as strong as I wanted to think it was. Two minutes in and I completely sagged against the counter.

"Fine. Eat your waffles and I'll tell you what happened." We both dug in as I recounted the night before. His enthusiasm cracked me up, oohing and ahhing at every little thing. When I got to the part about Thatcher and Beck, his eyes rolled so far back in his head, I thought he was on his way down to kiss the speckled tile floor.

"You said you were caught twice." He prompted.

"Yeah," I drew out the word, buying as much time as I could. What happened with Rhys was personal and something he wouldn't want spread around. It was bad enough I let my peculiar hobby get the best of me by invading his privacy. Even though Beck was there, I couldn't share his secrets. So now, what did I tell Ryan?

"I might have also been caught taking a picture of Rhys. But both he and Jonah asked me to delete them." I expected God to send a lightning bolt through the roof and smite me where I stood. But it didn't happen. Instead, I just told lie number one.

"Weird. I didn't see Rhys there at the party at all." He muttered to his golden brown waffle.

"You were probably too wrapped up in Pat to notice." I shrugged and shoved a bite of syrupy waffle into my mouth.

If he thought it was odd I suddenly had chipmunk cheeks, he didn't show it.

"Hmm. Yeah, probably." He nudged his phone around to check the time. "What do you need to do before we can leave?"

"Just straighten up. I did laundry yesterday." I glanced around the kitchen, noting the small pile of cups in the sink along with the toaster on the counter. A good wiping down and vacuuming would do it. Along with the dishes of course. Without the parentals here the house stayed much cleaner. Funny how that worked.

The dull grating of the garage door signaled the dreaded arrival of my parents.

Oh, fuck. My parents.

Shooting up off the stool, I made shooing motions for him to run out the back door. "You have to go! They can't see you here." They really couldn't. They'd never leave me alone again and that wasn't how I was trying to spend my last year here.

Ryan rolled his eyes like I was touched in the head as he stood up. "Astrid, my car is parked in the driveway. They know I'm here."

They did. There was no way they wouldn't have seen it. I was so fucked. "Sit. Let me grab my notebook. We're going to be studying." I was mostly talking to myself as I rushed to my backpack in the mudroom. It was a miracle I hadn't taken it upstairs like I normally would during the week.

My sketchbook spread out over the counter with half done sketches scattered around me, providing the perfect illusion of a teenager hard at work. Mother Dearest was the first through the doorway and her gaze darted suspiciously between Ryan and me. It was a little unnerving being on this end of the stare, knowing Ryan should not be here.

"Astrid." She greeted coolly. "Who's this?"

My dad walked in behind her with their suitcase. Whenever they went on their weekend trips, they were efficient and combined their stuff. Less work for both as my dad liked to put it.

"This is Ryan. He's in my art class." I rushed out. Not suspicious at all. *Yeah, right.*

"Hi, Mrs. Scott. Mr. Scott. It's nice to meet you." Ryan squared his shoulders and offered his hand out to my mother first. His smile was huge and friendly. He was good at this meeting the parents stuff. I definitely needed to take lessons from him on how not to be awkward. My mother's nose wrinkled but she took it. That had to be a good sign.

"Likewise. So what are you all doing this morning?" Her voice was extra nasally as she looked down her nose at my sketchbook. She wasn't fond of my art even at the best of times.

"We have a project coming up and we were brainstorming ideas." I went to grab my pencil to hold something in my hand, but there wasn't one. Great, I grabbed the sketchbook but not the pencil. No way would she think we were actually working on school assignments if she noticed. I pulled the first loose paper I could get my grubby hands on and held it up.

"We are working on..." I glanced at the sheet and saw my attempt at sketching the mannequins from our body form day. The pose of the mannequins was completely innocent, but my stellar skills made it look like someone was getting a good spanking. "The body form. We're supposed to study body language for our sketches." Lie number two this morning. I would be racking them up quickly if I kept on this sinful path. Not ideal, but better than the dreary alternative of being locked in my bedroom.

Her beady eyes squinted at the page before backing up a step into Dad. He steadied her and followed her line of sight.

"Well now, that's a little different than I thought they'd teach you in school." He cleared his throat.

"It's not what you're thinking, Mr. Scott. It only looks like that because Astrid lacks the basic skills of drawing. I'll be handling the actual project." Ryan puffed out his chest like he was actually proud of this fake project we were working on.

My dad laughed as my mother just glared at the picture like it smacked her on the butt in real life.

"It's true. I'm not any good at art." I sighed.

"We're going to put our stuff away. Say, I haven't seen you at church. Where does your family go?" If there was one thing my dad excelled at, it was small talk. He always seemed jovial and easy to talk to. Such a contradiction to the man I knew.

I must have got my people skills from my mother. Unfortunately.

"We don't go to church." Ryan supplied easily. I didn't believe he knew he signed the death slip of our friendship.

A frown line creased between his eyebrows. "Nowhere? You should come one Sunday with Astrid. She helps out with the Sunday School classes. You'd love it." He nodded his head like it was a done deal. He probably thought he'd converted another believer by merely making the invitation.

Ryan flicked his gaze my way before focusing back on my parents. I couldn't answer the question in his eyes because there wasn't a good answer here. Not unless he wanted to start passing out off brand cookies and mouth-wash sized cups of soda out for morning snack on Sundays. Too bad he was horrible at reading my dad's nonverbal cues, because he went on to dig himself deeper into the *bad for Astrid* grave.

"We don't believe in God. We've always been atheists." Ryan's cheeks tinged with color as Dad's demeanor changed drastically. It went from jolly and warm to stern and cold. He was the male version of my mother in this extreme moment.

"That's too bad, son. If you ever want to start attending and check it out for yourself, Astrid will bring you. Just say the word." His words were saying something different than his eyes. Those were saying I had poor taste in friends and he was about to remedy it quickly.

"Sure, I'll keep it in mind." Ryan's voice was polite but no one in the room bought it.

"It's probably best for you to go home now. We haven't seen Astrid all weekend and it's family time now." Mother Dearest shrugged out of my father's hold and set her purse on the counter.

"Yeah, no problem." Ryan cast me a nervous glance before he said goodbye and ran out.

When the door slammed behind him, I was left with this awkward, disapproving silence.

"How was the trip?" Nonchalance was plan A. Hopefully I wouldn't need a plan B. Because that would be very bad.

"Astrid, did that boy stay the night?" Mother growled. I had to appreciate her directness at the very least.

"No, he dropped by this morning about the project. I didn't even know he was coming." Sprinkle a little truth with the lie and maybe they'd actually buy it.

"I don't think I need to tell you that someone like him is not who you should be surrounding yourself with." Dad walked past me, carrying the suitcase. "If you're hard up for friends I'll connect you with some of the kids of my associates. Rhys and Trey would be good options."

His words hung in the air even after he was no longer in the room. I couldn't decide whether I should be embarrassed he thought I was such a loser or indignant at his condescending tone. If I was honest with myself, I was a bit of both.

"You're officially grounded. If you're having boys in the house when we're gone, you can't be trusted. I don't know how you screw up so much." Mother Dearest breezed past me like she hadn't taken the last bit of sunshine from me. On the upside, she kept her hands to herself this time.

Now how was I supposed to get amazing shots for my portfolio? I'd have to do it at school and hope that no one noticed me being a creeper. Because I was still going forward with my plan to win the scholarship. Now I had to get creative.

Chapter 14

Several weeks into my grounding and I was still trying to find a way to leave the house. Any other time, Dad would be oblivious in his study while Mother was working. But this time, they were both suspiciously home and eyeing me like I would escape at any second. And the funny thing was, I would have if I thought I could get away with it.

Now I had less than a month before I had to have my portfolio ready to review. Mr. Music started meeting me during lunch to give me an edge up on how to make an interesting composition. I'd also been working on Photoshop tutorials during art class. None of the other students seemed to care, which was good. If someone was butt hurt they could complain and get Mr. Music in all kinds of trouble for giving me special treatment. I didn't know if he knew I had a screwed up home life or if he saw a fierce determination he wanted to foster, but either way, I was grateful.

Mr. Music was out today, leaving me to work on the computer in class. Alone, I was comfortable enough to plug in the camera to view the pictures I'd taken of the Rhys, Jonah, and Beck. But here where other students could walk by, I always worried someone would see the pictures and recognize the subjects. Those shots were reserved for my laptop only. I'd studied the pictures so many times. I could see each one so clearly in my head, it was like they were permanently burned into the back of my eyelids.

Static crackled through the room as Ms. Hadley, the young vivacious secretary came over the speaker. I'd caught a nice little photo of her last week leaving the married principal's office with her shirt decidedly more wrinkled than when she went in. The funny thing. It was maybe five minutes.

These poor women and their minute men.

"Please report to the gymnasium for the homecoming rally. Do not leave your bags in the classroom. Thank you." It was short, sweet, and to the point.

The screen went black when I unplugged the USB cord. I used the utmost care as I placed the camera in the bag and rolled up the cord to stick in the side pocket. Footsteps pounded down the hallway as that wild feverish vibe spread through the passing students like wildfire.

On second thought, I could use this to get some good shots. Maybe the yearbook excuse would let me get close to the floor again.

With the camera in hand, I stepped into the hyped-up crowd, happy to be swept away. But this time was different. I wasn't fading into the background like every other time I'd walked the halls. People cast anxious glances in my direction before whispering behind their hands. The incessant buzzing of petty gossip swirled around me as I continued on my way.

The noise level was too intense for me to make out any of the conversations around me. I didn't like this. All of the random attention speared sharp needles of discomfort down my spine, leaving behind a surreal numbness.

Jonah's head bobbed up and down a little ways ahead of

me. He was the only one in the hallway I'd had any kind of conversation with, so I sped up to catch him. If I distracted myself with mundane conversation, I might be able to forget people were staring.

"Jonah," I grabbed his arm, pulling him to a complete stop. The crowd parted around us as he glanced down in confusion.

Yeah, I'd be confused too if the resident peeping tom suddenly wanted to chat.

"I can't be late." He pulled away and my fingers skidded over hard muscle.

That was unexpected. Jonah was a scholar, a nerd. How did someone so focused on academics get so toned, and how did he hide it so well? My gaze flicked down his body, catching on his tightly pressed khakis and navy-blue polo. At first glance, they were nice, preppy clothes. An outfit I'd expect to see at a chess tournament. But being this close, the worn material made it obvious the shirt had been washed many, many times. The sleeve closest to me even had a small tear close to the seam.

"Can I walk with you?" My voice cracked at the end. I sounded so uncomfortable, I winced at my own patheticness.

Someone jostled into me and Jonah pulled me closer before heading toward the gymnasium. I walked beside him as he glared down at me, seeming to simultaneously warn me away and dig my intentions out of my eyes.

"Why would you want to do that?" Apparently people didn't randomly talk to him, and given his not so pleasant disposition, I wasn't surprised.

"Listen, people are staring at me, and it's weirding me out. Can I just walk with you? It makes me feel better to share the attention with someone else."

"And you picked me to share it with? Thanks." He sneered and kept walking.

I increased my speed to keep up with his quick steps. "I don't mean I want you to be stared at too. I mean it distracts me if I'm not watching them watching me." I leaned so close my chin almost touched his shoulder.

He adjusted the straps on his back, the muscles flexing in his forearms. Did everyone else realize Jonah was sexy? Just me? Okay.

"I guess you can. If you try to humiliate me again, you'll regret it."

I faltered, then picked up the pace. "What do you mean? I haven't humiliated you."

"When you knocked the notes out of my hand. That rally gave me nightmares for days. I hate being unprepared." He sounded dead serious.

"Okay, Mr. Delirious. You ran into me too. That was no one's fault." Only one more hallway and we'd be at the gym.

"I blame you." He still wasn't looking at me.

I'd never wanted to trip someone so bad in my life. He must eat a lot of dick because he was the biggest one I'd ever met.

"Fine, whatever. It can be my fault. My mistake in thinking you were a decent person, when in reality you're just like *them*." I shouldered past him, making sure to check him as hard as I could. Fuck him. If he couldn't be civil then I wasn't going to waste my time. Let the fucktards stare at me.

I turned my death glare on one frizzy haired girl next to me, and took a sick satisfaction out of her glancing away first. That meant I was more dominant in the school food chain now. Only two thousand plus students to go.

Sweaty fingers slipped through mine to stop my

progression. When I turned around, Jonah was blank faced, gazing down at me. His black framed glasses slid down his nose.

"I'm having a shit day. Can we start that whole conversation over? You can walk with me." He released my hand and walked beside me. Someone knocked into me but Jonah steadied me with a hand to my back. What was so important about today that no one was safe from being trampled? The rough treatment was getting old.

"I'm sorry you're having such a bad day." I wanted to bump shoulders to show solidarity against the world, but it didn't feel like we'd reached that friend level yet.

Jonah shrugged and grabbed the door from the guy in front of us, motioning for me to go through. Same as last time, there was an electric undercurrent, rising in intensity with each person who entered. Today there was a platform rolled to the center of the floor with scarecrows and cornstalks decorating the cheap skirting. I could barely see the maroon cloth for all the decorations.

"What's this?" I stopped, looking for a place in the crowd to blend in. Only, I was late getting here and the bleachers were mostly full. At least in here people weren't staring at me. I breathed a little easier knowing I once again blended into the sea of youthful faces.

"Where have you been? The school's been preparing for this for the last week at least. Signs were everywhere." He pushed past me to head toward the front row. Most of Jonah's crew took up the first bench and rushed to make room for him when they saw him. Yet more proof that Jonah was the academic king.

"What's with the snide tone? I thought we'd just agreed to start over." I barked as I followed behind him.

"This *is* me calling a truce. How could you miss the

buildup of homecoming? Today they're announcing the king and queen candidates." He sat down in the newly opened gap, patting the spot next to him.

I could sit here, or I could try and climb the bleachers, looking for a discreet spot. But now, with people packed shoulder to shoulder on the stands, the thought of facing them as I climbed the steps was a little more daunting than I was comfortable with. Jonah was being enough of an ass that I would have happily left him here. Then on the flip side of that same coin, there was something magnetic about this geek from the wrong side of town.

"Excuse me for living my life. I don't follow the whims of the popular kids here." I dropped by backpack on the floor and plopped down. Our shoulders touched but our conversation died. No one would have figured we were actually sitting together.

Jonah pulled his phone out and started playing anagrams against some imaginary person. Even in his down time he was doing something to enrich his education. He probably had an SAT game on his phone to make sure his brain stayed in tiptop shape. I almost wished I had that kind of drive in school, but that didn't sound like fun at all.

After five minutes he spoke again. "That doesn't matter. It's been everywhere." His thumb slid over the screen, tapping letters and making words.

"Are you doing the talking today?" I discreetly watched his thumb zip around the screen to create words.

He glanced up, sliding his glasses back up with a forefinger. Thick lashes framed hazel brown eyes and his lips pursed in a frown. "No. Last year's junior king and queen make the announcements."

A hush fell over the stands as Rhys and a gorgeous blonde walked out to the center together. Big surprise. Rhys was every prom king stereotype from the pearly white smile, to the killer athletic ability and body to match. The girl had a dancer's body and glossy hair. She was obviously comfortable in the limelight.

"Why are we here again? It's not like either of us are going to be called up there." I whispered.

Jonah snickered. "I don't disagree with you. But I'm student body president. I have to attend these things. Unfortunately." We smiled at each other as Rhys kicked off the event.

"SRHS. It's that time again." His voice filled every empty crevice of the gym. "After several countless hours of voting, we are pleased to bring you the 2018 candidates for Fall Homecoming. Are you ready?"

The bench rocked so hard from the forceful stomping; I'd say they were ready. Beside me, Jonah looked completely disinterested, still playing anagrams on his phone. I sort of loved his ability to tune all this out. Rhys and the girl waited, not yet ready to reveal the candidates. This was a perfect moment to snap some school spirit photos, so I lifted my camera and adjusted some of my settings before clicking away. I grabbed Rhys, and the crowd. I even managed to sneak one in of Jonah.

The girl raised her hand. "It's time. First, the girls. If we announce your name, please come stand on the stage." Three names were called, and the girls were all your classic popular kids. Shiny hair, tight clothes, and a chip on their shoulder. Another girl was called, and she wasn't quite like the rest. She was petite, but all the way goth and currently mad as hell that she was being called. I snapped a picture of her snarl at the crowd. That was a keeper.

"Astrid Scott." The girl announced. Surprised, I

glanced back to the front in time to see an ugly smirk cross her face.

"Wait. Isn't that you?" Jonah straightened up in his seat, pushing his glasses up on his nose again.

I was paralyzed, not sure what to do. I mean, she announced my name, right with the names of other girls that were on stage, but I didn't have friends here. Only Ryan. And the only way those girls got up on the stage were by popular demand.

Rhys searched the crowd until his eyes landed on me. His face twisted in confusion and he bent down to ask the girl something I didn't have a chance of hearing, not even with the baffled silence of the crowd. Why wouldn't they be baffled? No one really knew who I was.

"Astrid, are you okay?" Jonah's warm palm landed on the back of my neck, grounding me enough that I sucked in a breath.

"I don't like being in the spotlight. It makes me nervous." I whispered as Rhys and I made eye contact again.

He looked almost apologetic, but I wasn't sure why.

"You need to get up there. It will be over quick." His nose grazed my ear.

"I –I can't," I stammered as Rhys broke away to start walking my way.

"Damn, you're shaking." Of course I was, this was every high school nightmare I could ever have dreamed up. "Sneak out the back, this is going to go on until school's over. Meet me at the park behind the grocery store and I'll fill you in."

Get out of here. That was a great idea. I needed to get out of here before people started to realize who I was. I stood and walked toward the doors, keeping my head down.

If I avoided eye contact with everyone, they might believe I was going to the bathroom.

"Astrid Scott," The girl said louder, getting impatient.

That was my cue to walk faster and once I reached the doors, I flat out sprinted down the hallway. For a second I was afraid someone had followed me, but I busted out of the school doors without hearing any shouting behind me.

Once I was behind the steering wheel of Freda and on my way out of the parking lot, I felt equally free and foolish. I escaped for a little while, but no doubt everyone would know who I was tomorrow. All I did was trade one spotlight for another. And wasn't that a bitch.

Chapter 15

One lone, bouncy toddler ran around the playground, stopping to pick up woodchips before discarding them again. Other than that, the rusty playground was completely empty as I got out of Freda and headed toward the swings. When I was in elementary school, I loved the swings. The wind in my hair was a tease to the freedom I thirsted for. It was a different kind of freedom I wanted, the seven-year-old version. I pushed off the ground and started swinging for all I was worth.

What was I doing? Did I really need to wait for Jonah? I was sure he was going to say everyone searched for me, and called my name. Some were probably curious to get a look at one of the homecoming candidates, maybe even wondering how someone they'd never heard of was nominated. I couldn't wait to get out of the hormonal cesspool of high school. Everyone was anonymous in college. I would blend in with the Starbucks lovers and essential oil nuts that thought they were saving the world one pair of yoga pants at a time. I liked Starbucks and yoga pants. I was already imagining myself as one with the masses.

"Astrid?"

Turning around, Beck and Thatcher were casually

walking my way. Wonderful. Jonah was going to arrive in time to spread my humiliation among these hot guys like the zika virus.

"Hey," I stopped pumping my legs on the swing, slowing down just enough so my hair wasn't flying in my face.

Beck grinned like I was the best friend he hadn't seen in ages. Thatcher smirked but was much more guarded. It was odd seeing these complete opposites together. Beck definitely exuded the bad boy persona, complete with a white, grease stained tee. Thatcher looked like he was ready to read some deep emotional, slam poetry after binging himself on cheap knockoff coffee. But who was I to judge their friendship? I barely knew how to hold one together. Especially given how little I kept in touch with Stace.

"Jail bait, what are you doing out here? Isn't it still school hours for you?" Beck shoved both hands in his pockets, just watching me swing back and forth, like a deadly, teenage pendulum.

"It was a little crowded. I needed a breath of fresh air." I almost asked him not to call me jail bait again, but it would have been useless. In his mind, it was already a thing. *Our thing,* apparently.

"Where's the camera? I've been dying to see some of your pictures." Thatcher startled me with his question and I narrowed my eyes, looking for any sign of mockery.

Genuine interest shown bright in his eyes. This whole time I hadn't hunted him down because I couldn't lower myself to accept pity help. *Yet.* But there was nothing in his expression except friendly curiosity and maybe something else I couldn't identify.

"It's in Freda. I haven't really taken anything good lately." Lie, lie, lie. I hadn't taken anything I was willing to share. He'd want me to scroll through all of my pictures and some, like the one of Rhys seemed too intimate to flaunt in the open daylight. Beck never saw the picture either. After we left, he didn't ask and if he had, I couldn't have shown it to him. These powerful moments were mine and I refused to share them.

"Freda?" He looked to Beck.

"Her car, man. She named her car Freda." Beck smirked, and it seemed to please him that he knew this detail about me when Thatcher hadn't.

Thatcher twisted around to see my dear Freda, parked all by her lonesome with a shiny new headlight and one slightly yellowed one. Courtesy of Beck's charity.

Two vehicles whipped around the corner of the shopping complex, one an old, canary yellow, beat up Honda, and a shiny black Range Rover. One parked on either side of my Jeep. The Range Rover flexed on every car in the lot, but Rhys acted like it wasn't anything special to drive such a nice SUV.

This ought to be fun.

Jonah climbed out of his car at the same time Rhys stepped down from his ride. With a hostile look at Rhys, Jonah approached us, faltering when he saw Beck with me. The things Beck said implied he hardly knew Jonah, but that didn't ring quite true. Not if Jonah was weary around Beck too.

"What's he doing here?" Beck growled.

What was his deal? I liked Beck, but he needed to get over what it was with Jonah. He was shooting hostile looks his way and being too judgy. Even I could see Jonah wasn't the criminal Beck thought him to be. Or would become. But we couldn't really judge people on who they *could* be, now could we?

Rhys completely ignored Jonah and only had eyes for me as he passed him. It seemed to knock him back to reality and he followed Rhys until they stood side-by-side, facing Beck and Thatcher.

It was weird and awkward having these guys together. I could have handled them better individually, but all together, the testosterone and hot guy vibes were too strong, threatening to melt me into a puddle of Astrid goo.

Rhys was the first to make any sort of move. He held his hand out to Beck, who took it without question.

"Beck, I would say it's good to see you, but both times it's been under less than favorable situations." Rhys, the serious Viking that he was, nodded to Thatcher and held out his hand. "I'm Rhys."

"Thatcher." He shook his hand and then held his out to Jonah, who begrudgingly took it. Jonah might have wanted to let me know what had happened at school, but he didn't seem crazy about walking into our unlikely circle.

"Jonah," he dropped clenched fists to his thighs. "Now that we've had awkward as fuck introductions, we'd like to speak with Astrid." He sent a less than thrilled look at Rhys, but he ignored it.

That made me wonder what went down between them at school. I'd never seen them together and shared no mutual friends as far as I knew.

"Wait, if Astrid's in some kind of trouble, then I insist on being here. I'm her partner in crime after all." Beck smoothed his hand down his chest.

I almost wanted to smile, before I remembered why Jonah was here. The real question was, why was Rhys? The possibilities were too numerous, and I couldn't torture myself by speculating. I'd rather they rip the band aid off so I could go ahead and start working on removing the ugly sticky residue from my skin. Or in this case, figure out a way to do damage control over what was bound to be a public fiasco when I got back to school. Just that thought caused my palms to sweat.

"I don't know," Rhys started, scratching his head. He glanced at me and I studied Beck and Thatcher.

Beck had crossed over into the friend realm, and since we bonded over trespassing, I didn't really mind him being here for the conversation. No, that was a lie. This was going to be awkward as hell and maybe even a bit humiliating. I would rather have as few people here as possible.

"It's about something at school. It would bore you guys to death. You don't have to stay." I shrugged like this was no big deal, but by the way Thatcher quirked a brow, I doubt he bought it.

"I think I'd like to stay. After all, I'm invested in your future now." His words were light, but his eyes were serious.

"Me too. Jail bait needs me."

Nice. Now he was spreading that little term of endearment far and wide.

Jonah looked to me as if asking for permission. Beck and Thatcher watched the other two, clearly not going anywhere. As much as it pained me, if I wanted to find out what was going on now, I was going to have to let them be here for this. It was either that, or try and get Jonah to meet me later. Or I could always sneak back over to Rhys house, he had as many if not more illicit details on the inner workings of the rally.

I sighed and motioned for Jonah to go ahead.

"After you left, the rally continued without you, obviously. I don't think anyone will really care about who you are. But that's not the important part. Rhys might want to take it from here." Jonah was even saltier than he was when

I met him in the hallway, so something must have happened at school. From the glares he kept shooting Rhys, I didn't need three guesses to know who was the cause.

Jonah's jaw flexed as he waited for Rhys to speak, and it was the completely wrong time for me to admire the understated masculinity of his features. The intense stare and flexing jaw was so sexy. I needed my camera.

"Astrid," Rhys pulled my attention back to him, and it pained me to witness the guilt weighing down his frame.

I tensed. Why was he guilty? It wasn't a trick of the lighting in the gym. He knew why I was nominated and for whatever reason, he felt guilty.

"It wasn't a mistake you were nominated. I talked to Ashley and she didn't even try to lie to me. Her group likes to pick on a random girl every year, it's never pretty and it's always messy. They've decided it's you this year." He grimaced.

I jumped up out of the swing in shock. Actually it was fury. I had to have misheard him. This wasn't some *Mean Girls* remake. Girls didn't actually bully other girls that way. Reality popped my righteous indignation, and I slumped over. Of course girls bullied other girls, I had seen that and worse over the years. I had never been naïve about the cruelty and manipulation that made the world go round. That's why I never really had any friends anyway. Well, that and my overbearing parents.

"That's unfortunate. But why would you feel any responsibility?"

His eyes widened. Was he surprised I could see him so clearly? He shouldn't have been, he hid his emotions about as well as my dad hid his disdain for gay people.

Beck and Thatcher stepped closer, crowding behind me

as if to offer comfort for whatever Rhys was about to lay at my canvas covered shoes.

Rhys ran his hand over his short hair, and I recognized it for the stalling tactic that it was. Admittedly, I didn't know him very well, but this seemed out of character for him. Steady and silent, definitely. Uncertain and spineless, no. I stepped forward, into his bubble and tried to give him the most reassuring face that I could.

"They didn't pick you at random. Trey told them to target you this year." He word vomited it all out in a rush and I wanted to say I was stunned, but really, something like this was in the back of my mind.

"What does that mean?" Thatcher stepped up to my side, the furious slant of his brow catching my attention. "Who the hell is Trey?"

"Trey is the ass wipe of the school. He thinks he reigns supreme because of who his family is." Jonah cut in bitterly.

And wasn't that curious. What had he done to Jonah for him to feel that harshly? A part of my heart went out to him, like me, he couldn't seem to catch a break when it came to the kids at school. He was now officially part of my friend circle. Only he didn't know it yet.

Rhys nodded his head in total agreement. There was apparently no love lost between him and his cousin.

"Trey's my cousin. He's been with us for two years and he's been a terror since day one." Rhys' lip curled. "I tried to keep him under control the first year, but it's useless. He does what he wants, and I can't even go to my parents. My dad encourages the behavior." He shook his head and leaned on the swing set pole as if he needed the support.

Beck placed a warm hand on my shoulder. "The question is, how are you going to fix this for Astrid?" His voice deepened and fun, playful Beck was gone. I glanced up and his fierce expression both warmed and scared me.

"I can't. These girls are ruthless once they get someone in their sights. I can't even rein in Trey." Rhys tossed his hands up and started pacing. "I can threaten Trey but he doesn't care. I could beat his ass, but he'd laugh like it was all one big joke."

He was clearly distraught and getting more agitated by the second.

"I've seen what they do to girls, but you're practically a recluse at school. Maybe they won't be able to do that much to you." Jonah sounded like he had about a thimble full of hope he was right.

"How do you know?" I hardly ever saw him except for a few passings in the hallway.

His cheeks tinged with pink and he looked away. "I see you around. I tend to haunt the library like you do, only I'm usually in the back."

"Damn. That sucks. I wish there was something we could do to help." Thatcher said absently as he glanced back toward the shopping center, like he'd find the answers in the filthy dumpster.

"Yeah, this is not a problem I can help you with, pretty girl." Beck turned me to face him, showing me with his eyes just how sorry he was that he couldn't help.

"It's not a big deal." It was totally a big deal. "I didn't expect you all to help me. Honestly, I'm grateful to have a heads up. That's more than I would have ever gotten before." At the old school, Stace and I would have had to fend for ourselves. There wasn't a sense of camaraderie at all. That was probably why I was so stunned by their strangely sweet behavior. Any minute I worried the punch-line would drop on my head.

Around me, these guys that barely knew anything about me showed more compassion and empathy than I'd ever received before. It was humbling and awe inspiring all at the same time. Were we friends? Did I want this friendship? As my gaze landed on each face, from Rhys' apology, to Jonah's determination, Beck's regret, and then finally, Thatcher's quiet anger, maybe I did.

If these girls were hell bent on destroying the calm senior year I'd hoped for, as I fought my way out of my parent's house, it would fatally divide my attention. I was strong and steady on the outside, mentally building a barbed fortress around my body. If I could fool everyone else, then maybe I could fool myself too. Lying to myself might just be the hardest lie of all.

16
Rhys

I shoved the door open to the cottage and tossed my keys on the counter. Rage simmered just below the surface as I opened the fridge so hard, the door slammed against the cabinets. If it wasn't a premium kitchen with fancy granite, it could have dented the countertop. I wished it would have. The satisfaction of destroying something tugged at my self-control, threatening to unravel everything I'd worked so hard for.

My hockey gear was in the corner, calling my name. That was what I needed. A few hours on the ice with guys that knew the score. I could shove them into the glass as hard as I could and no one cared. That was the game. I used to hate my dad for making me follow in his footsteps, but somewhere over the last year that changed. It provided an outlet for my rage every time I was tempted to bust Trey's face on the concrete, or ram my fist into my father's fucking face when he tore me down. And my mother was married to that fucker.

My sweet mother who cared too much about what everyone else had and not enough about what was really important in life. I would never tell her, but she probably knew he cheated. And she would never leave. He kept her in a lifestyle that paid for her Botox and spa days. That kind of life wasn't for me. If I ever turned into my father, I'd drive myself into the nearest brick wall.

Picking up my shit, I grabbed my keys and headed back to the rover. My gaze wandered to Astrid's house as I passed it, like it did every time I drove by. I could tell myself it didn't mean anything, but I'd always been real with myself. Not the world, they didn't want to know the truth, but to myself.

The drive was short and by the time I laced up my skates, I was ready to fuck shit up.

Thursdays were open days where practice wasn't mandatory, but we were still expected to get our laps in. Most of the time I loved it, it calmed me to go through the repetitive motions of skating. It was mindless and effortless. Just me and the burn of my thighs.

Today, there were a couple of the guys on the ice already. And what do you know. There was enemy number *fucking* one. Did I want to slam him face first into the glass as many times as I could, or confront him about what he was doing to Astrid?

It was a no brainer really. I could confront him later. Now I was going to get my shots in without coach.

"Trey, I need to work on some of my moves. You game? It will be ruthless." I yelled across the ice as I fastened my helmet. He turned around gracefully, like all the guys that played, he was smooth on the ice.

Take the bait. He never could resist a little foul play. It would also make him look weak if he refused. Not that it actually would, but in his mind he would be a pussy to back down from a challenge like the one I just threw down.

"Hell yeah. Give me your best." He cackled and the hairs on the back of my neck stood up. It wasn't from the cold, I was used to the temperature in the rink. No, it was from the furious waves of contempt, barreling over me like waves crashing against the shore.

A nasty smirk curled my lips as I made a show of cracking my neck. "Let's go, Dickwad." No build up, no slowly easing into the motions today. Zero to sixty in two seconds flat as I raced straight for him. He grinned and turned away, skating as if his life depended on it.

But it wouldn't do him any good. I was the better skater. I was the better player. And it grated on him. I'd often wondered if that was part of the reason he was such a dick. Where we should have been close like brothers due to our living situation, the only part of that relationship we had was rivalry. I didn't give a rat's ass about who was better or not, but it was everything to him.

Right now, I was glad I had the superior skills. I'd had private lessons much longer than he had and I was going to use my strengths to my advantage.

I caught up to Trey and rammed him so hard I'd be surprised if there wasn't a Trey sized indent in the glass.

"Fuck." He groaned and it slid over my body like the sweetest honey. "What's wrong with you man?"

You know what? Fuck it. I'd tell him right here what my problem was, and if he wanted to hash it out, I was damn ready to throw down the gloves.

"That was a fucked up thing to do, even for you." I growled, still holding him to the glass.

"What?" He acted like he had no idea what I was talking about.

Wasn't that a fucking lie? The curl of his mouth said he knew exactly what I was so worked up over, and he was *proud* of it.

"Astrid. That girl hasn't done anything to you. And let's

be honest bro, you're the worst kind of dick so you deserve it. Call off the girls or I'll make your life very hard." My breath came in deep pants, but it wasn't from the skating.

"Whatever, Rhys. You can't do jack shit. It's why you've never tried before." He rolled his eyes and my skin started to boil from the heat of my anger.

I'd never wanted to pummel someone so bad in my life. No one quite brought out these feelings like Dad or Trey. It must be a Bennet trait.

"I've never cared before. I care this time, so make it go away. Last warning." I shoved away from him and started to turn away.

"Oh-ho-ho. She's spreading it for you? I thought she lumped you in with the rest of us? Must be a pussy of gold for you get twisted like this." He spun around to face me.

Red covered my vision and images flashed before my eyes of blood on his face, his jersey, the ice. It was a very appealing picture and if it wasn't for the fear of conse-quences, I would have acted on it. But the last thing I needed was to get suspended from the team. That would almost guarantee a loss of interest from the scouts.

The cold from the ice chilled my skin, but did little to cool my temper. I curled my fingers into tight fists and used every bit of willpower to keep them by my sides.

"By tomorrow morning I want the girls called off." Without giving him a chance to respond, I turned around and darted off. His cackle echoed behind me and it only increased my hate for him.

The years he spent with us were years too many. I used to feel sorry for him, forced to move in with us after his dad went to prison and his mom ran off. If I had a penny for every time I tried to understand him, I could walk out and never look back, happily. But no matter what I tried, or how

I approached him, Trey did his best to make everyone miserable. Except for my dad. They were cut from the same cloth.

Over the years, I'd come to accept that Trey was not, and never would be a decent person. It wouldn't surprise me if he ended up following in his dad's footsteps.

I slammed the door to the locker room and started stripping off my gear, oblivious to the people surrounding me. It was always crowded in here, guys in all age groups changing for practice. Hockey was the big sport of Colorado and the rink was always packed. Even figure skating was fairly popular. I learned from a young age that if I didn't want to get an eyeful of dick all the time, to keep my eyes averted.

"Yo, Bennet. What was that out there?" Greg, the fullback of the team approached me cautiously. Even though I didn't spread it around, it was no secret I could barely tolerate Trey on the best of days.

"Nothing," I grunted and stuffed my gear in the team branded mesh bag. Proud to be a Grizzly stamped across one side and my dad's company logo on the other. Yeah... That was something to be proud of, how far my dad's money went to prove our family name owned everything.

"You sure? It looked intense. Trey is still fuming, racing insane circles around the rink." He shrugged, he didn't care what Trey was doing. He was firmly in the Trey hate camp too. As was most of the team.

"Yup. I'm outta here man. Let me know if Trey does anything stupid." I swung my bag over my shoulder and headed toward the door.

"You got it," Greg mumbled as I exited and the door closed behind me.

It would be a great day when Trey no longer graced my life. The dude was fucked in the head, thinking he owned everything and the general population owed him that and more.

He could be the son Dad always wanted. That was fine with me. The downside was Mom would probably always be with him too.

The ride home was slightly better, with cold air blasting me in the face. It worked wonders in cooling down my temper, at least after I had a go at Trey, the fucker.

I parked in my usual spot in the garage. Mom had a conniption whenever I parked by the cottage. She said my car was too filthy and needed a wash, and we were too well to do to be driving around in filthy cars.

For the most part, I did what I wanted, but when it came to small things like this, it was just easier to follow along. The Bentley was here, right next to me.

Great. Exactly what I needed. I could sneak through the side door of the garage and ignore my father ever existed. But somehow, that seemed like letting him win. Especially when he got the satisfied glint in his eye that said he knew what I was doing and was the weaker of the two of us. He acted like this was some kind of suburban alpha contest and he reveled in making me cower. Like that one night...

The night Astrid and her buddy Beck were spying on me. I should be furious my privacy was invaded like that. Indignant. Offended.

And those were my original reactions, but call me crazy, after I let them inside it was more of a comfort to not be alone than anything else. Astrid was gutsy to come over, but I hadn't sensed any malicious intent. More like curiosity and understanding.

Then there was that picture. I had lied. Being the star of the hockey team, people would recognize me, but I didn't have the heart to tell her to delete it. It was so powerful, it even spoke to me and I didn't have an artistic bone in my body. I was more of the brute, aching to settle my problems with my fists until the steam cleared.

I'd seen her around school a few times since that night. She hadn't known I was creeping on her, she was so oblivious to life. No, that wasn't right. Every time she came into view she had that damn camera in her hand, documenting some fucked up scenario at the school. If she ever released her photos, she'd start Silver Ranch Armageddon for sure. So far, I'd witnessed her snapping pictures of teacher affairs, back hallway fights, science room trysts.

It wasn't that she was obvious about it. In fact, she was damn near invisible, silently stalking the hallways and catching people unaware. But no one watched her the way I did. Besides the geek. He watched her just as much. He even gave me a chin lift here and there, acknowledging in some weird way that we both were low key obsessed with the hippie girl. Neither of us were willing to approach her, though. And I always made sure to duck out of the way if she started to turn toward me. I couldn't speak for the other guy, but she didn't need my kind of trouble in her life.

Now that she was the prime target for the twitch bitches, I'd have to figure a way to shield her. The geek, Jonah, might be a good ally. She only had one friend at school. Only one person to take her back. Astrid would need all the help she could get in the coming months.

Dad's voice rang through the hollow rooms as I entered through the laundry room. Mom's car was missing, so if she was gone, there was no reason he would have to be quiet.

"Yeah, baby I know. The weekend starts tomorrow and I can't wait." There was a pause and then a husky chuckle.

I gagged quietly. This was so disgusting. Not because he

was my dad, but because he was an open cheater. The urge to rip his face off was bubbling below the surface of my rage, but I wouldn't make the same mistake again. No father should ever put their hands on their sons like that. And I was trained to always respect him, not defending myself like I should have. He wanted to cheat? Fine. He could do what he damned well pleased, and as soon as I could, I wouldn't even be a memory for him.

"I'll call you when I get on the road. I know. See you soon." His voice dropped as I walked through the kitchen toward the back door.

His gaze tracked me as he hung up, an ugly smirk curling his mouth. I hoped I looked nothing like him. I'd disfigure myself to keep from looking like this man. If there was any kind of higher power in the universe, my mom cheated when she got pregnant with me. Actually, come to think of it, we didn't look *that* similar.

"Nothing to say, son?" He taunted, probably hoping for a repeat, another excuse for him to feel superior to me. It would come as a shock this time when I hit back, let the evidence of our family bond out for the world to see. Dad would never let that happen though. He'd lock me in the cottage and order tutors for school until the bruising faded.

"Nah, it's pointless. You're going to do what you want to do anyway."

He grinned. "Now see, that's the attitude you should have had all along. That's the Bennet way. We do what we want and no one cares, because we own half this town."

I gave him my best dead stare, but he ignored it.

"At some point, you're going to be just like me. You're going to want something so bad, you're going to take it and realize no one will stop you. They might not like it, but they'd rather be on our good side than cause waves." His face took on a fatherly expression as if he was imparting some deep life lesson on me.

And I guessed in a way he did. He was cementing my hate, sealing my determination to be everything he wasn't and nothing he was.

"And Mom? Isn't she one of us?"

He waved a soft hand in the air. "She isn't blood. And she doesn't care as long as her credit card bill is paid. You wait until you find the perfect woman for marriage. Wives are trophies only, good for making business deals and completing the American dream image everyone cares so much about. They look pretty when you take them down and show them around. Oh, you don't let them collect dust and let themselves go, but marriage is a lie. Not a partnership. The world is ours for the taking son, and not even our wives stand in the way of what we want."

The sad thing was, he really believed that. He thought I'd come around to his way of thinking and be just. Like. Him.

My biggest fear.

Dad could feed himself whatever lie he wanted to keep the dream alive, but at some point, when I didn't have to rely on him and his money, I was going to bust it wide open and he'd choke on the truth.

Chapter 17

O kay, so skipping school Friday and hiding out over the weekend seemed like a good idea at the time. I did a stellar job of convincing myself that everyone would forget about me being called as a homecoming candidate and I could face the school today, quietly sinking into the background like I always did.

Now I was sitting in Freda, clenching the steering wheel, watching students flow around my car to enter the school. The bell was about to ring, and I was absolutely terrified.

All through high school I'd seen people bullied and beat up and picked on. But it was never me. I was the observer only. The fear of the unknown was freaking me out right now and I couldn't bring myself to get out of the car.

I hadn't paid enough attention to the cheerleaders to know their secrets. Nope, instead I spent my time watching the hot guys. The perfect ones I was envious of. And now I was at a distinct disadvantage. I mean, I gave the girls as much attention as I gave everyone else but now I regretted not digging deeper into their lives.

Knuckles lightly rapped on my window and I screamed as I jumped in my seat.

What the...

Oh, it was Rhys. He wasn't looking at me, but at the crowd milling about. The way he squinted his eyes at each indifferent individual said, they were his enemies and he was short on mercy. And compassion. With that expression he looked stone cold.

I rolled down the dirty window enough that I could hear him clearly.

"Yes?"

"Come on. School's about to start." His voice was gruff but no less cultured than the first time I heard him speak at my house.

"I know. I think I can learn from here. If you really wanted to help a girl out, you could bring my assignments out to me." I raised my eyebrows.

He scowled and apparently didn't get my joke. I knew I fell short in the funny department, but considering the state of my emotions right now, I thought that was pretty good.

"I'm going to walk you in." He met my stare and my breath caught. His light blue eyes were beautifully calm and intensely captivating. My fingers twitched to snatch my phone for a picture.

Then what he said penetrated my musings and I held my breath for a different reason. He was helping me? If he publicly made a statement like that, would he get any backlash? He definitely seemed top tier in the high school echelon, but did that mean he was untouchable?

"Why would you do that?" I wasn't trying to sound bitchy, but I was genuinely curious.

"Because I'd like to think we're friends. Or we can be. And everyone should know it."

He was throwing down before it even got started. My insides were gooey mush and if he wasn't watching me so closely, I would have sighed dreamily. As it was, his offer went a long way to calm me down and I'd never admit it, but it was the push I needed to get out. I would take him up on his offer and lean on his unshakeable strength. He seemed like he had plenty extra to spare.

I gave him a closed lip smile and took my keys out of the ignition. He stepped back as I pushed the door open and grabbed my bag. Once I was out, the bag left my hands and Rhys threw it on his shoulder. I stared at him, surprised he'd taken it, then the picture it made actually sunk in. Rhys, the Ragnar hockey player, toting around my whimsical, royal blue and gold patterned backpack, with the gold tassels hanging off the bottom.

Laughter escaped past my lips before I could stop it, and I covered my mouth with a hand to keep as much in as I could.

Rhys' face scrunched up in confusion before he looked down. He must have realized what was so funny and found it equally as hilarious, because he grinned. It was a good look.

"Yeah, not exactly my style." He shrugged and turned toward the school. As we walked together, more and more people turned and stared.

I thought this was exactly what I needed to get over my fear, but I momentarily forgot that I hate being the center of attention, and there was no way walking with Rhys that gazes would not be drawn to us.

My hands started to shake, and I twisted my head to keep my attention on Rhys. If I couldn't see the looks, then I could pretend it wasn't happening. Bottom line, I had to get over this irrational stage fright. I had a feeling I'd need every tool in my arsenal over the next few months and this fear that shackled me did me no favors.

"What did you do this weekend?" Rhys glanced down and a blush heated my cheeks at getting caught staring at him. Why did I have to be so awkward?

"Uh, read in my text books about photography. Exciting, I know." I babbled.

"Oh yeah? That's cool. From that photo you showed me, you're crazy talented." He pulled the front door open and held it for me to pass through.

As soon as my feet crossed the threshold, it was like we were in some kind of play, where everyone was on the edge of their seats. Unsure of the plot twist, but waiting with bated breath to find out what happened next.

The girl who announced prom candidates was walking by with a group of identically dressed girls, but stopped dead center when she caught sight of us. Rhys' arm fell over the top of my shoulders as he tugged me toward the side hallway where senior lockers were.

"Come on. The bell's about to ring. Your locker isn't far from mine."

I let him lead me away, but before we got very far, the girl slid in front of us, blocking our path.

"Rhys. What's going on?" Her eyes darted to me before landing on Rhys. A flash of anger sparked in her make-up caked eyes.

Oh God. I hope this wasn't a past girlfriend. Or a current girlfriend. Rhys didn't seem like that kind of guy, but I didn't know him that well.

"What do you mean, Ashley?" His fingers dug into my skin.

Dang, his voice was so cold. Wait a minute. Ashley... Ashley, one of the girls that decided I was *her* play toy for the year? This was at least to my advantage. I glanced at her posse hovering by the wall, waiting and watching like the crowd of Botox vultures they were. They were perfect and plastic, and if I was being honest, they looked like they could use a sandwich. And I used the opportunity to memorize their features so I'd recognize them later.

"I see you found our homecoming candidate." Her nostrils flared and she cast a scathing look over me.

"About that..." Under Rhys' arm I found some of my backbone again, and I wrapped my arm around his back. I did not focus on his muscles flexing beneath my fingers as they glided over his shirt. "I withdraw. I'm not really that kind of girl."

Rhys nodded in approval and backed me up. "You can't make someone participate if they don't want to. In fact, I withdraw too."

He was nominated? That shouldn't be a surprise. By being the announcer, I knew he had won last year. The question of the hour was, why would he withdraw? Maybe he was showing his solidarity with me, or maybe he was sticking it to Ashley for some unknown reason.

"What? You can't do that! You always win and I'm always queen." She sputtered and a vein protruded from her forehead. It wasn't a pretty look for her.

Again, I wished I was in a position to use my phone.

"I can. I'm tired of all the politics of high school. I don't need to win to feel good about myself. Trey will be thrilled, though. He might actually have a chance at winning this year."

Burn! That was low. It was a double insult and delivered so smoothly. He didn't wait for a response, and guided me around her.

I wanted to ask him about his motives, but every possible way I thought to phrase my questions were lame. In the end, I stayed quiet until we reached my locker. How had he known which locker was mine? That was a question I could ask. When I turned to open my mouth, he beat me to it.

"I saw you here the other day. I'm not stalking you or anything." He adopted a squirrelly look and if I didn't know who he was and how important he was at the school, I would have thought he was lying to me.

"It's fine. It's not like it's a secret or anything." I opened the dented blue door to my locker and grabbed my backpack from him. He started talking again as I stuffed my English and chemistry book in the small, paint chipped space.

"I'm glad you withdrew. I was going to talk to you about it, but I know for some girls, the chance at being home-coming queen is a childhood dream. I didn't want you to think I was taking that away from you." The sincerity in his voice wrapped around me, pulling me toward him as if I were a withering planet in his orbit.

"You don't have to worry about that with me. I hate being the center of attention like that." I made a sour face and he laughed. Then I closed my locker door and faced him, bringing the conversation back to a serious level. "Thank you for what you did. I really appreciate it, and whether it makes a difference or not with those girls, it means the world to me that you'd do something like that. I hope this whole mess with me didn't influence you to back out of the running." After the last word fell from my lips, I lost my nerve and broke eye contact. Thoughts of fleeing danced through my head, but he didn't deserve me to run from him just because I was uncomfortable.

He shook his head and hitched his own backpack higher. "I'm happy to dip out. I hate those things. It was just a plus, adding a little insult to injury." He was referring to insulting both Ashley and Trey.

"Well, you're my new favorite person." I beamed and his eyes tracked the smile with unnerving intensity.

"Good, then maybe we can hang out sometime."

My heart skipped a beat at the idea, and it was a miracle I didn't jump up and down. Then, unfortunately, he continued.

"And hey, be careful. They were planning to mess with you during the homecoming events. Now that they don't have that, there's no telling what they'll be planning."

That shot my good mood straight down to the sticky hallway floor. "You don't think they'll stop?"

Rhys sighed and stepped closer. "Maybe? They know I'm on your side now, but those twitch bitches will do anything to make them feel like they're top of the food chain."

"Twitch bitches?"

He burst out laughing and slammed a hand on the lockers, scaring the guy behind him. "That's what I've always called the cheerleaders. They do all their dances and cheers so stiff, their routines look little better than uncontrollable twitching. Twitch bitch."

That was hilarious. Visions of Ashley and her posse literally twitching and spasming across the gym floor flooded my mind and I cracked up.

"That's the best visual ever." I wheezed.

The bell rang and I was sorry that our short time was over. Then again, if we stayed any longer, I was bound to embarrass myself with my awkwardness.

Rhys tapped my shoulder. "I'll see you later." And he was gone.

The rest of the day passed without any attacks from the twitch bitches. I figured they were regrouping and wouldn't have been ready to act again so soon, but it still didn't keep me from watching everyone around me with distrust and suspicion. The highlight of the day was reliving the pep rally with Ryan in art. Not. He thrived on drama, but when it was my own, it wasn't as much fun to indulge him.

"Girl, why didn't you call me?" Ryan huffed as he plopped down in the chair across from me.

"Why didn't *you* call *me*?" I retorted. It was actually surprising that he hadn't reached out.

"I had a stomach bug and left right before the pep rally. Then I missed Friday. I had no idea until first period where I overheard some girls' conversation, wondering who Astrid Scott was. I about fell out of my chair." He couldn't have looked more offended if I spilled red Kool-Aid on his Hollister shorts. You didn't mess with his style. He'd cut a bitch over that.

He had been out sick? I officially felt like the worst friend, being so absorbed in my own issues that I hadn't even thought anything was off when he hadn't contacted me.

"I'm sorry you had to hear that from someone else. But you know I don't like attention. I walked out of the rally and haven't been back until today either." I doodled mini cameras in the corner of my notebook to avoid his scrutiny.

He was very aware of my aversion to large groups of attention. One or two people, no problem. Even a small group wasn't a big deal. But large groups, like say the whole school, was enough to scar me for life. I did better in the background, and I was okay with that.

"Mmhm, and what's this about you walking into school with Rhys? I feel like I've missed two months of your life when it's only been about four days." He went straight to pouting and I couldn't hold in my laugh. That must have been exactly what he was looking for and he grinned.

Mr. Music breezed into the room and slammed the door, signaling the start to class and saving me from explaining *that* particular event.

After he set the expectations for today's class, I moved to the computer to continue playing with Photoshop. Mr. Music was essential in guiding me through the nuances, and it was one of those rabbit holes you could get lost in for hours if you weren't careful. You could tweak and change the photo to your heart's desire and still find tiny things to manipulate.

"Astrid, have you decided on the photos you'll use in your portfolio?" Mr. Music pulled out a chair to sit next to me. He tried to peer over my shoulder but unfortunately for him, I was working on a flower picture I took over the weekend. Just a little something to play with the tools of the program.

"No, not yet. I have some ideas though." And I did. I just hoped my ideas wouldn't upset anyone.

"Listen, you remember my buddy from the university?"

Like I could forget the guy that loaned me the Nikon. Pretty sure I would consider him a hero until the day I died.

"We've been in contact and he's offering up his star pupil to tutor you, if you're up for it?" He wagged his eyebrows in a non-creepy way.

"Isn't that what you've been doing for me?" Not that I was opposed to getting help, but did he think I needed extra help? I had been feeling pretty good about my skills but now I was questioning everything. My mood plummeted, making me feel like I was about two inches tall.

"I've been helping as much as I can, and I've probably helped more than I should. I can't be seen to show favorites." He leaned forward and winked conspiratorially, whispering, "although I'm rooting for you."

And with a few words he picked me right back up again.

"Thanks, Mr. Music." It sounded like I had a golf ball lodged in my throat and I coughed to hide it.

"What do you say? Are you willing to work with the tutor? You have about a week or so to get ready for the high school competition. A critique partner would be invaluable right now."

He really wanted me to say yes, and really, there was no reason I should say no. The last few months had been relatively calm, but my goal was the same. I needed to get out.

"I won't turn away free help."

The teacher grinned. "Perfect, he'll be here any minute. Every day until the competition, you'll come here for attendance and then go to the library to work with the tutor."

"*Right now?*" Wow, way to give a girl a heads up. My heart started banging against its cage as a knock sounded on the classroom door.

He couldn't have timed it any better.

A draft swirled around the room as the door opened, and the sound of footsteps came closer.

"Hi Mr. Music. We talked on the phone. I hope I'm not late."

I knew that voice. Why hadn't this popped into my head as a possibility?

Moving at the speed of molasses, I rotated in my chair and looked directly at the crotch of the new comer. Faded jeans slung low on narrow hips, a green and dark blue, soft plaid shirt sat on top, and I followed each button until I reached Thatcher's face. He smiled at me politely, like we hadn't been in each other's presence a hand full of times.

He looked at me like I hadn't walked in on him getting a blowjob.

Chapter 18

"Thatcher, nice to meet you. It was really kind of you to volunteer to help out Astrid." Mr. Music stood and laid a heavy palm on my shoulder.

They shook hands and I pushed out of the chair, partly to save my neck from a cramp and partly to avoid that weird feeling when everyone was much bigger than me.

"This is Astrid, she's the one we spoke about."

Thatcher's eyes lit with amusement as they landed on me. He extended his hand. "Nice to meet you."

"You too." I mumbled, shocked by the turn of the last five minutes.

He wiggled his hand as if to say hurry up, then I shoved mine in his.

"You'll be able to use one of the computers in the library. There's quite a few sections that will allow privacy as you help Astrid, and she's excused from class assignments while you're working with her. We'll chat after on her progress to get an independent study grade." Mr. Music propped himself up on his desk and crossed his arms.

Everything Mr. Music had done for me flashed before my eyes and I had a moment of mixed emotions. Sadness that not even my parents supported me the way this teacher did, and happiness that for whatever reason, Mr. Music was inspired to help me. He was the brother I never had, and I came really close to hugging him. I did manage to refrain because this was high school, and they loved nothing better than a scandal. Even if there wasn't one, gossip would spread and then it might as well be true.

"Let me grab my things, then we can go." I ducked between the two and stopped by the table I shared with Ryan.

"Girl, who *is* that?" Ryan whispered, but the way he tended to whisper, at least half the class heard him.

When I glanced at him, his eyes were large in his face as he kept alternating between my face and checking out Thatcher's butt. I discreetly looked over my shoulder and even I could acknowledge he had a great one. Although nothing could compare to the look on his face when I first saw him...

Where did that come from? I needed a distraction! Quick.

"Ms. Hadley is having an affair with the principal." I blurted so only Ryan could hear me.

"*What?*" His eyes got so wide it almost looked like he wore a pair of drunk goggles. "You can't walk out after sharing that bomb gossip."

I didn't answer and shoved my stuff in my backpack, instantly regretting the distraction that had popped into my head. Why had I said that? There were a million other things I could have said that would have had less impact. If someone accidentally overheard me, or Ryan mentioned it to Pat, two families could be ruined. I didn't doubt for a second that others would share it around because it was juicy and scandalous.

When I turned around, the attention of the whole class

was split between me and Thatcher. Wonderful. My heart-beat had calmed minutely, but started to speed back up again. A smug grin tugged at the corners of Thatcher's mouth. He must love the puppy adoration, as if he didn't get attention from the college girls. But he did, a much more satisfying kind of attention if I thought about it.

"I'm ready." I weaved between the tables, not bothering to look behind me to make sure Thatcher was following me. He'd figure out I wasn't playing when I disappeared through the door.

The door slammed behind me, then Thatcher was next to me, smiling.

"Nice to see you again."

"You too. Was this your idea or your professor's?" I squinted, trying to peel back enough of the fake Thatcher to see why he was really here. Growing up in church, I wanted to believe he offered his expertise out of the goodness of his heart, but the reality was no one did anything without a reason or personal gain.

"Mine. I told the professor I ran into you and that you had real talent. This way I can kill two birds with one stone." His gaze scanned the hallway looking for some unknown threat.

He must have forgotten what high school was like in his old age. He wasn't going to find any students out here when class was in session. Or very few anyway. They certainly wouldn't be planning to execute any devious plans of revenge on me when I was supposedly in class. If they watched me at all, they knew I never skipped.

"So you came because you think I need your help?" I slipped my thumbs beneath the straps of the bag.

His gaze snapped back to mine. He must have recognized the irritation in my voice. Then a teensy bit of guilt settled deep in the pit of my stomach. Thatcher was doing something nice for me that could tip the scales in my quest to leave my old life behind. I needed to remember that and not get so offended anytime anyone ever tried to help me. It never really bothered me before I moved here, but something about these perfect guys trying to help me, made me feel like they thought less of me. That I wouldn't be able to make it without their assistance.

The sad thing was, maybe I couldn't. And maybe they did have some villainous motives, but that didn't mean I couldn't get what I could out of them first.

"I didn't go to this school, but I remember what it's like. How cruel kids can be. So yeah, maybe I wanted to be here in any capacity I could, to make sure you were covered. But I didn't lie either, Astrid. I think you could have a real shot at winning. I could help." His eyes, those gold, green eyes implored me to believe him.

The same seed of guilt bloomed and crawled up my back. When had I become so cynical, believing everyone was out to get one over on someone else? It was the product of my love of photography. When you studied people so much, you started to see the parts of themselves they tried to hide from the world. Details that never would have caught my eye before were blaringly obvious and it both intrigued me and hardened my heart.

I took a deep breath. "I believe you. Here's the library." Two old wooden doors with greasy fingerprints smudged all over the glass, stood before us. He opened one and I filed through, heading for my favorite spot in the back corner. We didn't need to use the computers. I had my laptop with me and it had all of my pictures on it. When I started working on my portfolio, I started carrying my laptop with me everywhere. Mother Dearest had never invaded my privacy by searching my laptop, but I refused to give her an opportunity now with so much on the line.

We sat down and little dust particles flew in the air. Thatcher looked around while I pulled my laptop out, not hiding his distaste.

"Being back in a high school setting is making me itch. You're really lucky I like you." He tapped his fingers on the armrests.

Did he *like me* like me? Or as a friend. I found either hard to believe since our encounters had all lasted less than fifteen minutes. Would we have been friends if he were my age?

Just take what he's offering, Astrid. Don't go getting your hopes up that there could really be a friendship here.

"Is college any better?" He pulled his hands in his lap and studied his palms. I used the time to study him. Longish black hair tucked behind his ears gave him a very Jordan Catalano look. High cheekbones and a moody glare completed the artsy look I would expect on a male art student.

I quietly pulled my phone out and snapped a quick picture. As an observer, the level of emotions he felt was written all over his body. That was the powerful thing about photos. It brought out the empath in most everyone. By studying the slope of the shoulders, the tightening of their hands or the way the eyelids shaped around the eyes made a person hurt because they hurt, celebrate because they celebrated. To feel what the subject of the photo felt. That was why I loved photography. Only, I discovered secrets along the way.

"In some ways. But... your life is still your life. Your problems still follow you no matter where you go." He spoke to his lap.

His words rang with a truth I hadn't experienced in a while and touched me in a way that told me he might not be so perfect either. The moody, handsome, college art student had demons too.

"I can't believe nothing will change if I get this scholarship. If that's the case, then I'm working so hard for nothing." Thinking that way would only set me back and take the wind right out of my already weak sails.

He lifted his gaze and we once again locked eyes. I itched to reach out to him, hold his hand or touch his knee. I wanted to show him that I understood what he said. That I lived it? In the end, I kept my hands to myself and powered up my laptop.

"Maybe it will be different for you. Just don't expect for this to be the magic bullet that changes your life forever. Although for your sake, I hope it does."

He was so somber, I hurt looking at him. I nodded in acknowledgement, then pulled up the pictures I'd been working on. I rubbed my index finger over my slightly chapped bottom lip as I scrolled through the shots I thought about using. The theme could be anything I wanted it to be. And while that was awesome, it also sucked. I had originally wanted to use the guys as an anonymous type of revenge. They weren't supposed to know I used their images to further my agenda. The so-called perfect guys of Silver Ranch. But I needed something more solid than pictures of hot guys. I needed a well thought out theme. Something thought provoking.

There were so many choices that I would come up with an idea, only to discard it when I took some new inspiration shots of the guys. My pictures were all over the place and I felt like a dog chasing after eight different jazzed up squirrels. I did that over and over again until I was ready to go sit at the altar and ask for direction. Dad beat Jesus into me so much in my life, I resented the church a little bit. That was how I knew I was getting really desperate.

"Okay, so I don't really have a lot of time to come up with a solid plan. That's freaking me out." I stared him in the eyes as I used my *no bs* voice. "But I have some good shots if you want to take a look and tell me what you see."

He nodded and dragged his chair until the arms bumped against each other. "Show me what you're working with."

I selected several powerful pictures and displayed them side by side on the screen. The picture of Rhys on the ground, the picture of Jonah from the classroom, and a few others I'd taken since getting the camera.

His lips pursed as his brow furrowed, leaving a deep line between his eyebrows. Thatcher had shown so much emotion moments ago, and now he was sealed up tight. I couldn't tell if he was impressed or thought I was a one hit wonder and clearly it was a mistake by coming here.

Seconds went by. Long torturous seconds. That was it. He thought this was a waste of his time. It was a miracle he even wanted to be here in the first place.

"I can't take it anymore. Just spit it out already!" I burst out, then looked around wildly to make sure I hadn't disturbed anyone. The only person in sight was the aid for the period and it looked like he was catching a nap.

Bringing my attention back to Thatcher, I wasn't surprised to see he was staring at me. What shocked me was the amused smirk he was sporting like I was an adorable puppy trying to get his attention. Actually, make that a kitten. He seemed more like a cat person.

"Astrid," my name rolled off his tongue and I was

ashamed at how much I loved it. "Relax. I was in the zone, picking apart your pieces as a professor would in class."

That hadn't sounded good. Picking apart meant that he was thinking about all the things wrong with my stuff. He must have read the feelings on my face because he shook his head.

"I forgot, you don't do that in high school. At least I didn't. In college, the students bring out their work with the professors and critique each other. It helps make stronger pieces and it also makes you a better artist. It's good for the soul, I promise."

The little girl inside of me squealed at being referred to as an artist, even if indirectly. He had referred to me as an artist, hadn't he?

Feeling reinvigorated, I blew out a hard breath. Not in his face though, that would have been rude and a little weird. "Hit me with it."

"These are great shots. I want you to know that. But what you're missing is a connection between all of them. How many pieces are you allowed to put in your portfolio?"

That hadn't been so bad. It was a little disheartening, though. I felt these were my best shots, but it was better than saying something like his cat could take better pictures with its whiskers.

"Mr. Music said four to five was a perfect number. The person that picks the final winner of the scholarship was very specific that they didn't want to be looking at dozens and dozens of pictures of the same person's work. They wanted something small but powerful. There can be less than that, but no more."

"That's probably in your best interest anyway. The more pieces you have, the more work you have to put into the theme. What were you going for?" He adjusted on his heels and propped one arm over the side of my plush but ratty chair.

I looked between the different dramatic shots on my screen and winced. "Uh, emotion. I hadn't really given thought to a name or anything like that. These all seemed to evoke the same type of emotion from me." That was the lamest answer ever. From the look on his face, he must have thought so too.

"What emotion was that?" his lips twitched. If he laughed, I might play whack a mole with his balls.

I opened my mouth to answer but I didn't have any words to give him. What was the emotion I felt? The photos were all different types of compositions, some zoomed in, some larger scaled. Some dark and some light. There wasn't really a trend. But when I looked at them, I felt sympathy. I empathized with how they must have been feeling. Could that be a theme? Or would there need to be more uniform characteristics between each picture. Maybe they could tell a story? Collectively?

"I see where you're going with it. I sympathized with each person and what they must be feeling. And none of the photos are happy. That was the connection between the pictures I chose."

"Good. That's good." His fingers grazed the top of my knee for the briefest of moments, but it was enough to send a blaze of fire straight to my core. "But I don't think you're going to win with this. Or at least with all of these photos. You might be able to keep one or two and then add a few more that really drill into the specific mood that brings out the sympathy. Now, next question. What are your thoughts on photo editing?"

"I've been playing around with Photoshop at school, but

I haven't done anything other than play around with the lighting and contrast. Things like that."

"Good. Editing photography is one of those gray areas. They would probably prefer no editing at all, but you can get away with that little bit. Especially if it makes for a more dramatic composition. What you don't want to do is compromise the integrity of the picture so much, the final product is not recognizable compared to the original."

We spent the rest of the class period going over little details and talking through some potential themes. He even pulled up some of his favorite exhibits he'd seen in museums to discuss them with me.

The bell rang before I was ready. In the last hour, I connected with Thatcher on a level I never had before with anyone else. We shared a passion and it was exhilarating to hold an in-depth conversation about different concepts and techniques. It might have been his extensive knowledge or his feverish excitement that built the longer we were together.

I packed my laptop and stood up, stretching. The cheesy smile on my face felt like it was a permanent fixture, but I didn't care. He understood the art side of me. "Are you sure you don't want to study photography?" My mind went back to the day I met him.

He held a hand out for me to walk in front of him. There wasn't a lot I knew about Thatcher, but the little I did was pointing to him being a gentleman. Well... most of the time.

"I'm sure." The smile in his voice warmed his words until they were like sweet honey pouring over me. "I enjoyed the photography classes I took, but painting is my passion. There's something so addictive about shaping and sculpting a beautiful piece with your hands and your mind."

Visions of his hands running over my body assaulted me, and my body temperature rose twenty degrees. I was sure that wasn't what he meant but I couldn't get the images out of my head. It was fortunate I was walking in front so he couldn't see the thoughts written all over my face. Hell, probably my neck and chest too. When I blushed, it tended to turn into a full body affair.

"I'd love to see some of your work sometime." What was I doing? I had never been so forward before, but my curiosity wouldn't die until I had an insight into Thatcher's soul by way of his artwork. Wasn't that what art was? A window to the artist's soul, baring all of their hopes, dreams, and fears?

His arm shot out and pushed the door just as I was raising my own. The fabric of his rough, plaid shirt rubbed against the back of my arm as we stepped through the door, in an odd intimacy.

Thatcher gently caught my wrist and turned me to face him. We were standing in the middle of the hallway, blocking the entrance to the library with students swarming around us. They were blurry movements of color as I gazed at Thatcher, as if I focused on him through the lens of my Nikon.

"I can do better than that. Why don't you come watch me paint this weekend? I usually use one of the studios at the college when I really want to work on something. You can't beat the set up. At least I can't on a student budget." He grinned one dimple popped.

I nearly swooned where I stood.

"I... I think I'd love that. Depending on the time, I should be able to swing it." Or sneak out more likely, but I didn't want to share that with the handsome college student. It might have reminded him I was so much younger than he was.

"Great. Let's exchange numbers." He reached in his back pocket to grab his phone.

I went for mine, right as gross, nasty river water cascaded over my head.

I gasped, stunned, not sure what happened. Thatcher stood frozen with his mouth open.

Glancing down, two medium sized, pink and brownish green fish flopped around on the floor, clearly as upset as I was about their world being turned upside down.

Someone just poured fish water on me, and they cackled behind me.

Chapter 19

"What. The. Fuck." Thatcher snarled and darted around me.

Laughing. Laughing and gasping. Squeals and the well-known sound of the camera phone shutter.

Those were the competing sounds surrounding me. I wanted to shout and rage at the crowd to let them know this wasn't funny. It *wasn't* funny.

Instead, I watched the fish flail around the floor until they lost their bounce and their movements steadily slowed. Tears filled my eyes as I listened to people laugh and take pictures, not caring about the poor fish that suffocated on the dirty floor of the hallway. Kind of like me. I couldn't breathe; I was suffocating like those two small fish. But they were done. They didn't have to worry about people or predators anymore. At least they had that bittersweet peace.

Not like me. Sooner or later, I'd have to look away from the floor. To look up and see my tormentors' faces. They might not have been the ones to do this to me, but their excitement fed into the satisfaction of the twitch bitches. Because they were behind this. They had to be.

"Get away! You fucking people are worse than scum. There's nothing to see here." Hands gripped my shoulders and I was pulled against a hard chest. I closed my eyes as silent tears tracked down my face, although you'd never know it from the water dumped over my head.

"Shhh. It's okay." The scent of pine and bergamot with a slight smoky tang swirled around me. A hand petted the back of my head and I let this person comfort me. Too bad the person holding me would also smell like fish.

"Let's get out of here. I'm usually against skipping, but I think this calls for a break." A rough finger slid under my chin and tipped my head up. Dark hazel eyes seared me with their intensity. Jonah's mouth was set in a severe frown as he examined me. It was too much, he was seeing too much, so I jerked my chin back, breaking his hold.

He was probably gauging my sanity. I hated to tell him that it died on the floor with the fish. Oh look, he was standing on the tail of one.

"Move your foot," I mumbled through a sniff.

"What?" He sounded incredulous.

"The fish."

"What?" Jonah had no idea what I was telling him and I lacked the energy to give him any more words.

"Man, you're standing on a fish." Rhys stopped behind Jonah, his jaw clenched so hard, the muscles in his cheek popped out in stark relief.

"Fuck," Jonah cursed and shifted to the left without letting go of me.

"Those twats got away." Thatcher wheezed from behind me. I couldn't see him, but I imagined he was holding his side, from how out of breath he sounded.

"Who?" Rhys packed so much anger into that one word, it would have smashed through the wall if it were a physical thing.

"Bunch of punk ass kids." He moved around so I could see him.

I was right. He was holding his side.

"Let's get out of here. Astrid deserves a break." Jonah stroked the length of my hair as a few strands caught on a callous.

Silence fell as the three guys studied each other. They weren't friends, and they hadn't really known each other before the other day, I thought anyway. But now we were going to skip together. At least Rhys, Jonah, and me. Thatcher was along for the ride.

"Are you sure you can do that? You might burst into flames when you break a school rule." Rhys quirked an eyebrow, but his words were teasing instead of mean.

Jonah sneered without any heat. "Fuck off."

I had calmed down enough that I let my gaze wander outside my three protectors, but we were alone. Not another horrid soul still lingered in the hallway. Which brought up another thought.

"Where are the teachers?"

Rhys and Jonah exchanged a look before they both sighed heavily, almost in sync with each other. That was slightly eerie.

Rhys clenched his fists and answered. "They don't interfere when the twitch bitches set out to ruin someone. They never have, and even if you went to them, they wouldn't take any action. Ashley's dad is the superintendent."

Wonderful. Wonderfully awful for me.

I looked up to Jonah, who still held me close. "I'm ready to leave."

He waited a beat, then unwound his arms and snagged

my hand to lead me out of the school. Both Rhys and Thatcher followed.

It was weird. I was completely humiliated and weirdly exhausted, but with these guys at my back, I didn't feel alone. In fact. I felt like I was a part of something important. Which was odd, since we knew nothing of importance about any of us.

IN THE PARKING LOT, Rhys pointed out my car and Thatcher extracted me from Jonah when we reached Freda. I dug through my bag, reliving the last ten minutes all over again when I felt the dampness of the water inside my back-pack. Where my laptop was. I guessed it was a boon that I kept the camera bag over my shoulder. The case felt water-proof, but I'd have to check it in the car. Thatcher took the keys out of my hand and shuffled me to the passenger side. He apparently wanted the honors of bundling me into Freda.

"Let's go to my place. I can drive her if one of you guys can drop me back off later?" Thatcher buckled me in and closed my door before he faced the other two.

I immediately pulled my laptop out as I strained to hear the quiet whispering, but Freda was really good at muffling outside sound. Wait a minute. I could crack the window. Nope, too late, the guys had already broken up and Thatcher was rounding Freda to get in to the driver's side.

"You okay?" He didn't look at me and I didn't know if that was because he was learning a new car or trying to make me feel more at ease.

"Yeah," I croaked. "It's like I'm having an out of body experience but I'm starting to feel more like myself."

"People can be cruel. It doesn't say anything about you. It's about them and having small dicks."

I took off the outer layer of my shirt and tossed it in the backseat since it was soaked, and picked up an old dry shirt. The laptop escaped any major wetness, but I still used the shirt to wipe it off. When I opened it, the keyboard was dry and the password screen popped up. Thank God.

"I take it the ones that dumped the water on my head were guys?"

"Yeah," he grunted.

I studied his profile as he drove, appearing to be as comfortable as I was in Freda. "They were put up to this by those girls. You know that, right?"

"I know. But they were still weak enough to get talked into it. Either they thought the girls would put out if they did what they asked, or they enjoy messing with people. Both make them dickheads."

I guffawed without meaning to and he flicked his eyes my way.

"What?" he asked.

I shook my head. "You can't talk about girls putting out."

A cocky smile spread across his face. "I don't have to trade favors to get head. The ladies love me for my shining personality."

"I bet it has nothing to do with you being hot." I laughed again and then my words sunk in. I told him he was hot while I sat soaked in fish juice. For a second, I desperately wished I could crawl under a rock, but then... screw it. He was hot, and I was covered in dirty fish water, but so what. He treated me like a normal person regardless, and it was kind of addicting.

"Where's your place at?" I adjusted the vents and turned the air on to start drying off.

"By the college. It's not much. A small two-bedroom apartment off of Colfax, but it's all I need." He smoothed his hands over the steering wheel, almost unconsciously as if he needed to constantly move his hands.

"So not with your mom and dad?" The motion of his hands hypnotized me.

"Nope."

"Lucky." I laughed, but really, I was serious on the inside. He was now my real-life role model. If he was over twenty-one, I'd be shocked. Twenty-one and no parents. If luck were really on my side I would be eighteen and living on my own. As much as dorm living was on my own.

"Don't wish it away. Bills, cleaning, laundry," he made a sour face and I laughed. "It's not the dream you're thinking it is."

"Maybe, maybe not. I'm ready for a change and I've never minded laundry." It was like a bright, shiny light bulb popped into existence and blinded me with its light. I had a crazy, little slip of an idea. "Two bedrooms? You don't need a roommate, do you? I solemnly swear to do all your laundry. And pay rent." I looked down to my mostly dry lap and muttered to myself. "Although, I'd need to get a job."

He took my hand in his and gave a short squeeze before going back to the wheel. Dang, that felt like an apology.

"Sorry, Astrid. My little sister uses the room most of the time." He sounded sorry, like he hated letting me down.

He shouldn't have felt that way. He didn't know me, didn't owe me anything. I saw a possibility and asked about it. But I should have figured he had a roommate or something like that.

"Hey, it's fine. Is your sister in college with you?" Would she be there when we got to his place? She was probably cool like Thatcher, but after my run in with the twitch bitches, a small seed of fear had taken root in the pit of my stomach. I would be walking into his place smelling like I followed in Jonah's footsteps.

Not the Jonah following us. Jonah from the Bible who spent three days and nights inside the big fish before getting spat out.

He cleared his throat as if he was uncomfortable with my question. Odd. He seemed so self-assured every time I'd seen him. The change in behavior brought out the need to comfort him, but we weren't to that point in our friendship, if we ever would be.

"Our dad's not the best company, so she crashes with me whenever she can."

If I was reading in between the lines, that probably meant all the time. Which shed a new light on why he was hooking up in the closet. He wouldn't want little sis to hear his sexcapades in the apartment. Especially if it was small and crowded.

"That's really awesome of you. I've never really cared about being an only child or gave it much thought, but now I wish I had a big brother too. She's really lucky to have you." And I meant that. Thatcher had to really love her to have her in his space all the time.

He shrugged and fidgeted with the radio, finding an alternative station to fill the empty silence. That was the end of our conversation and *get to know you* session. Disappointment speared through me. The conversation had taken my mind off my problems—mostly—and it was nice to chat to a cute boy in a car. It was a bit of a novelty for me.

I turned my attention to the passenger window,

counting cars as they passed us. In the rearview mirror I could see Jonah's old beater directly behind us and Rhys' slick SUV behind him. Why were they all coming? Why did they even care for that matter?

I appreciated the support, and I couldn't lie to myself that it didn't make me feel like I truly had someone on my side. Only, bullying was a thing now. So many forms that affected so many people. What made me so special that these guys who didn't know each other, surrounded me?

Before I knew it, Thatcher was pulling into the parking lot of an old brownstone apartment building. It was a sketch area, and there was a questionable guy on the corner of the gas station who had a fear of grooming, but to me, it was perfect. It was freedom.

"We're here." Thatcher threw Freda in park, and as I climbed out of the passenger seat I made a face as my pants peeled from the seat. This was a good time to be grateful my old car at least had leather seats.

Chapter 20

I t was weird the way we all gelled together. No words were needed as we filed in and climbed two staircases to Thatcher's apartment. It was an old building with no elevator, with brittle leaves and paper trash in the stairwell. I certainly couldn't judge him for having what I so desperately wanted. And I loved that Jonah and Rhys hadn't said anything or given any sign that they cared either.

Rhys could have turned out to be an arrogant prick if he wanted to be. He had the house, the family, and the money. Jonah though, if Beck could be believed and I did believe him, probably lived very similar.

Everyone stopped and waited patiently for Thatcher to open the scuffed door. Once inside, Thatcher walked to the kitchen and opened the fridge. I slipped off my shoes and surveyed the place. It was small, as I figured it would be. But it was neat and though I couldn't really say it was decorated, there were a few pictures of Thatcher and a girl. I left the guys at the door and went to the wall where a collection of framed pictures peppered the wall. The girl had dark hair and eyes identical to Thatcher. If I hadn't known she was younger, I would have thought they were twins.

Where Thatcher was calm and content, like the surface

of a lake at sunrise, his sister was forceful and vivacious, like the waves crashing and lapping against the shore at sunset. That was the funny thing about pictures, you could gain so much about a person from the way they smiled or held their body, even down to the way she interacted with the people or things around her.

"That's Trinity." Thatcher said over my shoulder. He was so close, his body heat soaked into my back.

Which reminded me, I was still sopping and gross.

"Do you mind if I change into something and use your washer and dryer?" I spun, careful not to touch him or get fish juice on the pictures by accidentally touching them.

"Yeah, you can borrow something of Trinity's. I don't have a washer or dryer though." He winced and stepped back. "We use the ones in the basement for tenants. I can throw your stuff in if you want."

I nodded. Anything was better than staying in wet clothes.

"Come on, I'll show you the bathroom and you can take a shower." He jerked his head toward the hallway and I followed him.

It was a short walk since his living room, dining room and kitchen was all one big—or small—room. I smiled a little at Rhys and Jonah as I passed them, to let them know I was good. Dreading what I had to have looked like, I probably resembled the guy on the corner. Only wet.

Thatcher stopped at the first door on the right and flipped the switch. "Go ahead and get cleaned up. I'll knock before I bring clothes. Washcloths and towels are under the sink."

I shuffled past him, sucking in my breath so we didn't brush against each other in the doorway. He didn't stick around, slamming the door as he fled. I would wonder if I stunk, but you know, I did.

The bathroom was tiny. The four of us couldn't have fit in here if we tried. It was old but clean and I was stalling. I needed to go ahead and get it over with. One deep breath later, I lifted my eyes and met my reflection.

"Ugh..." I groaned. It was as bad as I had feared. Half of my hair was wet and slightly curling, but the other half was dry. The little bit of make-up I did wear, mainly the mascara, ran down my face. I had always hated the water-proof stuff, it broke off my lashes when I tried to get it off. But now, I was rethinking my choice of make-up. I should be better prepared for next time.

I stripped down, but left the door unlocked. The guys wouldn't come in on me, right? I needed Thatcher to be able to set my clothes down when I was in the shower.

The hot water was amazing, pelting my chilled skin, beating down and erasing the last hour. I couldn't believe it had only been an hour since those stupid guys did that to me. With every minute I stood under the spray, my anger ratcheted up a little higher.

Those girls didn't know who they were messing with. I had my flaws, I hated being under so many pairs of eyes, I preferred the background to the stage, and I had been incredibly sheltered all of my life. But I was not the person to fuck with. Maybe the girls in the past hadn't ever stood up to them, but that was about to change. The only thing was, I needed to figure out a way to bring them down without jeopardizing my scholarship. Or my potential chance at a scholarship.

A soft knock came at the door. Clean clothes never excited me so much.

"Come in." I called and stuck my head around the curtain, holding it to my chest to cover the rest of my body.

And then it happened.

I was not a clumsy person. Maybe today just wasn't my day.

Right as Thatcher opened the door, I stepped on the shower curtain, falling forward and taking the curtain with me.

I screamed as my knees and elbows slammed into the creamy linoleum, droplets of water hitting my back now that the curtain wasn't containing the spray.

"God, Astrid!" Thatcher maneuvered hands under my armpits and lifted me up against him.

Jonah busted into the bathroom and slid around us to turn off the water. Rhys also joined us, blocking the entrance completely with his massive frame.

My breathing was the loudest, followed by Thatcher and Jonah. I didn't think Rhys was breathing at all. That was it. The rest was silence. Heavy, heavy silence as my situation actually penetrated the fog of my mind.

"Fuck, I'm naked!"

Thatcher failed to pick up the curtain with me, so I burrowed deeper into him to hide my nudity. His arms twined around me, rubbing soothing circles on my wet back. He turned, pressing me into the wall, so there was that.

"We heard you scream and we were worried something happened. Like you fell." Jonah pointed out the obvious.

"Yes, and you got a nice eyeful of my ass as payment for your concern." I snapped.

Jonah's lips twitched. He was laughing at me. Bastard.

Just you wait, nerd man. I narrowed my eyes into slits and apparently it wasn't intimidating at all, because he lost his battle and beamed us with a bright smile.

Rhys smiled sheepishly as his gaze trailed down the side of my body. When our gazes locked, his eyes widened and he tried to step back.

Tried, because he stepped on Beck in the process.

Please don't tell me one of the guys, most likely Thatcher, called in Beck. How did I get into this situation? All I wanted was to leave school and go sit in silence somewhere after I showered and found clean clothes. Instead, I was cursed to continually embarrass myself all afternoon.

"Watch it there, Goliath. You're going to break my goddamned toe." He peeked around Rhys and if I wasn't mortified, I would have laughed at the way his face went completely slack.

"Damn," he whistled. "I didn't realize it was like that, but I'm game." He grinned and winked at me.

No one laughed. Although, there were some grins going around. They tried to hide them by turning away or covering their mouths, but I saw them.

"I fell. They wanted to rescue me. I think I'm good now guys." I really needed to get them out of here so I could forget this ever happened.

"All right. You guys go on out and I'll follow behind you." Thatcher used an authoritative voice. Beck tossed me one last wink as he disappeared.

"Don't look so embarrassed. I'm glad you weren't actually hurt." Rhys raised a hand as if he was going to pet my hair, then thought better of it and backed out of the bathroom.

Jonah didn't say anything, he only smirked and shook his head as he left.

Now that we were alone, the position we were in was doing crazy things to my body. I glanced up and the heat in

Thatcher's eyes assaulted me like a heat wave in the heart of a Louisiana summer.

His arm that was wrapped around my back tightened, bringing me flush against him and my hands went to his shoulders. The smell of man and oil paint was almost as intoxicating as the feel of his hard body against mine. Something hard pressed into my stomach and I gasped.

So, so slowly, he started to lower his head and my eyelids fluttered shut.

I knew Thatcher the least of all the guys, but I couldn't snap out of it. I didn't want to. I was numb to the real world as I waited for my first kiss. One that would count.

"Hey, wh—" Beck popped back into the small room that seemed to be shrinking by the second.

Thatcher jumped back. Cold air rushed over me and I crouched to grab the curtain. It was under Thatcher's foot and I gave a good yank to get it loose. I wrapped it toga style around me as quickly as I could, but it hadn't even mattered.

Thatcher and Beck were locked in a death stare, not paying attention to me at all. Against my will, my gaze dropped to Thatcher's dick to see the thick outline in his jeans. I did that. He had that reaction from being close to *me*.

I swallowed hard and forced myself to intervene, although it was the last thing I wanted to do right then.

"I need to get dressed." I prompted them to leave, hoping they would take the hint. They did.

They exited and instead of going toward the living room, they went into the room across the hall. Whatever, as long as they weren't fighting it wasn't an issue. Right?

The cheap wooden door closed on its own. I made sure it was locked this time with shaking hands. Water covered the floor and a few of the clips that held the shower curtain up, lay bent by the tub. Those were now trash, unfortunately. Whenever I got around to making cookies for Beck, I'd add a few extra batches for Thatcher and the mess I'd made in this bathroom. At least I'd already washed my hair and body. I wasn't in the mood to jump back in the shower.

Taking my time, I got dressed in a pair of old sweats and fixed the shower curtain as much as I could. Four clips had fallen casualty to my accident; I guessed that wasn't *that* horrible. There was a hairbrush under the sink, but I used my fingers instead. I wouldn't have minded using her stuff, but she might. This way I wouldn't make an enemy before we even met.

"Astrid, are you okay in there?" A bang on the other side sounded like Rhys dropped his forehead on the door.

I walked over and did the same, the texture of the wood grounding me.

"I'm okay. Embarrassed, but okay."

"It's okay to come out. We aren't going to make fun of you. Well, Jonah might laugh because he's a dick, and Beck might smile or wink at you because he seems like a player. But I think they're both harmless and care about you." The more he talked, the more he lowered his voice. If I hadn't been leaning on the door, I wouldn't have been able to understand his muffled words.

"I know. Today has been a shit day. I can't tell you how glad I am that you guys are here. I feel fine with you guys, like what happened at school was a million years ago. It's so far removed from my present. If I was alone, I know it would be different. I'm sure I'd be bawling my eyes out." I could say these things when I didn't have to look him in the eyes. Courage was abundant when people couldn't see me.

The door moved again, but I had no idea what he did.

"Come out?" He left it at that. As a request.

I'd have to get it over with sooner or later. As much as I wanted to hide in the bathroom forever, I didn't believe Thatcher would feed me Gogurts through the gap under the door.

In my mind, I imagined I was strong and I was confident. I was trying that whole fake it 'til you make it motto. I twisted the lock and opened the door, slowly lifting my gaze to his. Rhys was there with his hands locked on the doorframe above my head.

A look of relief and something else passed through his eyes as he nodded. "Jonah went through the cabinets and pulled out snacks." He smiled and went back to the living room.

Was he afraid I was going to run? I couldn't do that with him blocking the way.

It was only Rhys and Jonah in the big room, sitting at the table with wavy chips and ranch dip. My stomach rumbled as I approached the table.

"Hey," Jonah said. I studied him for signs of any assholery, but he seemed to be attempting to bring us back to normal ground.

"Hey." I pulled out a chair and immediately dug in after I settled. Where our silence was companionable earlier, now it was awkward. We all studiously ignored each other while picking at the snacks.

A few minutes later, Beck and Thatcher walked in, expressions eerily blank.

I started to ask what was wrong, but Rhys decided to go in another direction.

"What are we going to do about the twitch bitches?"

The other guys were confused, so I explained. It was

nice being on the inside of a friend circle for once. *Were* we friends?

"Back to the question, what are we going to do?" A hard glint entered Rhys' eyes, and if I hadn't known the softer side of him, I would have been afraid.

Jonah straightened in his seat and pushed his glasses up. "Is there anything we can do? I'm all for protecting Astrid, but I have scholarships on the line. I can't be enacting revenge. I'd lose everything."

Beck made a noise at the back of his throat. "Then why are you here?"

That was harsh. I really liked Beck, but he had a chip on his shoulder when it came to Jonah. I scowled at Beck until he met my gaze, then he shrugged and looked away. He was completely unrepentant about how he treated Jonah. I'd have to corner him at some point and have a *Come to Jesus* chat. We had this flimsy circle of friendship we were building between the five of us, and if he didn't stop his antics it could break. I had a feeling once it broke, there would be no fixing it.

"I'm her friend. And what they're doing to her is wrong." Jonah growled, bending aggressively toward Beck.

It was time for me to wade in before they decided to whip their dicks out. If this conversation kept going, someone was going to open the measuring app on their phone. "Guys. No one has to get revenge on my behalf." Because that was my mission. "I don't want anyone to get in trouble over me." I made eye contact with Rhys, remembering the words I told him through the door. Even though it was weird to profess my gratitude, they deserved to hear it. "Thank you all for coming to my rescue. It means a lot to me. You all don't know me, and I don't know why you would even bother."

That wasn't how I wanted my thank you to come across. I wanted it to be heartfelt, but it sounded like I was fishing.

"I'm just really grateful." I made eye contact with each of them to make sure that they knew I appreciated what they had done, but I didn't expect anything else.

Thatcher stepped forward but stopped. He pivoted and bent down to reach in my bag by the entry door. One of the guys must have brought it in, because I hadn't.

He pulled out my phone, which was manically buzzing.

No one ever called me. Hardly ever.

Maybe it was Ryan. He could have heard what happened at school.

The phone stopped as Thatcher reached the table and immediately it started again. Trepidation trickled down my back as I held out my hand.

Mother flashed across the screen. That could mean nothing good.

I got up and robotically walked toward the door. This was going to be so bad.

"Hello?" I tried to hold my voice steady.

"Astrid Elizabeth Scott! Of all the foolish things you've ever done, it shouldn't even surprise me." My mother's harsh tone beat at me.

"What, Mom?" Did she know about what happened at school? I didn't see how she could but somehow she found out.

"Skipping is for delinquents. I told your father we should have shipped you off, but he didn't want to. It would *look bad*. Well, guess what. He'll have to face what a stupid girl you are. It's better if you were gone than to allow you to ruin our reputation like this."

I felt the same exact way, but in an entirely different context. What did I say to her? Logic dictated I tell her what happened, but she wouldn't care. She'd believe I did something to deserve it. Dad wasn't the greatest dad, but if I could get to him, he might understand.

"Nothing to say for yourself? I didn't think so. If you're not home in fifteen minutes... You don't want to know what will happen." The phone went dead.

Fuck. This was a fuck moment.

Fuck, fuck, fuck.

I slowly turned around to face the guys. When I answered, I had meant to slip out the door and take the call in the hallway, but it happened so fast, I was too stunned to move. Or even speak.

"What's going on?" A thunderous expression darkened Beck's face.

Was he angry something bad had happened?

"It's nothing to do with school. Or not with the girls. My mom found out I skipped this afternoon. I have to get home." I rubbed my shoes together, afraid and nervous about what they heard and what waited for me at home.

The importance of following orders plowed into me and I raced back to the bathroom. Luckily my clothes were still there. Did I change and wear my wet clothes home? No, I couldn't handle that. Mother Dearest was on a warpath regardless of what clothes I wore. Maybe this way I could shove the fish smell in her face. Even then it was doubtful she'd believe me.

All four guys were standing and facing the hallway in some kind of line of protection. My own barrier to keep the bad at bay. Too bad it wouldn't work on my mother. She was immune to almost everything.

"I'm so sorry. I really have to go. Thank you. All of you." I ran past them and scooped up my bag.

"Wait!" Thatcher rushed to the cabinet and pulled out

a grocery bag. "Here, so the clothes don't get your backpack wet." He helped me shove the clothes in the bag and handed me the keys to Freda. "We'll talk tomorrow at school."

Oh, yeah. He was my tutor. I couldn't stand here wasting any more time, so with a wave, I raced down the stairs.

21
Thatcher

W hat the fuck was that?
One minute, we were about to tackle the messed up situation that surrounded Astrid. Then she got a phone call from her mom and acted like she got caught peddling meth to toddlers. Now she was gone.

I glanced around at the others and they looked even more confused than I was. At least I knew it was her mom that called.

"Does Astrid have bigger problems than just the cunts at school?" Beck said as he prowled to the window to watch her back out.

I had the least amount of information here, so I waited to see if the other two knuckleheads would answer. They couldn't have been more different from each other if they tried. Were those two actually friends?

When no one offered anything up, I shared what I knew. A small twinge of guilt passed through me at the idea I might be betraying her trust, but I ignored it. I couldn't be there at school or in her personal life the way the nerd and jock could. They needed to know what to watch for so they could keep her safe. I hadn't had a good feeling during our chat in the car.

It got awkward because I hadn't known how to answer her without feeling like an asshole. So I turned up the music and ignored what she wasn't saying.

She didn't have a good home life. Not now. Maybe not ever, but I was too chicken shit to ask her. Astrid wouldn't have shared anyway. She was young and naïve. She was also guarded and prickly.

"Her mom called. You guys know anything about her home life?" I swiped a hand through my hair, pulling it away from my eyes.

Jonah had no idea. He seemed like a bright guy, but he impersonated a deer in headlights flawlessly.

Rhys was the only one that might know something. He gritted his teeth and went to stand next to Beck. Astrid was long gone by now, so I didn't know what he was looking for. Beck took the opportunity and smacked him in the shoulder in an *out with it* gesture. With a cut of the eyes, Rhys growled something too low for me to hear and Beck rolled his eyes. That guy wasn't ever phased by much.

"I've had dinner with her family. Our dads do some kind of work together, but I don't know why, unless it's some kind of charity donation my dad can write off."

"And..." Jonah leaned forward, very interested in this answer.

"It was weird. There wasn't anything that said she was abused or anything like that. It was just *weird*. I can't explain it." He scrubbed a hand down his face and sat on the window ledge.

"I don't think it's a good situation. They wouldn't air that shit in front of others anyway." And I would know. So did Trinity, even with as much as I tried to shield her. "On the way over, when I mentioned I had a two bedroom, she asked about filling it. She wants away from her house bad."

The air kicked on, the low screeching filling the silence and dying off after a minute. By then the shock seemed to wear off and I motioned toward the table. We might as well take advantage of everyone being here.

The wooden chair creaked when Rhys sat down. If we formed some kind of friendship like it felt we were, I'd need to get a stronger chair for his fat ass.

"Okay." I met everyone's eyes. "What's her situation at school. Does she have friends? Is she well liked? What's the deal?"

"She's new this year. Doesn't really talk to anyone, but that Ryan kid. She's going to have a much harder time with those girls making her life hell because she doesn't have a lot of people to stand up for her. I don't even think anyone knew who she was before the rally." The sneer he wore so well fell away, and real concern shone through.

Rhys tapped agitated fingers on the table. "I know people didn't know her. I had a front view of the crowd, and everyone was confused when her name was announced."

"Cunts like the girls you described last time don't go away. They also get angry when anyone tries to interfere with their plans." I knew that too.

Rhys cleared his throat and his face scrunched up in a grimace. "I'll keep working on Trey, since he's my problem. He's had a hate-on for her ever since she turned him down the first week of school."

"He hit on her?" Jonah's head jerked back before he bent forward. "That doesn't even surprise me. But I imagine he hits on a lot of girls that turn him down." He finished as if Rhys' reasoning didn't quite jive.

Everyone looked to Rhys to see if there was more to this story, but he shook his head.

"True, but no one else turned him down quite like

Astrid. He didn't like her attitude. Like I said, I'll deal with him."

A smirk threatened to burst free as I thought about sassy Astrid. Good for her. Not a lot of girls could stand up to school jerks like that.

"What can we do? I mean, me and you, Thatch, we can't hang out in the high school to protect her from either the cunts or Trey." Beck worried his lip as his *good time guy* persona completely leaked out of him into a sad puddle on the floor, leaving behind the caring guy he tried to hide.

"You can't. I can. I set it up so I'm tutoring her for the scholarship competition."

"Which is next week. So you can protect her for a week." Jonah raised his brows daring me to object. "I can hang out with her in my free time. Our schedules have us in the same parts of the school at the same time. She's in the library any time I'm in there." He was smug as he glanced at Beck. Instead of the reaction he thought he'd get, Beck only nodded. Looked like Beck was putting aside whatever he had against Jonah.

I doubt he'd give it up for good.

I also didn't like that way Jonah brought up the date of the competition. Like I was temporary.

"I'll work it out. There's the final competition later in the year if she wins. And she will." I was sure of it. She had an eye that wasn't often seen in high school. Mr. Music had referred to her as an old soul.

"Why are you here anyway? Don't you have drugs to run or something like that?" Beck taunted Jonah. And there it was. He made it all of two minutes.

A deep crimson creeped up Jonah's neck as he snarled at Beck. "You'd like to think that wouldn't you. Afraid your mom's on the client list?"

Rhys and I exchanged *oh shit* looks as Beck jumped out of his seat. I shoved him back in his chair with a hand to his chest.

"You don't know shit." Beck spat and tried to stand up again.

"Beck, man. Stop. Jonah's trying to help and like it or not, he can help Astrid. Probably more than you can." It was the truth, but it would cut him.

He looked up at me with wounded eyes but stayed down this time. What was his deal with Jonah? The guy had to be a few years younger than Beck. Not many ways they could have crossed paths. Especially not with Rockstar Beck and Bookworm Jonah. Nothing about Jonah said drugs of any kind. He was more like pocket protectors and *Lord of the Rings*.

"I walked into school with her today. It was an attempt to make a statement, but it didn't matter. They still came after her." Rhys broke the tension by getting us back on track.

"So what, between the three of us, we stay with her as much as we can to protect her?" We could try, but I couldn't stop the guys today. Maybe now that I know what we were up against I could be more vigilant.

"That's great for you guys, but she's my friend too. I know her better than any of you." Beck glared at me, daring me to say anything to dispute his claim. I raised my hands. Just because he knew her better didn't mean she hadn't wanted me too. She did. Just as much as I wanted her. He witnessed it and hated it.

"I can take her to school and bring her home." Beck nodded like it was decided.

Should I point out that her mom was not happy and she'd probably be grounded? I doubted her parents would be cool with her riding in his mustang, or on the back of his bike. Call me crazy, but I didn't see it happening.

"Let's grab numbers and we can stay up to date on Astrid. That way everyone's in the loop." I brought my phone and waited for them to get theirs.

Everyone complied, even Beck, grudgingly.

"So that's it. We stay with Astrid as much as we can?" Jonah asked as he stood.

Shoving his phone in his back pocket, Rhys said, "There's nothing else we can do yet. If we hang with her, people will see she has friends. Once we get a feel for how they plan to torment her, then we can talk strategy. But it's going to take a few days. The twitch bitches never do their own dirty work."

I sighed. Revenge was messy work, and from the expressions on all three faces, that's exactly where their minds had gone. Not that I blamed them, but I had a lot to lose, for me *and* Trinity. As much as I wanted to help, I might have to take a back seat on that.

Everyone shuffled to the door, lost in their own thoughts. Beck slapped a hand over the door when Rhys tried to open it.

"Wait." Beck turned around and squared his shoulders. "We need to talk about what kind of friend we plan to be to Astrid." His eyes darted to me before going back to the other two. "I know why I'm helping and what I want. What do you guys want?"

I stayed silent. I already shared exactly what I wanted. Astrid wasn't exactly my type, but I was drawn to her. When she looked at me, she had a way of making me feel like I was her hero. Outside of Trinity, I'd never had that and it was addicting. Beck hadn't liked that answer.

"What do you want?" Rhys hedged, looking uncomfortable in front of all of us.

Again, Beck looked at me. "Astrid is a sweet, beautiful girl. A lot different from the ones who usually throw themselves at me. It's refreshing. I like her. I'd like to see where that leads."

Rhys stared at him for a beat then shifting on his feet uncomfortably. "I like her. But I'm helping from a true friend perspective right now. My life is too crazy to want to seriously date anyone." Regret rang clear in his words. Beck looked slightly relieved, until he continued. "I think you'd have a hard time with her family. Her dad's a pastor and her mom seems just as stuck up as the women in my family's circles. No offense, but you aren't exactly the take home type."

The relief slipped, then Beck's expression completely blanked as he looked at Jonah. He was including him in this discussion? If he was willing to include him, even as little not biting his head off, maybe there was still hope for them.

Wait. What was I saying? It wasn't like we were going to all gallop into the sunset, and live happily ever after with a girl that may or may not even like us. I shook the thoughts from my head and focused back on Jonah. After all, I needed to know where my competition was.

"I barely know her. I can't answer that. But I can tell you that I can't stand the group of kids that are targeting her. More than that, I hate to see someone bullied and tore down for no good reason." He nailed Beck to the door with his gaze.

No need to wonder who he referred to there.

Jonah continued. "Astrid and I haven't really been friends. Not until the rally anyway. And I'll do everything I can to protect her. As long as it doesn't jeopardize my future."

Beck nodded and so did I. I could sympathize with him. We weren't like The Hulk over here with buckets of money to burn. We wanted to protect Astrid, but we couldn't risk ourselves to do it.

"That's cool. I don't think there will be much competition then. I'm the only one with nothing to lose by doing whatever it takes, to take down those cunts." His smile was ugly. It said more self-deprecating than happy at having little perceived competition.

As soon as the door shut, I pulled up all their contacts and created a group chat. What should I name it? Astrid's boys? No that was lame. Astrid's men? Still lame. Astrid's protectors. Astrid's heroes. There wasn't a great choice. The options were all cheesy so I settled on Astrid's heroes.

Beck: cheesy dude

Rhys: 100 agree

Jonah: now I feel all special

What, were they all sitting in their cars texting each other within seeing distance? That was cheesy.

Oh, fuck. My car was at Astrid's school. I darted through the door and down the steps but every one of those douche canoes were already gone.

"Thatch?" Trinity appeared around the corner, a huge grin on her face. "Why do you look like you lost your car and aren't sure how to get it back?"

That was Trinity. Always amazingly adept, even when she had no idea how true her words were.

"Because I did. Do you have time to run me to get it?"

She rolled her eyes and grinned. "Where did you leave it? At some hookup's house?" She laughed and I cringed.

"Don't speak those things. It makes me uncomfortable." I shoved her away from me playfully, before throwing my arm around her shoulder. "My car's at Silver Ranch High School."

"That's random, what's at Silver Ranch? Oh God, you're picking up high school girls now? Gross." She did a face palm, but I wasn't laughing.

If she only knew how close she was to the truth with her comment. I wasn't about to admit it though.

She unlocked her pride and joy, swiping a loving hand over the hood before she got in. She'd been working at the Bonnie Brae ice cream shop, saving up. One of the main reasons she thought I walked on water was because I helped her along by putting down two grand on this baby. It was straight out of my grants, but she needed a way to escape if she needed it.

"One of my professors asked me to tutor a student that has a lot of potential." I didn't bother telling her about the scholarship. She was the furthest thing from artsy fartsy. Trinity excelled at science, and dreamed of being a nurse her whole life. Unlike me, the weird son who would probably end up using an art degree to work in a daycare or at some place where they painted and drank wine. Not really the winning career someone aspired to. But I loved what I loved, and painting was where my passion lay. Maybe she would return the favor and support me when she got a killer nursing job. One could hope.

"Oh cool. How did you leave your car there though?"

Shit, I had forgotten about that part. When in doubt, the truth was the best option. Add in a little hope that she wouldn't read too much into it, and it would sound legit. "I was walking out with the girl I'm tutoring and some punk ass kids decided it would be a good idea to dump a cooler over her head with fish and dank river water. I drove her car here with some of her friends here so she could shower and escape the school for a bit. They guys just left and I forgot my car wasn't here." Why did I sound like I was explaining myself? I didn't have to do that. Trinity sure didn't expect it, but it still felt weird.

Fire lit her eyes as she looked away. "I hate people like that. I'm sorry that happened to her."

"Me too. I gave her a pair of your sweats." I reached up and grabbed the handle, rotating it back and forth.

"Yeah, that's cool. I would have offered if I'd been here."

Astrid didn't have a lot of friends, but she'd like Trinity. I could connect them and give her another reason to be around. Another reason to not feel like the world was against her. That would make me happy, like I'd given her some hope that there were actually good people in the world.

I pushed the seat back to give myself legroom. She must cart around middle schoolers. Justin Bieber blared through the speakers when she started the car, and I had to rethink my idea. Astrid wasn't the Belieber type. Actually, that might be a good thing. She could help my sister find better listening options than boy bands.

"How's Dad? He been bothering you?"

Trinity's lips pressed tight and she hesitated. That was never a good sign. She only hesitated when it got bad.

"You're staying with me the next week. If he's drinking and letting his buddies in the house then you have no business being there."

I'd never tell Trinity, but I purposely stayed close to take care of her. I could have gone out of state just as cheap—or not cheap—as DU was. And saved a hell of a lot more money. My apartment was shit but even shit in the city was expensive.

"I planned on it." Her hands gripped the steering wheel so tight and my heart clenched.

Astrid wasn't the only one with a bad home life. I got out, and nothing could drag me back. If it broke me, I'd make sure Trinity got out too.

Damn, Astrid had issues. I liked her, she was different. But did I want to take on someone else's problems too? Rhys might have the right idea, just help her until she gets free of the bullies. Then be distant friends. My sanity would thank me for it.

Chapter 22

Both Mother Dearest and Dad were home. This could be a really good thing, or it could be a really bad thing. In the past, my infractions were all imaginary, a product of my crazy mother's imagination. Now my mother had a real reason to be angry, and I doubt she'd listen to the reason even though it was a good one.

Dad was the wildcard. Ninety-five percent of the time, he never interfered in her punishments or tongue lashings. After the moment we shared a few weeks ago, he might wade in. At least long enough for me to share what happened.

The curtain moved, so I took that as a cue to hurry the heck up. If she was waiting by the window, I didn't need to hand her any more ammunition by taking my sweet time. I already drove as slow as I could without getting pulled over for breaking the speed limit backwards. Ryan called three times during my drive, but I didn't have the right state of mind to assuage his totally founded fears of what happened, or indulge his gossip addiction.

Sweat coated my palms and my traitorous heart beat an ugly staccato in my chest. It was time, and as much as I didn't want to face them, I needed to get this confrontation over with.

The door opened as my foot hit the chipper welcome mat, my mother practically vibrated with rage as I squeezed past her. I would have stayed on the porch until she stepped back, but knowing her, it would have infuriated her more that I was trying to air our business in the neighborhood.

"So where were you that it took you so long to come home? The school's a ten-minute car ride." She followed me as I went to the kitchen. The dining room table had always been where we had our serious discussions, so not to prolong our time together, I headed directly to my seat.

Dad wasn't here. This was a mistake. I should have gone directly to his office to make him listen. With only Mother Dearest I wouldn't get a word in between her spewing.

I played the one golden card I could. She wasn't as hot on them as dad had been, but it was worth trying. "I went to one of Rhys' friends place to change, I—"

"You skipped with boys?" She nearly shouted. "You had sex didn't you? You had sex with those boys and you're going to end up pregnant, like a whore." Her upper lip curled in distaste as she drew out the word whore.

I jumped up as she advanced. She was unpredictable right now and I couldn't let her stand over me. "Mom, something happened at school. I—"

Her hand cracked across my cheek and my head whipped to the side. I had the strange urge to spit. Would there be blood?

She grabbed my shoulders and shook me.

"I've asked one thing of you. Keep your reputation clean. Don't ruin ours. This is a new town and you're jeopardizing your father's position in church by acting like a righteous slut." Spit dotted my face as she punctuated each word.

"Mom!" I screamed as loud as I could, hoping Dad would hear.

Sadly, no footsteps made it my way.

"Keep your voice down," she rattled me again.

A knock came at the front door. Holy hell, was that a beloved blessing or a veiled curse? Tears filled my eyes, but not from relief or emotional pain. The sting in my cheek was too close to my eye not to react. She'd want me to stay here. That way no one would get a look at her handy work.

Another knock.

Mother Dearest looked torn. Finally, she released me and walked calmly to the door, the picture of the perfect Mary Sue. A breeze slid through the room when she opened the door. I couldn't see her from my spot and I knew better than to chance someone seeing me.

"Mrs. Scott, hi. Is Mr. Scott home?" Rhys' deep voice paralyzed me.

What was he doing here? I told her I was with him! She was going to grill him and find out that I told the truth, or believe I lied if he tried to cover for me.

"I'm afraid now isn't a good time. I'll let him know you stopped by." The door shuffled over the floor as she tried to close it, but then the sound suddenly stopped.

"I'm afraid that isn't going to work. You both need to know what happened at school today."

I was going to kill him. It happened to me, and I needed to be the one to share it. He could screw everything up by not understanding my parents.

"I said this isn't a good time—"

"I will come back with my father if you don't want to talk to me now. I'll let him know you weren't interested in listening to what I had to say, even after I let you know it was important. He won't be happy." The hairs on my arms stood up with his threat.

Did he know something about the church that I didn't? Whatever it was, Dad heard him because he came rushing through the kitchen toward the front entrance without even sparing me a glance.

"Rhys, it's great to see you. Of course we'll let you in." All jolly, pretending he hadn't heard me scream.

There must have been a small scuffle as my dad forced the door open, but eventually my parents and Rhys entered the kitchen. When Rhys' gaze found me, his fists balled up by his thighs and he broke eye contact. Other than that, there was no sign that he noticed anything. The handprint must be noticeable. I mean, my cheek was still on fire like a thousand suns burned under my skin.

"Should we go to the living room?" My dad said as he turned to me, then stuttered. His gaze whipped to his wife, who had the good grace to look uncomfortable. Not remorseful, but uncomfortable.

"You know what, let's just chat here." Dad took the seat on my right, and my mother immediately moved to take the seat across from me.

These weren't their usual spots, but the seating arrangements forced Rhys to sit on my left. My current good side.

"Thank you for having me," Rhys said like he hadn't threatened them minutes ago. Although, he wasn't doing a very good job of hiding his distaste of the situation. Or even my parents.

"No problem, son. What did you need to tell us?" My mother stayed quiet, which was pretty unusual for her. She must have felt the displeasure rolling off Dad.

I'd love to say it was because he hated seeing me abused.

It was more like he hated that someone else saw me abused. Their reputation was now at risk. I was sure Mother Dearest would blame it on me.

Rhys' gaze burned into the side of my head, but I kept my own on the table. Counting the lines of the wood was actually kind of soothing in this tense situation. There were twenty rings around the knot in front of me.

"Sir, there's a group of girls targeting Astrid at school. Some kids pulled a really mean prank today and poured a cooler with live fish over Astrid's head. I hope you don't mind, I took her out of school to get her cleaned up. She was pretty shaken up." Rhys' voice was always cultured and smooth, but now it was distant and a little snotty. He truly sounded pretentious right then as he addressed my parents.

I chanced a glance across the table to see my mother mew in concern. Fake. She was completely fake. She probably thought I slept with those girls' boyfriends or something for them to retaliate.

"That's horrible! I can't believe that happened. Were the teachers notified?" Dad's hand grabbed mine and I looked up at him. He actually did look sorry. "Are you okay?"

I nodded, not sure what I should or shouldn't say with Rhys here.

"I plan to go to the office tomorrow. Astrid was embarrassed and kids were laughing. It seemed like the best decision to get her out of there as quickly as possible."

Thanks, Rhys. You're doing an excellent job of helping me relive it all over again.

"Of course. Thank you for taking care of her. I'll be sure to let your father know what kindness you've shown to my Astrid."

Rhys nodded. "No problem, sir. If it's all right with you,

me or one of my friends will take Astrid to school and bring her home. We plan to be with her in school as much as possible so she can't be targeted again."

"That's a very nice offer of you, but I don't think that's necessary." My mother interjected.

"Now dear. If they're willing to look after Astrid, why not let them? If these girls are as serious as Rhys believes, it wouldn't be a bad thing." Dad gently chastised Mom.

"You're right," she conceded but her eyes said he'd be sorry later.

"I need to get back home, but can I have a minute with Astrid?" Rhys pushed back his chair.

The tension that had slowly dissipated, thickened again. Dad squeezed the hand he still held and I looked at him. His eyes traced my cheek, probably to make sure it wasn't very noticeable now. He nodded. It must have passed his inspection.

"She can walk with you to the street. Thank you for coming."

Rhys stood and lightly touched my forearm as if he was helping me up. He followed me out and shut the door quietly behind him. Why had he come here? Was he really that concerned? He also deserved cookies for saving me, even if only temporarily. I kept walking until we were about ten feet from the house, then I turned and tipped my head back.

"I don't know whether to kiss you or kick you in the shin."

He smirked and glanced back at the house. The smirk was gone when he faced me again. "Are you okay?"

I couldn't lie to him. He'd seen the evidence of how my relationship with my mother was evolving. "I'm fine now.

Thank you. I don't think she would have listened to me if you hadn't come over."

A car drove by and it took me a second to realize it was Thatcher. He nodded and kept driving. How had he known where I lived?

"Give me your phone. Beck has called your rides to and from school." He held his hand out, assuming I'd pass it over without a fight. I would have if I understood what he was saying.

"What?" I couldn't have heard that right.

"Your number."

Another car drove by from the opposite direction, and Jonah waved. I laughed at the dorky gesture. It fit with his personality, but not, all at the same time.

"Is Beck going to drive by next?" I smiled.

"Probably. Phone?" This time it came as a request, so I gave it to him, and watched as he called himself and saved my info.

"Beck will get you in the morning. When do your parents leave for work?"

The curtains were still. No one was watching us. As nosy as my mother was, that was surprising. Dad must be having a word with her.

"They're usually sleeping still when I leave."

"Great. See you tomorrow." He strolled off with his hands in his pockets.

"Bye." I called. For such a big guy, he had a swagger that other guys could only dream about. And he didn't care. He really didn't care that he was so hot, or wanted, or cool.

Sighing, I jogged back up to the house.

Raised voices filtered through the door.

Fuck. Please don't let it be about me. Please be about

the mail, or the mortgage, or something that had nothing to do with me.

I pushed the door open.

"And I can't go?" Mother Dearest was pacing around the kitchen, coming into sight every few seconds.

"No, Trina. I already explained. This is a guys' trip from the church. You wouldn't have fun anyway. You hate being outdoors. It's glorified camping." Dad's voice took on a reedy quality in his exasperation.

They were clearly done with me, thankfully. I snuck past them toward the stairs on stealthy tiptoes.

"What am I supposed to do?" She acted like she couldn't survive without him.

"Go see your friends back home. Stay here and make up to Astrid for the smack you landed on her." He sounded like he didn't care either way.

"Right. Leave her here alone or make her think she wasn't in the wrong when she clearly was."

I pressed my back against the wall when I reached the top of the stairs. Up here, their voices carried enough that I could make out their words, and get to my room if they started to come this way.

"It sounds like you were in the wrong." A cabinet slammed shut as someone moved around the kitchen. Probably Dad. I bet Mother Dearest was trailing behind him, flailing her hands wildly around her head.

"You believe that boy? They're probably having sex, and now you gave him free rein to spend more time with her."

"Trina! Give it up. Not everyone is after sex. You of all people should know that. I'm done with this conversation. Go see your friends. Who knows what you'd do if you were left alone with Astrid."

They'd always seemed solid growing up. Every once in

a while, they'd have a shitty attitude toward each other, but not anymore. Arguments and angry hand gestures were the new norm. When had that changed? When we moved, or before? It was a sweet karma that they were doing a stellar job of making each other miserable.

I edged down the hallway. Their conversation wound down, and I wanted to get caught like I wanted to spend quality time with my mother.

Residual adrenaline thrummed through my body and I needed something to do. Too bad I was stuck in my room. There was always my laptop. With the portfolio review next week, I needed to get my stuff sorted anyway. At least now I didn't have to worry about my parents and the guys were trying to help with the bitches at school. That allowed me enough headspace that I could spend the night looking through my collection of pictures, planning my portfolio and plotting my revenge.

Chapter
23

Balls of lead piled up in my stomach, and I seriously considered waking my parents and telling them I was sick. My fear of school was almost worse than my fear of my parentals. Almost.

In the end, it was a text message that gave me the courage to leave the house.

Beck: I'll be there in ten, pretty girl.

It was weird. There wasn't any logic behind it, other than the fact he reminded me I wasn't alone. I went down the checklist of things I couldn't forget before I could go outside.

My homework, my laptop, my camera.

The hallway was quiet other than my dad's snores. No noises floated up from the kitchen, so I was in the clear. I tiptoed down the stairs and out the front door to an empty driveway. Empty outside of Freda anyway. It had been at least ten minutes. Where was Beck?

Pulling out my phone, I opened his text string.

"Psst."

What was that? I surveyed the street for the noise, and finally my gaze caught onto Beck, hiding behind the huge aspen tree at the edge of our yard. Hiding might be the wrong word. He leaned against it, but on the other side.

"What are you doing here?" I whispered when I reached his side.

"I brought my bike. Rhys mentioned your parents were hardcore, so I didn't want to get you in trouble. Come on." He grabbed my hand and winked.

Goosebumps trailed up my arm, lifting the tiny white hairs. The charm he exuded on the stage was much more subdued in the bright morning light, but he still had the power to turn me inside out with his attention.

He led me over to a motorcycle. I wished I could describe it, but I had zero about motorcycles. At least I knew this was the part where he expected me to get on. Too bad for him I hadn't ever ridden one before.

"What are you waiting for?" He grinned and handed me a sparkly black helmet.

"For a tutorial."

He laughed and started going over the basics. *Don't touch this, hold on to that, keep your mouth closed.*

"Got it." I nodded and fixed my camera bag crossways so there was zero chance I would drop it.

Beck swung on, holding out his hand for me. I slipped mine into his and climbed on behind him, using his shoulder to steady myself until I was situated. He paused and I waited for him to start up and get moving. Was he a meditator? It was like he was taking a moment to appreciate the beauty of the early Colorado morning, as it gently caressed the street with strong fingers of light.

"Astrid."

"Yes?"

"Are you going to hold on to me or what?" His voice shook with laughter.

I was waiting until he at least turned it on. Now he was making it awkward.

"Sure." I slid my arms around his waist and locked my hands together. It was a loose hold but still tight enough that my upper chest pressed against the thin white fabric of his T-shirt and his warmth seeped into me, rolling a shiver down my spine. If the helmet weren't so big and clunky on my head I would have rested my cheek on his back, secretly sniffing his soft cotton shirt.

"Astrid," he sighed as if he were dealing with a misbehaving puppy.

Beck separated my hands and tugged until I was completely flush against him, and he placed my hands over his chest. I gasped as a million butterflies started doing meth inside my stomach. Tingles shot down my arms and legs.

If he noticed my reaction, he didn't let on. We slowly eased onto the road, and the cool morning air coasted over my skin. Another, different taste of freedom, and it was glorious.

By the time we were pulling into the school, I was so high on life, it wasn't until he stopped right up front that I remembered to be anxious.

Girls were openly gawking at Beck, and one girl started to walk toward us until her friend jerked her back.

"Thanks for the ride," my voice was low and revealing way too much of the emotion trickling its way back to the forefront of my mind.

"No worries, pretty girl." Beck grinned over his shoulder.

"Hey." Jonah appeared at my side, holding the straps to his backpack as he waited for me to get off.

"Hey." I smiled, ignoring the growing crowd. They weren't there. I *did not* notice a forming group of gawkers.

I took my helmet off and the whispers started. People were pointing and laughing. Okay, I was crap at pretending and I needed something different to focus on.

"What are you all looking at?" Beck yelled at the crowd. "Pathetic. The lot of you." He grumbled as he got off the bike too.

He took the helmet from my hands and stepped close to Jonah. Anger rolled off him as Jonah sneered in the direction of the students clustered between us and the school entrance.

"Do you need me to stay?" Beck whispered.

Jonah shook his head and pushed his fingers under the strap of my bag, pulling me close. "No. These jerks are harmless. They're sheep. Laughing and pointing because they think that's the cool thing to do." He looked down at me, and his glasses slipped down the bridge of his nose. "They'll stop. You aren't going to be this popular for long." It was a promise. Only, he didn't have the power to follow through with it.

"I hope you're right." If this was my new norm, the twitch bitches would get a whole new normal too. One they would never see coming.

"I am. Beck, see you this afternoon." He pulled me toward the doors so fast, I didn't have time to say goodbye.

The hallway was just as bad. Jonah speed walked me to my locker and stood at my back, blocking the world out. Since I started watching Jonah, he never put on a friendly face. If anything, he mean mugged everyone because he knew he was smarter than they were. How did he get voted to Student Body President with that attitude? I was grateful for it now. If anyone thought about approaching me, they'd think twice. The intimidation vibes coming off Jonah were much stronger than I would have thought the school geek capable of. Quite the surprise.

"I'm not going to break down and cry in the corner." I spoke into my locker.

"I know. But these assholes are pissing me off." He was so much more crass than any other time we'd talked. I liked it. This was like the real him bleeding through.

"What's the plan? You and Rhys are going to shadow me every second of the day?" I smiled, amused their grand plan was to babysit me.

"Yes." Stern. Confident.

"And when I have to go to the bathroom? You can't follow me there." I shut my locker and pivoted on my heel.

There was so much determination in his eyes, my amusement changed into a different kind of warmth I didn't want to examine too closely.

"You can go in the boys. Rhys and I can both stand guard." He was dead serious.

They were being downright ridiculous. Now that I knew how dirty they were willing to play, I could be more careful, more observant. I wasn't going to cower in the boys' bathroom everything I had to pee.

"Why do you both look like someone pissed in your shoes?" Rhys fell on the locker beside us.

Great analogy, considering our bathroom talk.

"Astrid thinks she can go to the girls' bathroom on her own." Jonah's tone said I was poorly mistaken.

"Absolutely not." Rhys straightened up.

"Whatever. We'll play it your way for a while until it settles down." But it wouldn't, not until I did something about it.

Satisfied with my answer, they both walked me to class. True to their word, one or both were always waiting outside my room, ready to escort me to the next one. Jonah was even my shadow during lunch. He invaded my favorite corner and started studying, not paying attention to me, but content to do his thing while glaring at anyone who came within ten feet of us.

Any other time it would have been hilarious, but today, it was comforting. He provided a sense of safety in the bitch-infested waters of high school.

Ryan about died when I entered the art room with Rhys on one side and Thatcher on the other. He was shocked enough; he didn't say one word about how I ghosted him the night before.

"Girl." He said, but sealed his lips when Thatcher sat at our table.

Ryan gave me big eyes continuously as Mr. Music opened class, until Thatcher and I were excused.

"I'm calling you later. Make sure you answer." Ryan pointed at me as I snatched my stuff and left.

I loved Ryan, and he was the friend I needed when I had no one. But I wasn't looking forward to the conversation he wanted to have. He'd want to rehash everything that happened, but I was happy to leave everything that had happened in the past. It might make me a bad friend, but I was going to push that particular conversation off for as long as I could. When it no longer stung to think about, then I'd retell my story.

"How's your day going so far?" Thatcher bumped me with his shoulder.

"Fine. The worst offense has been pointing and laughing. It could be worse." I shrugged.

"Do we *need* to go to the library today?" He asked.

"No. It's usually deserted so it's a good choice." I tipped my head, trying to figure out what his game was.

"Will you get in trouble if we sit outside on the lawn?" He turned around and walked backward toward a side door leading to the courtyard.

"I guess not."

"Good." He grinned before pushing the door open and letting me through first.

The sun was bright sitting in the middle of a light blue, cloudless sky. I inhaled a deep breath of fresh air. It was a good day to sit outside. I didn't even need my sweater in the sporadic fall temperatures.

Thatcher took off his messenger bag and pulled out a thin beach towel first. He motioned for me to take a seat as he sat on the other half, taking out a broken-down easel, and assembling it back together with a serene expression on his face. Whatever he planned to do, he was in the zone. I wanted to get lost like that. When I escaped into my work, I was never completely free of the real world. Thatcher looked like he was the master at shoving life to the side while working on his art.

I opened my laptop and scrolled through the database I'd amassed over the last month or so of school as he worked next to me.

About ten minutes later he leaned over my shoulder to see what I was doing.

"That doesn't look like portfolio options. Those look like camera phone shots."

"They are. I'm working on something else at the moment." I slowly toggled browsers so it didn't seem suspicious.

Don't ask. I won't tell you.

"Okay, well for today only, since you probably aren't going to be allowed out of the house anytime soon, instead of you coming to watch me paint, I thought I would bring the painting to you." He was extremely proud of himself.

"You're treating me by letting me watch you paint?" I quirked a brow.

He sobered up after my question. "Uh, I mean... uh."

I busted up laughing and leaned into him. "I was joking. I'd love to see you in action. Please carry on. I'll keep working as I watch you. Cool?"

He slouched in relief. "Yeah, cool."

I got through maybe five pictures before I looked up to see what he was doing, and was immediately mesmerized by the way he moved the thin paint brush over the canvas. It was like one of the do it yourself craft videos where you get sucked in, watching nothing turn into something that you desperately needed in your life.

For Thatcher, he started with a couple lines and kept adding more and more depth, texture, and color. He was completely in the zone. If he forgot I was behind him, it wouldn't have surprised me. I moved around him and snapped pictures at different angles, using the sun as a prop. If even a little bit of his magic came through the lens, I would be ecstatic.

By the end of the class hour, I had eight new pictures of Thatcher and a new appreciation for his craft. The paint he used was acrylic, so it dried fairly quick after he applied it. When he turned, he smiled huge and I snapped one more picture.

"Hey now..." He grinned. "What do you think?"

I was stunned. I scooted up next to him and really studied the painting. He had painted me, holding the camera over my face, the flash going off. You couldn't see my features, the only reason I knew it was me was because of my hair, and who else would he be painting with a camera? I loved it.

"I have to go over it again later and fill out some more details, but you can have it when it's done." He wiped the paint off his hand with some wet wipes from his bag.

"I would love that." I bent close to the painting. The smell of the acrylic seared my brain with this forever memory. I knew whenever I smelled this type of paint again, I'd be reminded of this moment. When a cute college boy shared his art with me, and created something beautiful.

The next few days went by smooth. Almost too smooth. The girls would glare at me anytime I passed by their little clique and they did nothing to hide the fact they were planning something big.

On the bright side, my parents were on the outs, barely home, and when they were, they weren't talking to each other or to me. I mentioned one time to Dad that I was hanging out with Rhys, and he gave his permission. Not waiting for Mother Dearest to weigh in, I booked it to Rhys' house where he was waiting in his SUV.

I got some great shots of Rhys playing hockey, and his team winning. Then of Jonah and the debate team as they killed the other school. The whole week was surreal. By the time Friday rolled around, I was ready to take my life into my own hands and commence operation take down the twitch bitches.

Only, Friday hadn't gone exactly as planned. My whole life flipped upside down and there wasn't anything I could do about it.

Chapter 24

It was going to be hard to sneak out this morning. It wasn't even seven and my parents were arguing. Again. For the most part they ignored each other but the few times they were actually in each other's space, it was like Revelations all over again. I wouldn't be surprised if Mother Dearest threw out a reference to the Whore of Babylon. She was actually doing most of the arguing. Dad played defense through the whole thing. If he could ignore her, he did.

Hopefully I could catch Beck before he got here.

Me: I better drive myself today. My parents are up and would definitely notice you on your bike.

Beck: That blows. You want to meet me at the end of the street?

Me: Nah. It's too risky. I don't want to upset the balance I have with the parentals right now.

Beck: : (

I laughed and shoved the phone in my backpack along with the camera bag. The boho backpack looked ridiculous so stuffed, but I didn't want them to question why I had a camera bag with me all the time. They knew I was using it for art, but they were unpredictable this week.

It was actually a good thing I wasn't riding with Beck today. I had a plan, and it would go much smoother if I didn't have a shadow. Beck must let the others know the exact time I'd be arriving at the school, because someone was always there to greet us and escort me inside. Not that I hadn't enjoyed the last week, I had. For the first time in my life, I felt like I was a part of a real group, even as weird as our group was.

The school nerd, the star hockey player, the moody college art student, the heartthrob musician. And then me, the weird boho chick who had a penchant for documenting people's stupidity.

The energy in the parking lot was wired when I pulled in. Did someone somehow find out my plan for today?

No, no one knew, not even my shadows. And that made me even more nervous. Was today the day the twitch bitches decided to put another phase of their plan into motion? A week of peace was longer than I had hoped for, so maybe.

I got out of Freda and zipped to the front doors. The less time people had to see me, the less chance someone would do something stupid.

Inside, the hallway was popping with guys bouncing all over the place and girls giggling. Someone bumped into me but I grabbed them.

"Hey, why is everyone so excited this morning?"

The girl jerked her arm out of my grip and shoved a hand through her hair.

"It's senior prank day. All the seniors harass the under-classmen today. Don't get caught in the hallways or bathrooms." Her eyes rolled around in her head as she watched who was around us. Clearly, she was an unfortunate under-classman.

"Jesus." I muttered. "Thanks." She scurried down the hallway and then I noticed it. The majority of the people in the hallway were fighting to get to class, and the seniors were living it up, feeding off of the fear.

Senior prank day put a kink in my plans. It was now or never. Did I want to play it nice and warn the bitches away, or did I want to ruin their precious reputations?

There wasn't a lot of time to think about it. I was a senior, but if I was right, they'd do something else horrible today. They'd lock me in the bathroom, strip me down or beat me up. Who knew what these girls were capable of? The only thing I knew with any certainty was that it would be worse than dumping fish and dirty water over my head.

I forced my way through the crowd, to the back hallway where they liked to hang out. It was all huge windows and blinding sunlight. Premium space in the school so they called it as theirs.

Their cackling reached me before I saw them. Miniskirts, heavy make-up, and stick straight hair, a great impersonation of a slut barbie.

"Ashley, look who's here. Just in time." The short blonde next to Ashley snickered.

Another round of grating cackles and then I was in Ashley's face. Pushing her back. Pushing hard.

"We need to have a chat." No one would ever have known the insanity of emotions twisting inside me right then. Fear, anxiety, satisfaction at finally standing up for myself. And a little glee to get mine back.

"Watch it, slut. The school already thinks you're a whore with all the guys you have watching out for you. It's pretty pathetic."

I rolled my eyes. "Whatever. If anything, the girls are jealous because they're all hot guys and don't pay attention to anyone else." That was a bluff. Maybe they did when I wasn't around? I couldn't dwell on that right now.

She started to open her mouth, but I pushed past her.

"You don't want to have this conversation out here." The bathroom was right behind her, and that was where I was heading. Rhys and Jonah would be freaking out any minute when they realized Beck hadn't dropped me off and I wasn't in my car. This way, they couldn't interfere.

I walked to the back of the bathroom and spun to see the last of the girls follow me in. She shut the door and braced herself in front of it. Five girls blocking my exit. This had to go my way. If it didn't, they had less brain cells than my camera. Although my camera at least served one hell of a purpose.

"Are you trying to prolong your surprise?" Ashley crossed her arms, pushing her boobs up.

"Actually no. I didn't know you were going to do anything. I thought we were past that." I deadpanned. Of course, I knew they were planning something else.

"It won't work you know. In about five minutes the freshman guys are going to do it, all to avoid senior prank day. They'll get immunity." Her face twisted with sick satisfaction. She felt powerful.

Oh, how I wanted to watch as she was knocked a few rungs down the school's pecking ladder.

"And that would be?" I was in here. If it was something directed at me but not me specifically, were they targeting Rhys? No, he was too popular. Jonah? That was a possibility.

"That's our little secret. You'll have to wait to find out."

I opened my bag and pulled out a folder. "Maybe, maybe not. If I were you, I would call the guys and tell them not to follow through."

"Please. Like you could threaten us?" Her group giggled and wiped their eyes dramatically, like the idea of me threatening them drew tears to their eyes.

This was it. The moment I'd been building up to. And it was so sweet.

"This is just a teaser. You have your secrets and I have mine. So this is the only teaser you'll get. Just know, I have more. On every one of you." I met each of their eyes and put every ounce of anger and contempt in my gaze that I could.

It worked. At least on a few of them. The girl next to Ashley swallowed hard. Perfect. She was my teaser anyway.

Ashley snatched the folder from my fingers. "What crap is this?" She opened it and it took her a minute to realize what she was looking at. Teaser girl knew immediately because she gasped and backed up, nearly knocking over two of the other girls.

"Bella!" She spun and shoved the folder in the girls face. "That's my fucking boyfriend!" she screeched and I had to cover my ears.

The twitch bitches dissolved into a catfight, complete with slapping and hair pulling. True to my nature, I pulled out my phone and snapped picture after picture.

Oh. That shot showed a nipple. These girls were getting vicious.

I sent the pictures—minus the one with the nipple—to Beck since he was the last person in my messages along with a text to tell him I would explain soon, then I shoved my phone in my back pocket.

It was fun, now it was time to let them know I was not to be messed with. "All right. So you saw one picture. I have many. Pictures you wouldn't want to see the light of day." I projected my voice and the fighting stopped. Laughter threatened to knock me out of my fierce mode, but I pushed it down. These girls looked like extras from *Thriller*. "Call the guys. Tell them to stop whatever they were planning. If you don't, if you try to fuck with me again, or any of my friends, I'll release the pictures to the school blog."

"What's to stop us from busting your phone?" Ashley huffed.

They really were stupid.

"Because the pictures aren't stored on my phone and a friend out of state has the pictures and the blog name. If I say the word, she'll upload all of them." I spoke slowly so they could understand the words coming out of my mouth. Stace was horrified to hear what happened and jumped on the chance to get revenge.

"Astrid!" Pounding startled the girl leaning on the door.

"That's Rhys. Does he need to know you went through with your plan?" I raised my eyebrows. Five minutes was almost up. If they didn't call off their freshmen, it would be too late.

"Ann, call Heath. Tell him it's a no go." Ashley did the best she could to smooth out her makeup in the mirror, completely ignoring the continuous banging and screaming. It sounded like Jonah had joined him.

"Got it." Ann, a short brunette, who looked too innocent for the likes of these bitches, started texting.

"You lucked out, Astrid. You aren't our target anymore. For the first time ever, it's changed in the school year." She raised a hand to unlock the door, but twisted her head and looked back over her shoulder. "Watch yourself, Bella." Then she was gone and Jonah, Rhys and Beck fell into the room.

Hands patted me down, but they weren't going to find any sign of injury.

I beamed. They scowled.

"What the actual fuck?" Beck yelled. His face was red and he eyes were wide. "You scared the fuck out of me. Fuck!" He spun and banged a fist on the dirty green concrete wall.

"Guys, it's okay. I fixed it all." I bent down to pick up the picture that had fluttered to the floor, flipping it so they could see.

Jonah squinted, the thunderous expression totally blanking out. Seconds ticked by as he and the others studied the shot. Then he grabbed it out of my hands, laughing his butt off. "This is great! I hate that guy." He wrapped his arms around me, lifting me in a hug. "This is epic, Astrid."

"No, it's not. You scared the shit out of us." Rhys remained three feet away, hands fisted at his sides.

My good mood plummeted when I met his gaze. He was scared for me. And now angry because I went off on my own.

"Rhys," my voice was almost a whisper. It wasn't an apology, but it was close.

He sighed. "If you want revenge or if you're doing anything at all, with or about the twitch bitches, let us know. We could have helped."

With each word, I shrunk until I felt two inches tall. It wasn't a big deal. Or I hadn't thought it was. The fact that he was disappointed in me turned my stomach in a weird way. I didn't like it. This kind of friendship was new to me, but I already knew I didn't want anything to happen to mess it up. If it was important to him to be involved, I would let him.

"Okay. If I'm ever planning to do anything like this again, I'll tell you and you can be my accomplice." That was what it really boiled down to. I wanted to protect them and keep them out of trouble. It seemed, at least Rhys hadn't wanted that.

He nodded. "Let's get out of here. We can go to my place."

"I can't." Beck waved at a girl that tried to come in, but she backpedaled as soon as she got a look at who all was inside. "I have to work. I'll text you later." He trailed his fingers down my arm and left.

"I can't skip. It looks bad, especially as the class president." Jonah shook his head. "Sorry, man. We'll catch up later." He turned to me and grinned. "That was awesome. I'm always happy to help you on the back end when you're causing mayhem. I would appreciate a live video feed so I can live it through you, though."

We laughed and then he left too.

"Want to get out of here?" Rhys stuffed his hands in his back pocket.

My mother would get a call again. But right now, that was the last thing I cared about. I wanted to leave with Rhys and forget about senior prank day. If I wasn't here, then no one could prank me. Just in case they decided to follow through on whatever lame plan they cooked up.

"Let's do it." I closed my eyes tight, then opened them and grinned. Today, it would be worth the trouble.

He smiled, releasing the tension from his shoulders. After a moment of staring at each other, he reached out a hand and I took it. His rough calluses slid across my palm, and he squeezed.

People literally stopped walking to watch us leave together. It was because I was with Rhys, and we hadn't held hands before so this was news to them. This time, it didn't bother me. I still avoided making eye contact, but I didn't feel like my skin was crawling.

We parted ways as we climbed into our own vehicles, and I followed him back to his place. He must have realized my car couldn't be seen, as he pulled around the back of the house where we parked behind the cottage. It was bad enough I was skipping for real. Parking where Mother Dearest could see would be asking to get caught.

"Hey, my parents should be gone. Let's go grab some food from the house." He tapped the hood of his car and walked to the side door of the garage.

He stopped in the doorway and I plowed into him.

"What the heck? Move." I shoved my way around him because he was still frozen.

The sight that greeted me. I was frozen too.

Rhys' dad had another man bent over the hood of his car with their pants down.

And that man... That man was my dad.

Chapter 25

I couldn't see anything indecent, except this whole thing was indecent. The sides of their hips, butt and thighs were all on display and Mr. Bennet was pressed tight to dad. This wasn't right. This wasn't actually what I was looking at, was it?

"Astrid," My dad spluttered, pushing off the car to grab his pants, effectively flashing his dick and taking the cover from Mr. Bennet's. They both had raging erections. Old man, hairy ball erections.

"Ahhh!" I covered my eyes and Rhys pulled me around until I face planted in his chest. "Rhys, tell me our dads aren't doing what I think they're doing." I demanded. Because if my eyes weren't lying, they were having sex on the hood of Mr. Bennet's car.

He rubbed a soothing hand over my back, cradling my head with the other. It was his dad and my dad. *Together.* Was he as grossed out as I was? His muscles spasmed, but he remained quiet, keeping his cool. Shouldn't he be shouting the house down right now? This was an insane turn in my life, and I didn't want to process it right now. Maybe after a few weeks or months, I could contemplate how this could change the world as I know it.

"I can't tell you that." He growled. "We'll be in the house, Dad. Waiting for an explanation."

Okay, that hadn't sounded as calm as I had first thought. He shuffled me past them but I kept my eyes closed. Hopefully they had their pants up now, but just in case, I didn't want to see their dicks again. Rhys reached around me and pushed the door open. It was safe, so I could finally see where I was going without fear.

The door slammed and Rhys punched the wall, making a fist sized hole in the plaster. Pieces of light gray drywall flaked off the wall, as he shook his hand out. When he turned around, I sucked in a sharp breath. His face was murderous, and he narrowed his eyes as I took a step back.

"Hey, hey. Come in here with me." Away from anything else he could damage. The kitchen was right off the mudroom and very open. Perfect.

"Remember that night you and Beck came to the cottage?" He walked to the island, and pounded his fists down on the speckled granite. He grunted under his breath, dropping his head to his chest.

Not good. If I didn't calm him down, he was going to do serious damage to his house or his hands.

"How could I forget the night you caught me trespassing?" I sidled up close to him and pulled his hands in mine, linking our fingers. I doubted he would slam my fists against anything. For all the restrained anger boiling under his skin, he wasn't a violent person. Unless it was on a rink. Rhys would never hurt me on purpose.

"I overheard Dad on the phone. That was the first real proof I had that he was cheating. Mom was upstairs." He glared at the door.

I remembered he said he caught his dad. At the time, I was an outside observer. Now, we bonded by this bizarre experience. His own dad betrayed him. I should have felt the same way. Why didn't I? Because I hated my mom? Because my dad wasn't any kind of dad at all?

It was like I was numb to the whole situation. Where I should have been outraged and hurt, I was simply surprised. I was watching through a weird film, dulling my senses to the whole thing. My empathy for Rhys was much stronger in that moment than my own feelings.

I was more shocked he was with a man, rather than him cheating. Mother Dearest must have suspected something with the way she'd been acting lately. Projecting her fear of what her husband was doing onto me.

"I assumed it would have been a woman. He never gave any indication that he liked... men." Rhys furrowed his brow in confusion.

From the few times I had seen Mr. Bennet, he seemed completely straight. Then there was the whole marriage thing throwing me off.

"Is that more upsetting to you?" I hesitantly edged closer.

My dad was a pastor. While they didn't outright say being gay was a sin, my dad's disapproval was tangible anytime it was brought up in conversation. Where I was numb at first, all these thoughts pelted my mental shield until I started to question everything my father had done and said my whole life.

Was this the first time? Were there other men, or women? Did my mother know? If she did, that was probably a large cause of why she was such a screaming bitch. Not to mention, she didn't seem like the type of person that would stick around in that type of relationship.

"No?" Rhys' voice brought me back to the present. "I don't think that bothers me more. It makes me angry he would cheat at all. He thinks he rules the world, and Mom's nothing but a trophy and body for him to use." His lip lifted in disgust.

"I'm sorry." Then it hit me. We were friends. We'd started building this friendship and this could tear it all down. I gasped and curled my fingers around his hands as tight as I could. "Is this going to change how you feel about me?"

"What?" He reared back. "Why would you say that?"

He looked at me like I was one song short of a full hymnal.

"Because he's cheating with my dad. My *dad*." I bent forward and pressed my forehead into the hard plains of his chest.

I shouldn't have pointed it out if he hadn't put it together before. With my eyes closed, I saw the proverbial ties of our friendship severed by my dad and his philandering ways. Definitely cutting the string between Rhys and me. Maybe the others too if they thought I was anything like my dad.

He gently pushed my shoulders back until I looked up at him.

"You're being ridiculous."

My mouth popped open.

"If I would have found out before I knew you, really knew you, then I might have said or felt things I'm not proud of. But it didn't happen that way. I know you. I know you aren't your dad. Like I'm nothing like my father." How did he manage to solidify my feelings for him with each word? No one had ever seen me like Rhys, or the other guys. As someone completely separate from my family. It was amazing and scary all at the same time.

No matter what happened between our dads, we would

be okay. The question of the hour, was what did we do about this whole mess? After talking to Rhys, my rising emotions settled back down, and I was pretty sure his did too. Tension in his shoulders eased until he appeared relaxed.

I released a breath and leaned back against the counter as the door opened to the garage.

Both men filed through, put together in a way no one would ever know what they'd been doing. If they tried to convince us we misunderstood what we saw, I'd stab them with one of my charcoal pencils.

How would they try to spin this against us? An idiot could see they had something working behind their eyes. Mr. Bennet wore arrogance like a cheap cologne. And my dad held more of a righteous posture, daring me to go against him. Part of me wondered if they would try and play it off like we misunderstood. *Oh, Dad was showing Mr. Bennet how to kneel and pray.*

"Son, I don't think we have to discuss how you never speak of what you walked in on." Mr. Bennet made a statement. Not a request, a demand. They were going for the authority card. Like we would fall in line because we were their children and still in dependent of them.

I glared at my father and his eyes shuttered like he was at least a little guilty.

"Are you going to leave Mom?" I asked, stepping away from Rhys.

Dad's mouth went slack before he responded. "Astrid. No."

"Are you in love with him?" I jerked my head at Mr. Bennet. Okay, so I *did* care a teensy bit. I *was* angry. I knew Mom was crazy and hard to live with, but if he wasn't happy he should have *left*. Not cheated.

"No!" Both men shouted.

"That's not what this is, Astrid." Dad tried to use his pastor voice, the voice of reason. It fell flat.

I exchanged a glance with Rhys. Then what was it?

"We aren't gay." Mr. Bennet said.

Rhys nor I said anything.

"We aren't." Dad parroted.

"Sure. We believe you." The way Rhys said that meant we totally didn't believe them.

"Listen, honey." Dad stepped closer but still not in touching distance. I wouldn't be able to stomach his touch right now anyway. "Your Mom can't know. This would break her." He tried playing on heartstrings, I didn't have for my mother.

I sneered. Then an idea started forming in my head. It would harden my heart if I went through with it. But at the same time, how could I not take advantage of this? I was angry with Dad, but they didn't deserve my sympathy. They weren't good parents and really, they deserved each other. This was my shot.

"I can keep a secret... But I want something in return." Several somethings but I started with one.

He sucked in a breath and narrowed his eyes. Mr. Bennet and Rhys ceased to exist.

"What do you want?" He lost the sweetness to his voice and a hardness I never heard from him before replaced it.

"I want live a normal life for my senior year. I want to have friends, and go out to the movies, and be *normal*. I want you to keep Mom from verbally and *physically* abusing me." I didn't blink as I conveyed how important this was to me.

Rhys placed his hand in mine and held on. Offering me comfort. I confirmed what he suspected. He knew about the one time he came to save me. But I had never shared if it had happened before. Now he knew it had.

"I can do that." He agreed.

"And I want to go to any college I want, and study any major I want. Possibly art." This time he wasn't as willing to agree.

"Astrid. Your college education is important. What would you do with art? You wouldn't be able to support yourself. Who would marry an art graduate with a minimum wage job?"

Dad acted like he was rolling in money. He wasn't that much better off than the jobs he constantly put down.

"I would. There are a million guys out there that would." Rhys interjected. "Just because you have hang ups doesn't mean the rest of us do."

If our dads hadn't put us in this awkward as hell situation, I would have swooned.

"Thanks," I twisted and smiled up at him.

He returned it.

"That's my ask. You want me to lie for you? Well, our whole life is a pretty lie. Ours. The Bennets. If you want to keep living it, you need to help me get what *I* want. So *I* can be happy." I covered my heart with my palm. It beat so fast under my hand, I needed to contain it. Any second it would burst out of my chest and gallop around the room.

This was it. Freedom, and a real shot at happiness were so close, I could taste the sweetness on my tongue already.

Dad's nostrils flared. His gaze darted between Mr. Bennet and me before he spoke. "Fine." He said through clenched teeth.

"Yeah?" I couldn't keep the radiant smile off my face. He probably hated me right now. His career and way of life were on the line, but I was exuberant.

"I agree. Your mother won't give you any problems and you can choose your major." Still through clenched teeth.

"Perfect. I'll keep the pretty lies alive and you can keep banging Mr. Bennet." Rhys snorted behind me.

"Rhys?" Mr. Bennet locked on his son.

I glanced over my shoulder and winced. Hopefully he wasn't too offended by my last thoughtless comment. The longer I thought about it; I truly didn't care if they carried on with their affair. Although, Rhys probably did.

Rhys was glaring at his dad, but his eyes softened when they came back to me. They moved back and forth between my own, before he eventually turned back to his dad. "Stay out of my way, and I'll stay out of yours. Your secret's safe with me as long as you follow that rule." His gaze never left mine.

I jumped when the door slammed, and I turned around to see both men were gone. This was why Mom couldn't go on the weekend trip with him. It all made so much sense now.

"Can you believe that?" I jumped around which was completely out of character for me, but I couldn't contain the excitement thrumming through my entire body.

"I can." He laughed. "Wait until the others hear about it."

I laughed with him as we walked out a different back door to the cottage. I had been my own hero today, and it provided me with the deepest sense of self-worth I'd ever had. Technically, I didn't need the guys anymore. I took care of the twitch bitches all on my own. With my dad agreeing to pay for my college, I really didn't need the scholarship either. It was nice to know we would all still be friends.

"THANK you guys for doing this for me." I linked arms with Thatcher and Jonah.

The five of us were walking into the auditorium to view the portfolios that had been submitted for the scholarship. Even though the pressure wasn't what used to be, I still wanted to do well. This was the first time I had ever entered anything like this, and I spilled so much of myself for the world to see. Or a very small group of viewers. But it was a start.

Now that I wasn't the one with anything on the line. Jonah was the one I was worried about. He was tugging at his shirt collar like it was doing it's best to put him out of his misery.

"Don't mention it," his voice was strained.

I stopped and faced him. "Jonah. I don't have to play the audio."

He shook his head. "They told you the judges were the only ones going to be in the room when you play it. That's fine."

"Are you sure?" I really wanted to play it, but I cared about our friendship more.

"Sure." He tucked a strand of hair behind my ear and started walking again.

"Can I just say, this whole last few days has been insane?" Beck was referring to the fight, our dads, and their concessions.

It felt like a dream that any minute I would wake up, and it would all be taken away from me. Sometimes, I even felt like the guys were too good to be true.

"One hundred percent, man. One hundred percent." Rhys smiled and threw an arm around Beck.

Tonight, the participants were invited to view their competitor's work, then when the judges were ready, they walked room to room to review each portfolio. They designated a classroom to each student so there was a level of privacy.

Which was perfect for what I had in mind.

The next hour passed at a slug's pace, and I waited patiently for the judges. The guys had already gone back out to the lawn to wait for me, each leaving me with a hand caress or shoulder squeeze. Once I showed my work, I was free to leave.

Moving around the room, I made sure each piece was perfectly level and dust free. The first picture was Thatcher in profile, painting in the sun. His features were hard to see, but from the way he held his body, he was serene and happy. Jonah was next. It was the back of him when he was at the podium, kicking butt at the school debate. He came across as confident and strong. Again, the light was blaring down and distorting some of the picture. Then Rhys, with his fist raised and mask on. The buzzer had signaled the end of the game and he won. I used Photoshop to increase the contrast, which removed some of his recognizable features. He wasn't serene but pumped and excited. Last, there was Beck. The night of the concert, under the stage lights. Not the one where he was crouched in front of me. That one was private and wouldn't be shared with the public. No, this one was where he was crooning into the microphone and living his dream.

There was a knock on the door, and then four people walked into the room. Three men and one woman. I didn't know any of them, thankfully.

"Are you ready... Astrid?" The short, stout woman asked as she glanced at her clipboard.

"Yes." I smiled. "I hope you don't mind, my piece tonight is both visual and audible." I went to the wall and turned off the lights. The guys—mainly Jonah—had helped me rig lights over each framed photograph so they were highlighted. "Let me know when you're ready for the next part."

They took several minutes inspecting each photograph and making notes. My hands shook as they leaned close to really look at each shot. I was suddenly glad I had taken Thatcher's advice and not used Photoshop in any significant way. They would have noticed.

"We're ready." one of the men said.

They stepped back and formed a line, silently absorb the show.

I grabbed the remote Jonah had given me and pressed the button to start the presentation.

All the lights clicked off except for the one above Thatcher.

His strong and steady voice projected through the room. "I come from a broken home with an abusive father, doing my best to shield my little sister from his filth."

The light switched off, and the next one brightened Jonah's picture. "I live on the wrong side of the tracks, constantly looking over my shoulder, trying to rise above the gang life."

Then Rhys. "I come from an affluent family, with an arrogant father that expects me to be just like him, doling out insults and condescension to hurt the ones that love us most."

Lastly, Beck. "I take care of my druggie mother and because of my weakness for a woman that never loved me, I can't afford to go to college."

All the lights pop on. Altogether they said, "But that's not what the world sees. They see..."

Thatcher says, "an artist."

"The debate captain."

"Star hockey player."

"Rock star."

Then all at once to finish. "And these are our pretty lies."

The room was engulfed in darkness as all the lights went out. I waited a few moments for dramatic effect, and then hit the switch to turn the regular lights on.

The four judges clapped. As they exited the room, they each smiled and said, "well done."

I couldn't help but smile to myself and think of my friends. This would have been impossible without them. We really did work well together.

26
Jonah

I'd left the guys after dropping off Astrid. There was so much studying to do. I shouldn't have taken so much time off tonight, but I refused to let Astrid down. In the end, I was glad we were all able to be there for her. She was glowing, ready to show the world what she could do. Astrid was going to be something special. She already was.

And what did I have? I had a trailer I shared with my aunt, who worked all the time. When she wasn't, she could be found on the couch with one of her fuck buddies.

I shouldn't be so bitter about it. She'd taken me in when my mom went to jail. The fact she could even afford to do that was a miracle. But we didn't often have food, so it wasn't that much of a miracle.

The metal door banged against the wall as I entered the trailer. Clouds of smoke hung in the air. Great. She was here.

The bathroom door opened as the toilet flushed and Reaper walked out. That wasn't his real name, obviously. It was his gang name that was supposed to instill fear in the general population.

He wasn't shit though. I could take him easily if it wasn't for the gang backing him up. If it came to a fight,

Rhys, Beck, and Thatcher would back me up. Wasn't that something? The most unlikely group of friends. But they were solid. And we all came together because of a hippie chick.

We still had Trey to take care of. Astrid thought everything was over, but it wasn't. We just didn't have the heart to tell her.

"Jonah, kid." He slurred. "The boss has a job for you. He's been waiting and you don't want to make him angry." He wagged his porky finger in my face.

"Sorry, I don't take jobs anymore. I'll be out of here soon." I pushed past him, but he slammed me into the wall.

"Jare, you hear this?" Reaper laughed until he wheezed, then started coughing.

"Hear what?" She called from the back.

"Jonah said he's going to be gone soon. You know anything about that?" Reaper braced a hand in the middle of my chest, and I didn't know if it was to keep me in place or keep him standing. Probably both. It would be so easy to feed him my fist, but I was smarter than that. He would call in his buddies and beat the shit out of me. That was not part of my five-year plan. Anything that could fuck up getting out of this shithole wasn't part of the plan.

"Yeah right." She walked through the door smirking, the bags under her eyes wrinkling as her cheeks lifted. "You might want to check the mail. I laid it on your bed."

She was joking. It was a cruel joke. What she was insinuating wouldn't have happened.

Reaper stumbled down the hallway, likely for his next fix, leaving me alone. I spun and burst into my room. Three letters were on my bed. Opened. The bitch opened my mail.

With trembling fingers, I pulled each letter out. I was

waiting for one specific college. I'd already been accepted to a few, and received some piddly scholarships. Nothing that was worthwhile or would really help me out. I had one more school I pinned all my hopes on.

An acceptance letter to DU. That was great. *Amazing.* She was bluffing.

The second letter was the amount of scholar ships the school was awarding me. Okay, I could work with that.

The third letter.

The difference I would have to pay after scholarships to go to college there.

Ten grand a year. I didn't have that kind of money. I couldn't even finance it. Jare had horrible credit and even if she didn't, she said she wouldn't sign the FAFSA for me. And the rule was, someone over the age of twenty-four had to be a co-signer for the loans. I'd have to do some research about grants. Did they need a family member to apply with me? With everything going on, and with stellar grades and a well-rounded application, the thought never entered my mind that it wouldn't be enough.

"Fuck!" I threw the letters and they harmlessly fluttered to the floor like little maple seeds.

Reaper pushed the bedroom door open, the creaking straight out of a horror movie. "Jare told me what was in the letters. Go see boss. He can give you enough jobs to make up the difference." He smirked before letting it close.

There had to be a better option to get out of here. Surely, doing illegal runs wasn't the way I would finally get out. Michael was right, you never leave after you start. It's a deadly sort of quicksand that pulls you under until you suffocate.

Damn.

TO BE CONTINUED IN UGLY TRUTHS...

Thank you for reading! I hope you enjoyed Astrid and her fellas as much as I did! If you did, please consider leaving a review as it helps promote the books you love.

You can stalk me on my Facebook Author Page, Bookbub and you can also find me in my closed reading group the Lusty Legion. In the LL you can interact with me directly, find excerpts and information on upcoming releases, as well as play games and enter for giveaways. I'd love to have you join me!

Turn the page for a sneak peek of **_Marks of the Mazza_**, a fun, light, reverse harem paranormal romance. If you like paranormal and #whychoose, this book is for you.

Please note, this is a med-fast burn, and there may be times where you laugh out loud.

MARKS OF THE MAZZA

Thunder booms in the distance as rain pours down from the heavens.

Damn.

Damn, damn, and double *damn*.

If there is truly a god out there, he's spitting on me right now. That's how bad my day sucked. The rain is coming down in torrents where only moments ago there wasn't even a sprinkle in sight. Ducking into the closest alcove, I shake off the water as best as I can. Water seeps through my light-weight hoodie to my skin.

In the last hour, a rando walked into the book store and wouldn't leave. Normally I wouldn't mind, but this man walked around for twenty-five long minutes *after we were closed* and didn't even buy anything. I waited to balance the drawer until after he checked out but no, he left empty handed. Someone should teach him common etiquette. If you are going to make someone stay late, you should at least support their business.

Then when I balanced, the drawer was fifty dollars short, emptying most of the cash from my wallet. We aren't

294 MARKS OF THE MAZZA

supposed to replace missing funds, but you get written up for coming up short, and there is no way I can afford to possibly lose my job. I'll take the small loss now.

My current options: wait for the rain to stop or order an Uber. At 11 p.m. I don't really want to take my chances and wait it out, but I also don't want to waste any of the last twenty dollars in my account either. I enter the address of my studio apartment in the app to gauge the cost. I'm going to do it. Only seven dollars, and I waitress tomorrow at the diner, so I'll at least refill my cash stash a little bit.

Two minutes. Not bad. I blow out a sigh, slide my phone back in my bag, and glance up and down the street. Fog rolling in from the mountains slowly blankets the town. Shivering, I wrap my hoodie tighter around my body as a sleek black car pulls up to the curb.

Sweet! My ride's here.

Running out through the rain, I pull the door open a crack and slide into the back seat. Already I feel better in the heat that's on full blast. I take a few seconds to check out the car and notice two guys sitting in the front seat. Two very good looking guys. Both are turned around and staring at me with somewhat confused expressions.

"Umm... Hi." Wow. So eloquent. Internally, I give myself an eye roll.

A warm blush creeps up my cheeks. Good thing it's so dark back here and these two don't have a clear view of me. I get the distinct feeling that something isn't quite right.

Clearing my throat, I ask, "This is an Uber, right?"

The man in the passenger seat gives a smile that's friendly if a bit mischievous. I take him in for the first time. Shoulder-length, wavy blond hair is tucked behind his ears. At least I think it's blond.

The driver does not have the same welcoming reaction.

I feel like he is staring right into me and definitely finding me wanting. Where the passenger is light, the driver is dark. Dark hair, dark eyes, dark expression. Yeesh. Someone must have taken a sharpie to his fancy Italian loafers. My body temperature starts to rise as we sit here in silence. I run my fingers along the seat on either side of me, flitting across the seams.

Both men are still staring at me. I clear my throat again, dig my phone out without looking, and unlock it. Finally breaking eye contact in this bizarre stare down, I glance down at the app.

"Ughhh..." I groan and drop my head on the back of the seat. Looks like I missed my real Uber while participating in this little...whatever this is here. Wonderful. I still get charged five dollars even though I missed the ride. "Look, sorry I barged in on you here. I'll...ah...I'll just be going." I hook my thumb back at the street. Scooting over toward the door, I reach for the handle. Before I make contact, the door swings open, and a third man jumps in and slams right into me.

"What the..." The man grabs my shoulders to keep me from falling over. His weight pins my leg, forcing me to shift away from him. I twist my shoulders to disconnect the unnerving contact. His voice is deep and has a slight accent that I can't place. Either he is from somewhere I don't recognize, or his accent is weak.

"Sorry! I jumped in the car by accident. I thought this was my Uber." I'm mumbling because there is most definitely something going on here, and I don't know how to escape the situation. They don't have any lights on. At all. No headlights. No interior lights, not even when the doors opened. The only light is the glow of the clock on the dash.

I turn on my phone again and check the time.

11:08 p.m.

The last eight minutes feel like an eternity has passed and yet no time at all.

The man next to me sucks in a breath as he stares. I scoot away and grab the handle on the opposite side of the car. Again, my attempt to escape is thwarted. It's the guy next to me again, this time with his hand on my arm. It's a gentle grip, but tight enough to show that he absolutely means to keep me here. I whip around and look at him with my heart running a stampede inside my chest.

The glow of the street light filters in behind him. I can barely make out any of his features, but his hair is a burnished red, or appears to be in this light. His hair is short on the sides but has a longer wave on top. His ears are actually pretty adorable, as they stick out a bit with almost pointed tips.

He raises a hand, and the tip of his index finger grazes the strange, purplish birthmark under the outer corner of my left eye. It resembles a fuzzy letter K. There is a vertical line, with the little arms fanning out toward my left ear.

It generally gets attention when people notice it, but nothing so...reverent as this.

"Wait. Let us at least take you where you were trying to go." He drops his hand to the seat, brushing my arm and maintaining contact.

"That's okay. I didn't mean to intrude." I jump out on the side facing the street and briskly walk around the back of the car to the sidewalk. The rain has tapered off to barely anything at all. Just the way my luck runs. If I had stuck it out with the rain, I would have stayed five dollars richer.

Damn you, Uber, and your missed-ride fee.

As I dart up the block, I think I hear a car door close. Turning around for another peek at the car before I round the corner, I notice it's gone. Strange. The car didn't pass me or even make any noise. I suppose it could have left in the opposite direction.

An odd tingle runs down my back, and I quicken my pace. Every few steps, I glance behind me, but I see nothing and no one out of place. Just a quiet, deserted business street with a haze of fog hovering around the streetlights. Every so often, I pass a glow of lights behind a window shop, but nothing alarming.

I make it to the apartment complex after about a fifteen-minute walk. Trucking it up the three floors, I suck in a deep breath as I slam the door, lean my forehead against it, and at the same time engage the lock.

What a strange night.

IN THE MIND OF BLAKE

It never fails to amaze me, how far a book comes from its rough draft! I seriously could not have done it without the help of my alphas, Dom Whit and Maya Riley. Then Sue Ryan and Angela Greene followed them as trusty betas, helping to spot inconsistencies and pick out teasers.

This story was so much fun to write and started out as a challenge to myself. My first series was a mediumish burn, some may even think it on the fast side. I wanted to see if I could write a slow burn. It was easier than I thought! But don't worry, I can't hold out for too long. There will definitely be some steam in book two. 😊

Thank you all for reading!

WHO IS BLAKE?

Blake Blessing is new on the Indie scene and ecstatic to embark on this new chapter in life. She is a mom, wife, art enthusiast, and author.

She attended ten different schools growing up, so books became her constant friend. Escaping into books of all different genres made life fun and exciting. Blake was also raised on music and still blasts it through the house and car at every opportunity.

She has a weird sense of humor and a penchant for chocolate milk. It only makes sense she would one day go on to write her own stories.

Made in the USA
Middletown, DE
01 March 2023